Recent Books by Mignon G. Eberhart

El Rancho Rio
Two Little Rich Girls
Murder in Waiting
Danger Money
Family Fortune
Nine O'Clock Tide
The Bayou Road
Casa Madrone
Family Affair
Next of Kin
The Patient in Cabin C
Alpine Condo Crossfire

Alpine Condo Crossfire

Mignon G. Eberhart

Random House New York

Published in the United States by Random House, Inc., New York, and simultaneously in Canada by Random House of Canada Limited, Toronto.

Library of Congress Cataloging in Publication Data
Eberhart, Mignon Good, 1899–
Alpine condo crossfire.
I. Title.
PS3509.B453A79 1984 813'.52 84–42527
ISBN 0–394–53766–1

Manufactured in the United States of America
9 8 7 6 5 4 3 2
First Edition

Alpine Condo Crossfire

Alpine Condo Crossfire

All the persons and events in this book are entirely imaginary. Nothing in it derives from anything that ever happened.

One

In the pale glow of her headlights Emily Brace caught a view of the sign, ALPINE VILLAGE. It was a very discreet sign but its wooden frame had a carefully rustic air.

The shades of night were falling fast, when through an Alpine village passed—the rhyming lines repeated themselves in Emmy's head as she approached the turn into what was euphemistically called Alpine Village. She bore, however, no strange device, only a strange demand.

The road wound around in an artistic, very, very rural way, designed, she surmised, by the architect who had designed all the houses. She had never seen the Judge's house; she had never visited the condominiums.

It had been a demanding message that brought her here now.

He had telephoned her, getting straight through the switchboard, naturally, reaching the cubbyhole they called her office, although she shared it with anybody who needed space. The Judge was not one to wait while a message was taken or other, far more important calls were suitably answered. Probably he had thundered into the ear of the girl at the switchboard, nearly breaking her eardrum with his usual courtroom voice. But then when Emmy herself replied, he ordered her to get out to his house at once. No reason given, although she did have the temerity to ask why. He

had been about to hang up, apparently feeling that his few words of peremptory command were quite sufficient, when China's flutey voice came on. She could imagine China's pretty hand snatching the telephone from the Judge, in the very act of dropping it with a commanding thud on his desk. "Better bring some clothes, Emmy," China said hurriedly. "It's cold out here. You may have to—"

Then there was the hard thump of the telephone being put down. So Emmy knew that the Judge had taken it from China.

China probably did not know why the Judge had demanded Emmy's presence; the Judge merely issued fiats which were obeyed. It was Friday—a free weekend stretched ahead. Emmy had no intention of staying over the weekend. But in view of the cold December weather she did take a small supply of clothing: a very small supply. She didn't want to risk the loss of her job simply because the Judge had a whim.

The Judge was not a whimsical man. However, he had softened to some extent since his marriage to China, young and pretty China. She and Emmy had been schoolmates, had shared dates and giggles and secret trips to the city for the theater and as much shopping as their purses would permit, and stealthy trips back to school without being detected. The school was not a strict one; it claimed, indeed, to have one of the more permissive regimes. However, unauthorized trips cityward had not been smiled upon.

Emmy grinned a little to herself, thinking of China's smiling face, her dimple going and coming when some of the boys from Harvard or Princeton or Yale turned up to meet them. China, with an unsuspected gift for guile and wile in getting her own way, had arranged these encounters, and the boys were always only too pleased to meet the girls and buy them as lavish a dinner as their own pockets could provide. There would then remain only the problem of getting back to school without being discovered, and China could always manage that. Emmy had followed her lead with zest, no getting around that. She wasn't as good or convincing at lying as China. China could open her forget-me-not blue eyes wide and look like an innocent child who cannot understand why she is being scolded, and eventually the problem of discipline would dissolve. Somehow, Emmy herself merely profited by

China's guile. As far as she could remember, however, she did so without the slightest qualm.

Through the early, heavy December twilight a light flashed ahead of her. It outlined the window of the guardhouse, which someone, her sister Kate probably, had told her about. To encourage the necessary pause before entering the grounds of Alpine Village, there was a carefully constructed bump of concrete at the guardhouse; it was painted in black and white stripes in the charitable hope of protecting brakes and axles.

She checked her own small car. There were lights dotted around in the woods and slopes ahead. The woods and rocky slopes were probably the reason, or at least the excuse, for naming the cluster of houses Alpine Village.

As she brought the car to a slow halt, a uniformed guard loomed up beside her. Above a glistening raincoat and below a heavy cap, a warm, red and vastly friendly face grinned happily at her. "It's me."

She gasped. "Why, Mac! I didn't know you were here—" She leaned past her suitcase and thrust her hand out the opened window toward him.

Mac took it in his rough and strong hands. "I knew you were coming! How have you been? Making great strides in the city, I hear."

"But, Mac, how does it happen you're here?"

"Oh, Mrs. Slocumb bought one of these places. She had to sell her big house. But she said she couldn't get along anywhere without me. Poor lady!" The red beaming face sobered. He touched his cap. "Gone now. But"—he cheered up—"it's great to see you."

She laughed. "Remember the time you spanked me?"

"Now, now! Wasn't much of a spank. Besides, you shouldn't have been fishing there at the edge of that pond. Too dangerous. But you were"—he chuckled—"a very headstrong child. Somebody had to take action."

"It didn't really hurt!" Even now Emmy knew she was being defiant.

Mac chuckled again. "The Judge tells me you are doing fine in your television job."

"I'm a very small cog in a big organization."

"That's not the way the Judge tells it. Fact is, though, he's not too pleased with you right now. A few days ago I asked how you were getting along and he nearly had a fit. Said you were digging into a murder case—"

"Research, only."

"—and he didn't like it."

"I can't help that, Mac."

Mac shook his head. "You can't fool around with the Judge. You ought to know that by now."

Emmy later remembered her carefree and laughing reply. "Oh, Mac! Why, I have all the notes for the case right here with me. I'm going to work them up into something presentable—I hope—during the weekend."

Mac shook his head rather glumly but brightened as a tall, very familiar figure came up beside him. "Here's Bar."

"Hi, Emmy." Bar leaned into the car, took her chin in one hand and kissed her warmly on the lips.

"Bar!" She was almost shocked, not so much by his unexpected appearance as by the memory of his lips upon her own. But that was in the distant past, she told herself hastily, and caught her breath.

Bar laughed. "The same, Hezekial Barselious Slocumb. It's great to see you, Emmy."

Mac was beaming. "Sure like old times to see you two together."

"But—" Emmy began. She had to get control of herself and her suddenly thudding heart.

"Too long," Bar said lightly. "Must be all of two years."

Since China's marriage to the Judge. Emmy did not say it aloud.

Mac's red face was troubled. "I thought you two would have made a wedding of it by now. Of course, I know you haven't. You'd have told me. But—"

Bar said again quickly, "Emmy, it's great to see you. The Judge told me you were coming and sent me to show you the way to his house. These roads are a little bewildering, aren't they?"

Mac still seemed troubled but was diverted and shook his head. "Ought to have cleared out all these big boulders and those rickety stone fences. Wander all over the place . . ."

Bar nodded. "Must be rural if it kills us." He was dressed for

the weather in a heavy sheepskin-lined jacket and heavy boots. His head, however, was bare, and his thick black hair frosted with snow flakes. "They think these old farm walls give the place an authentic, old-time rustic air."

"Poor idea," said Mac, who liked everything about any place to be in perfect order. Bar had once said that Mac measured the grass to a fraction of an inch for cutting. It must have hurt him to give up his long-held position as gardener and, indeed, as an all-round caretaker, not only of the Slocumb place but the whole neighborhood where Emmy and Bar and Kate and Archie had spent their childhood. Archie Callser had been a neighbor, too, for a time. The memory seemed at the same instant something that had happened long ago and only yesterday as well. Mac's ruddy face suddenly stilled as a long car with blackened windows drew up beside Emmy's car.

Emmy was immediately sure that the same car had paused near her once or twice at toll gates all the way out from the city. The blackened windows were both annoying and weirdly puzzling. She felt now, and each time she had seen the car earlier, as though someone inside it, invisible to her, was peering out from the shelter of those windows and noting everything about her, from her gloved hand on the wheel to the small suitcase on the seat beside her. Of course, the car was at her left, and the invisible passenger couldn't have seen straight through her to the suitcase, but all the same there was a kind of disturbing something emanating from the blackened windows. She dismissed that as an absurd notion but wished there were a law against such cars; indeed, she had a vague memory of such a law having been considered at the strong request of the police. Mac, his expression disapproving, barely touched his cap. The car glided on, rather sinisterly, it seemed to Emmy. Bar was watching as the long car's red taillight swerved into another road.

"Who was that?" she asked.

Bar shrugged. "His nibs."

She looked questioningly at Mac, who rubbed his chin grumpily. "He means Mr. Manders. Thinks he owns the place."

"He has a lot of clout," Bar said cheerfully and slid into the seat beside Emmy after tossing her suitcase onto the back seat. "We take the first curve left."

By this time Emmy had gotten herself and her treacherous heart under control. "Bar, what are you doing here?"

"My mother's house. Settling things." His voice was sober. "Actually, I'm trying to sell the place. Prices have gone up fantastically for these condominiums. See you, Mac."

Mac, however, was staring behind them, looking definitely surprised. Another automobile, long and blatantly white, had drawn up behind Emmy's car. After a moment Mac touched his cap, and the white car went swiftly on, turning right as the limousine had done.

Bar said, "Who's that?"

Mac sounded puzzled. "I thought it was his nibs in the first car. But no, it was Mr. Manders driving the white job. The limo must have been driven by that man of his, secretary or whatever. Anyway, his name is Guy something—Wilkins, I think. Comes down here sometimes, evenings. Talks a lot, but doesn't say much. Can't see why he'd want to skulk behind black windows. Manders is the one who—" Mac paused and continued discreetly, "Manders just might have enemies."

"Good," Bar said heartily. "I can't stand Manders. We'd better get along to the Judge's. Ready, Emmy? See you, Mac."

Mac grinned from ear to ear. "Good to see you both," he repeated with a twinkle in his blue eyes. "And it's time you made a match of it, remember! Wouldn't have thought either of you would turn out so well. Or, that Archie. You know he's living here too."

"Oh, sure. Go ahead, Emmy." Bar leaned out to wave at Mac, who waved his cap happily after them.

Emmy nodded thanks to Mac and put her foot on the gas pedal. "Who is Mr. Manders really?"

Bar, slouching down comfortably beside her, said, "Tsar of the place, near as I can make out. Clout, as I say. He owns one of the houses. He spends enough time and money to induce a certain respect."

"Do I turn here?"

"Right. I mean left. I mean yes, you do, but not so fast."

Blue stones had clattered up under the wheels of her car. Emmy said, startled, "Dear me! They do go in for luxury here."

"You haven't seen the half of it. Well, you haven't seen any of it, have you? The Judge said this was your first trip here."

Emmy nodded, fascinated by the glimpses of lights shining among trees and shrubbery. The condominiums looked very, very elegant, and if she knew the Judge, they were elegant.

Bar rubbed his hand across his hair, which she seemed to have known for years and years, black, thick and unruly; she knew his face, too, not handsome but a good face with strong features, a mouth which could smile and eyes which could—she stopped herself. Eyes could tell lies, couldn't they? They certainly had at one time. She stiffened her spine a bit and said, in spite of herself, "I'm surprised to see that you are apparently on such good terms with China and the Judge."

There was, she felt, some swift speculation and perhaps some amusement in his quick look at her. She wasn't sure that he was smiling but thought it likely.

"Sure," he said, "why not?"

"You know perfectly well why not!" she snapped, responding to a sudden urge.

She felt the look he gave her again. She also felt, rather than saw, a little smile; it was in his voice, however, when he said, "You mean because China married the Judge instead of me. My dear, I have no control over China. No—look out! Turn left again."

She jerked the wheel around, barely avoiding a cluster of mailboxes that loomed up in the headlights.

"China is very happily married to your uncle," Bar said. "He is very happy married to her. Call it a June-and-January marriage if you like, but they are really very pleased with each other. Especially," Bar added thoughtfully, "since China is such a perfectly fabulous cook."

"Cook! China?" China had many gifts, but as far as Emmy knew, cooking was not one of them. "Now where?"

"Just keep going. That's Kate's house over there."

"Oh yes. I'm going to stay with her. That is, I phoned her and she said all right."

"Kate?" He sounded surprised.

"Of course, she is my sister."

"Yes, well—but—I don't think you are going to want to stay there."

"If you mean that Kate and I don't always get along—"

"I didn't mean that. I know you like dogs, but . . ."

"Dogs!" She braked, stopped the car and stared at him. "What on earth do you mean! People or—"

"Oh, I mean animals," Bar said hastily. "You see, Kate is in one of her do-good moods."

"I don't understand you . . ."

"Just what I said. There was a loving little bitch who was too loving at the wrong time, apparently. Seven puppies. They are not allowed here."

"Oh, come on, Bar! Explain—"

"That's all, really. No, it isn't quite all. You see, there's an Alpine Village Board, elected by the owners of the condos. One of their rules is: no more than two dogs (if that) to a house. The puppies, along with their mother, were found by Kate on a sofa in The Barn. They were about to be—well, sent to the happy hunting ground, if you want to put it that way. Anyway, Kate adopted the whole batch, mother and all. They have the entire use of her only spare bedroom. Aside from hundreds of leaflets and newspapers."

"But Kate isn't such a reader—"

"Oh, the newspapers are for the puppies. On the floor. She's paper-training them."

"Kate! But Kate is—"

"I know. Finically tidy. But she feels that if the puppies are at least paper-trained, if not housebroken, she'll have a better chance of wishing them off on her friends." He paused. "I bet you're slated for one of them. You'd think they had different fathers. Not one looks at all like any other. If I were you, I'd choose a kind of poodle-collie mix. Of course, the mother has a quite unidentifiable bloodline. Nice dog, though."

Emmy cried, "But I can't take a puppy!" Bar had never even seen her apartment. "Dogs are not permitted where I live."

After a pause he said mildly, "Oh, I imagine you can get around that. After you've seen the puppies. Of course, though, the poodle-collie is the runt. Big bones that he'll grow into eventually but hasn't yet, and the other pups seem to hassle him a bit."

She wished her heart wouldn't soften puppyward. She didn't intend it to soften in any direction. "Well, I can't have a dog. What are the leaflets for?"

"You'll hear all about those. If I know Kate, she'll have you

addressing them. Really, she's been having a fine time in Alpine Village. All sorts of city boards in Appledown, near here. You must have driven through it. But the puppies—you see, my house is next to Kate's and the puppies are growing fast. They've reached the barking stage and make a bit of a racket. Rather discourages interested buyers, and I do want to sell that house, as I told you."

Kate Brace, almost ten years older than Emmy, had already come into her share of what was left of the family estate. Emmy would have to wait two more years before she received her share. Kate had put much of her inheritance into real estate. Emmy knew that Bar spoke the truth about the Alpine Village condominiums, which had appreciated almost preposterously in value.

Bar sighed. "I've been renting Mother's house for the last year and a half. A fine high rent, too, I will say that. Very welcome to a young but brilliant upcoming lawyer."

"It's fine to speak well of yourself. One likes to know."

Bar chuckled. "Thought that would interest you. Well, the catch to that lovely rental is that it is taxable. So it simmers down to not such a beautiful rental. I really do want to sell the place," he said seriously. "It isn't as if it has much sentimental pull for me. My mother bought it because she wanted to get rid of that white elephant of a house where I was born—at least I wasn't precisely born there, a hospital no less. But I loved it and so did she. It was simply too much expense, too much care—in short, too much. So —oh, you know all this . . ."

She thought back over two years. Bar gone to work in Boston, true. She had been in New York—not far from Boston. Yet if or when he was in New York, he had never so much as invited her to—oh, even to a movie, let alone dinner. But there was a time, not too long ago, when she'd have been—*no,* she told herself firmly, as she had for what seemed a long time, *no,* she had not, positively not, been heartbroken by his defection. Actually, her common sense had always told her that nobody, *nobody* could resist China's loveliness and vivacious charm. Certainly two years ago Bar hadn't tried, apparently, to resist. But then China married the Judge, Emmy's uncle. Emmy herself had introduced them.

She did not really approve of the marriage even if it cut short Bar's liberally displayed infatuation with China. He did not, in fact, jilt Emmy, but his sudden lack of interest, once he met China, amounted to the same thing. He had certainly given all his time and devotion to China.

Emmy had been in love with Bar . . . how long? Probably since she was a child, certainly by the time she reached seventeen or eighteen. Bar had liked her. He came to see her; he took her dancing, skating, everywhere—for a while. Then he met China.

Even if she had had a hope that after China's marriage to the Judge, Bar would come back to her, it had been a faint hope. Also, she knew, a very humble and forgiving hope. It was a hope which she could not approve of herself.

She had been wrong, the whole time. Bar had been faithful to China; at least she certainly had heard nothing at all from him even after China's wedding. It was so quiet a ceremony, in some other judge's chambers, that not even Emmy or Kate had been invited.

Bar said almost absently, as if thinking of something else, "I'm coming to New York now, if arrangements don't fall apart. I hope eventually to become a partner in a well-established firm. Meanwhile, I'd like to sell this house. It's been a good investment. That is, it should prove to be a good investment. The money value of a house is always only the price one gets for it. Turn right."

Through the trees, bright lights were winding nearer. Bar laughed softly. "See that! China has put on all the lights. I'll bet the Judge is telling her off for spending so much on electricity. On second thought, probably not." He added seriously, "He really is devoted to her, Emmy. And she to him. Slow down. That's right. Here we are. Turn into this driveway. Now then, wait a minute."

He fumbled in a pocket, drew out a small white box and pressed a button. The door of a large garage slid upward, slowly and majestically; it rolled smoothly out of sight.

"Dear, dear," said Emmy.

The garage lit up as the door glided upward. There were commodious spaces for three automobiles: a long car, probably the Judge's, a smaller car, probably China's, and an empty space for Emmy's car or a visitor's. She slid into it, shut off the motor, looked around at the rigidly neat garage—with its carefully coiled garden hose on its standard, a sundial, stored for the winter, in one corner, and the tidy doors of what appeared to be a long cupboard along a wall—and sighed. "Dear, dear," she said again. "Home was never like this." Her mind flashed back to the ancient red barn, made over with rather uneven car spaces, of her childhood.

"Wait till you see the house. Everything that can work by itself does."

"What heaven!" Emmy said. "That one little box. Works by—"

"Remote control, naturally. Come on. They know you're here. There's China."

China came running, laughing, into a stream of light from an open door of the house. Bar pulled out the small suitcase Emmy had brought and went ahead toward the lit doorway. China had flung herself at Emmy. "Emmy! It is simply great, great, great to have you here! Just wait till you see the house. It's like something out of a fairy tale."

"Come in," the Judge bellowed from the doorway. "You two little idiots, don't you know it's turning very cold! Oh, thank you, Bar. How about dinner with us?"

China, hugging Emmy, put out one arm suddenly and took Bar's hand. "Of course Bar will stay for dinner."

There was a proprietorial tone in her voice and gesture which stiffened Emmy. If China wanted both Bar and the Judge, she'd try to keep them.

But Bar was shaking his head, smiling but firm.

China let go of Emmy to put both her hands on Bar's arms. "Please stay, Bar," she whispered. "That awful man is here."

Before she could continue, the Judge entered the garage and said warmly, "Nobody is more welcome, Bar—do stay."

Two

Bar said, "No, thank you." He deposited the suitcase and Emmy's forgotten handbag inside the entrance door. He bid a pleasant "Good night" in a general way and started walking down the driveway. The crisp rattle of his footsteps made a kind of period to the few moments of talk he and Emmy had had. China drew Emmy quickly into the light and warmth of the house. China looked, as always, very, very pretty.

The Judge had followed and was beaming, although he was not a man who often beamed. He was as dapper, as neat and precise, even more youthful-looking than formerly; obviously he was a happy man. China wore a substantial white apron over her ruffly blue dress; she turned her delicate little nose toward what must be the kitchen, for fragrant odors were wafting along the hall from that direction. The Judge embraced Emily heartily (smelling, as always, of after-shave lotion and cigar smoke). China said, "You can go to your room later, Emmy. There's a washroom over there, under the stairs." She disappeared at a graceful little trot. The Judge waved his neat, small hand toward a door. "In there, Emmy. Drinks are waiting. You are a little late . . ."

Emmy had a flashing glimpse of elegance and luxury; it seemed to be a small but beautifully decorated house. Lights were everywhere; a familiar painting, a Utrillo which she remembered had always pleased the Judge, hung in a conspicuous spot along the hall. She let herself into a washroom which was so lavishly and luxuriously appointed, including the soaps and hand-lotion bottles, that she thought rather coldly of her own small bathroom, efficient, yes, but never with gold (or at least gilded) faucets. There was an agreeable scent from the soaps.

When she emerged she was led by the crackling of a fire to a room off the almost manorial hall—almost manorial if on a very small scale. It proved to be the Judge's library. Beaming again, he ushered her in and shoved a chair at her—or rather, Emmy thought, amused—he shoved Emmy at a chair. "Now then, martinis still?"

She nodded and then saw a man standing in a corner, simply looking at her, but also looking rather out of place and faintly awkward. China's "awful man" probably, whoever he was. But the Judge indicated an introduction merely by waving the hand which was not occupied in mixing cocktails in a handsome silver pitcher.

Nobody could be more suave and graceful socially than the Judge when he chose to be. At the same time, nobody could be more autocratic in setting up his own rules, one of which was that any guests in his home ought to be able to introduce themselves; his invitation alone should suffice as to their qualifications, so he expected them to introduce themselves. It was not always a convenient or helpful rule.

The "awful man"—if he *was* the awful man China had complained about—probably was not accustomed to the Judge's arbitrary way with his guests. He looked embarrassed and nodded. Emmy nodded in return and the thought crossed her mind that he looked vaguely familiar, but before she could consider it further the Judge came to her, smiling. "I think it's the way you like it, Emmy." He watched anxiously as she sipped. She was pleased because he remembered that she liked martinis. She wondered briefly what could be so awful about her fellow guest.

"Expect you get plenty of these in your job," the Judge said, but not quite so pleasantly.

"Well, no," Emmy said honestly, "there's not much time for drinking. It's a hard job, you know, Uncle."

The Judge was legally her uncle, a younger stepbrother of her father's, and thus her father had left Emmy in the Judge's care, as trustee of his estate. Emmy was very young at the time her mother and then her father died and the Judge, rather young himself then, undertook that position with great and, Emmy felt sure, sincere affection. He had encouraged her to call him Uncle and indeed he did give her what parental care and advice she had ever had, aside from Kate's rather acid and condescending admonitions to a much younger (and certainly in Kate's view, a bothersome) sister.

"Now then!" The Judge settled himself in a big brown leather chair which Emmy also recognized from his bachelor library in the years past. "I sent for you to tell you that you must give up this ridiculous job of yours."

Emmy swallowed too hastily and sputtered. The Judge kept on beaming, but there was a steely glint in his gray eyes which forbade undignified behavior. "But, Uncle, it's not a ridiculous job at all. It is very hard work."

"I never *see* you working very hard," he said pleasantly but still with underlying disapproval.

"But of course you don't! You don't see half—a tenth—you wouldn't believe the staff that makes that program possible!"

"Really?" The Judge twirled his own glass, eying it, Emmy couldn't help thinking, suspiciously. She was beginning to feel a little suspicious herself. She knew the Judge was up to something and couldn't guess what, unless he felt that the whole television world was something rather vulgar as, incredibly, some people still appeared to do. She did know that for years he had hidden a small, inconspicuous television set behind a sofa but near enough to a comfortable armchair to watch any program that interested him. But surely now—she glanced around and saw that indeed his secret affection for television had been permitted to emerge into the open—there was the machine snugly ensconced against a wall opposite the Judge's armchair. An excellent set, too, she noted, with a quick glimpse at the make. He had seen her glance and smiled.

"Oh, yes. I'm not such an old dodo as you seem to think, Emmy. I like television. Yes," he said thoughtfully as if delivering a judicial opinion, "I like it very much. Some of it. Mainly I listen to the news. And that is what I do not understand, Emmy. You have a job there, I know, being your trustee and overseeing your financial affairs, and—well, in any event, I know that you are paid very well. Exceedingly well for a young woman," he added.

He hadn't intended to express condescension; he had intended to compliment her, Emmy knew. All the same, the little note of patronization irritated her. She downed more of her martini. The somewhat pallid young man sat in a corner, apparently brooding over a very elegant oxford, and didn't seem to like his drink, which was a colorless liquid of some kind. Straight vodka, she decided, not even on the rocks; but surely there must be some kind of soda or quinine water added to it; nobody could even sip straight vodka without showing signs of having been unexpectedly bitten, as Emmy had discovered in her one experimental gesture.

He was a rather slight, pale young man, thirtyish—no, perhaps forty—not a young face but not an old one either; he was handsomely tailored, so impressively unwrinkled that his black slacks and neat white turtleneck sweater and good tweed jacket looked almost as if he had purchased them that day. His thin brown hair shone neatly as if watered down; his pale eyes seemed melancholy, but he listened with interest as the Judge spoke. His ears were practically sticking out, Emmy thought; he must be a devoted television viewer. There was a vast audience for television, as Emmy saw when she made the slightest, smallest error in the material she researched, wrote up, then submitted to writers and editors who didn't trust anybody, it seemed to her, not to make errors.

"Yes. I expect it is a large staff," the Judge said pensively, as if following her own thoughts, which as a rule he was all too likely to do. But then his years on the bench, as well as his youthful years as prosecuting attorney, had developed in him powers of observation as alert as those of a wild animal, instinctively wary of any slight sound or movement.

Emmy nodded. "We get letters if I—if anyone goes wrong on the backgrounds. This is a very good martini, Uncle Judge."

He sprang up. He was so neatly articulated in every motion that he moved like a young and active man. He was energetic, no question of that. She said, "Still playing golf, Uncle?"

He frowned. "Really, Emmy! I'm not in my dotage. Of course I'm still playing golf. There's a fine course right here on the grounds. Tennis, too. A couple of courts. Oh, we have everything here in Alpine Village."

"How did you happen to buy the condominium?" She had seen China rarely since her marriage. The latest meeting was a hurried lunch a few weeks ago.

"Oh, it was Kate." The Judge brought Emmy a second drink and China came in, her cheeks pink, bearing a handsome plate of hors d'oeuvres, which she set on a table.

"You'll have to help yourselves unless you want to pass them, Judge."

Emmy wondered vaguely if China always called her husband Judge. Probably she did. Emmy herself would have to rummage in her memory to dig out the Judge's Christian name. Ah, there she had it: Harry. Judge Harry Doane. His opponents, or at least the people who didn't like some of his decisions, had called him Handsome Harry. And he had handed out some very stiff sentences, Emmy knew; she also knew that he was completely, utterly intrepid on the bench.

"Don't just let them stand there," China said and vanished kitchenward again. The Judge smiled under his neat gray mustache. "Here, my dear Emmy—oh, thank you." This he addressed to the silent young man who had stirred himself to pass the appetizers, which proved to be smoked salmon on thin slices of toast and red caviar on tiny rounds of rye bread. Very fine and very extravagant, Emmy couldn't help noting.

She asked, munching, "What did Kate have to do with your buying this house?"

"Glad you call it a house." The Judge seated himself again. "People around here call them condos. Only that! A *condo*!" He growled over it and took another slice of rye bread and caviar.

"But it's easier than 'condominium.' " Emmy reached for more smoked salmon.

The pale man settled himself again near the wall.

"Surely you knew that Kate had used part of her inheritance to buy property here—very wisely, I might add," the Judge continued.

"Oh, yes. That is, I know her address. But I've never seen her"—out of consideration for the Judge's feelings she avoided the word "condo," which indeed seemed very sensible to her, and said "—house. But I've never actually been here, as you know."

The Judge's neat mustache twitched as if he'd like to smile but thought it indiscreet. "Well, I know that you and Kate are not precisely bosom friends."

"Please, Uncle Judge! We *are* sisters. She knows I'm coming. I phoned her."

"But China is expecting you to stay with us," the Judge said severely.

"Thank you. But I haven't seen Kate for quite a long time and somehow I didn't expect these—these houses to have many bedrooms. I'll explain to China. I'll stay with Kate." If the puppies permit, she thought, remembering Bar's warning.

"Her house is charming. When we came back from England, we drove out here to see her. I had some business to transact with her, giving up my duties as her trustee and so forth. I think China had had enough of cold, damp baronial houses while we visited in England. Some very pleasant people, my—our friends there, but their houses . . ." He shivered realistically. "Cold! We saw Kate's place. Everything so comfortable, so easy. Fireplaces and warmth if you only touch a tiny little switch." He nodded toward the hall. "Just give it a flick and set the temperature to whatever you want and there it is, by the time I get the newspaper in. Or in hot weather, a flick the other way, set the temperature to whatever is comfortable and the whole place is cool. Comfort," he said thoughtfully, "is a great thing."

"Yes." Emmy concurred with feeling. Her own apartment in the city had reluctant and clanking radiators which sent up heat twice a day, early in the morning and at six o'clock at night. No persuasion of any kind could induce the superintendent to undertake any other plan, no persuasion and no weather. He had explained, on far too numerous occasions, that the thermometer was outside the building (on the second floor level as it happened; Emmy's apartment was on the twelfth floor and got the north and west winds). And, said the superintendent, the law was that only when the outdoor thermometer showed fifty-five could he allow extra heat —or indeed, any heat. She had tried to reason with him about that, but when she commented adversely on the position of the thermometer at the second floor, protected from wind by other buildings, he had shown no yielding. All the same, it was an attractive (if hideously expensive) place, small but large enough for occasional little dinner parties.

"Tomorrow you'll see the grounds for yourself," the Judge went on. "Every effort was made by the builder to preserve the natural contours of the land. Luckily, toward the north they contrived to fit in a golf course. Otherwise the hills, woods are just as they were in the time the Indians hunted here. Of course, I'll admit the name Alpine Village is a bit fanciful, but still there are some pretty rugged hills about here. The roads connecting the houses are planned carefully. No house can see into another house. Oh, every possible privacy is provided." He paused. "I'm not trying to sell you a house, Emmy. But if you should want to invest—and a good investment it has been, I must say—there's Bar's house. He wants to sell and you can take the money from your present investments. Those bonds you have—of course, as your adviser I'm afraid you'd have to get my consent before you change any major investments. Now, Kate—"

China came in, minus the apron, her cheeks pink. "Kate!" she said scornfully. Then she giggled. "Emmy, you'd never guess her latest hobby. It's selling bras in New Zealand or—no, perhaps some of the African countries or—"

"China!" The Judge exclaimed. But it was in feigned reproach. His eyes were dancing. "You're making that up. Kate is no fool. She came to talk to me the other day. She's going to try for politics."

China blinked. "All the same, from what we see on television sometimes, bras are very much needed—here and there," she added hurriedly. "Politics! How will she start that? What is she aiming for? President?"

"China," the Judge said reproachfully but still fondly. "You know better than that. If she's really serious about it, and I think she is, she'll have to start at a very low level. Doorbell-ringing, that kind of thing. Speaking at every possible occasion—"

"She's very good at that," China said irrepressibly. "Tells people just what to do."

Emmy agreed, but silently. "Kate has a good brain," she said loyally and added rather wistfully, "and more energy in her little finger than I have in my whole body."

"You're not so dumb," China flashed. "Or lazy! You went out and got a job and your own apartment, all on your own. Oh, dinner is ready. And I will say, it's a good one."

It was more than a good dinner; it was practically a great dinner. Emmy thought with distaste of her own usual hurried, on-the-go meals, sometimes dinners at a little restaurant near her apartment, or her own efforts at scrambled eggs or anything, in fact, that could be prepared quickly and still satisfy hunger. The little parties she sometimes planned had to be catered—and paid for!

The soup was green turtle, liberally laced with sherry. Next came a small serving of sole, which, Emmy believed, tasting it, had been poached in white wine. The roast was precisely rare enough; pickled walnuts turned up with that, also a Yorkshire pudding which was so good that its British cousins would have fallen even soggier than their custom at its look and taste; the endive and blanched-almond salad couldn't have been better, and then—oh, then China produced her masterpiece, a chocolate mousse which had to be sampled to be believed. She said as much to China, who glowed.

The Judge, probably in deference to the delectable food, did not again bring up his absurd suggestion that Emmy leave her cherished job, not even his reasons for making such a recommendation. Of course, coming from the Judge, it had sounded more like a command than a mere suggestion, but that, Emmy told herself between bites, was only the way the Judge sometimes spoke. There was a little talk about Alpine Village: its nearness to New York, yet its completely countrylike living.

"But we've fallen into a nest of splendid cooks," China said rather pensively. "Nobody has a professional cook around here. Can't find one. We are too near White Plains, Mount Kisco and Greenwich, and anyway, I'm not sure there *are* any cooks anywhere. In these days. Everybody cooks for herself. So," she concluded with well-earned pride, "I went to cooking school. And I really like it."

"So do we," Emmy said warmly.

The Judge nodded, his mouth full of chocolate mousse. But then he talked again, although in a rather desultory way, about the condominium situation. "Everybody I know has sold a big house —not so much trouble here—everything done for us."

"Expensive," China said gently.

"But worth it. You'll see, Emmy. We live in a kind of enclave here. It's really a cul-de-sac. Kate has one of the houses. Bar's mother left him her house. Archie Callser has one—you remember Archie." He didn't wait for Emmy's reply but went on, "And our house. No other close neighbors. You can see lights through the trees and shrubbery, but our little area is quite protected—yes, yes —excellent dinner, my dear."

Naturally, in view of the food, there was not much conversation.

The thin young man didn't say a word; he ate, however, as if he'd never had another meal and was afraid he would never have one again. It seemed strange to Emmy that so thin and cadaverous-looking a young man could store away so much food. But she was doing pretty well herself, too.

The Judge had brought out what China said happily was his very best Burgundy; it certainly did not detract from the pleasure of the dinner. Neither, however, did it seem to promote anything but torporous satisfaction.

Later China served coffee and brandy in the living room. The Judge lit the fire already laid. It snapped and crackled. The young man sat against the wall, digesting probably, Emmy thought. China, with a curiously serious look on her pretty face, vanished, murmuring excuses. Nobody could help; she had everything organized. Nobody was to move. She trotted away, happy about the dinner she had achieved, and it was indeed an achievement, but there was a certain expediency about her departure. So, Emmy thought, the Judge had something serious to say to her.

Yet the pale young man remained.

The flaming row between the Judge and Emmy began abruptly. It ended abruptly too, with Emmy's slamming out the door, remembering barely in time to snatch her coat. She started out to find Kate's house, having not the least idea where, amid the circles of roads, the crowding shrubbery, the looming shapes of boulders, it might be.

There were scattered low lights along the roads, set discreetly at about waist height. There were dimly shining lights from other houses, but they, too, were so discreetly situated that they seemed very far from one another. Somewhere in the darkness a dog barked.

Kate's dog? It might be. Emmy tried to discover the direction of the bark, and a man's figure loomed up near her, coming rapidly along the road.

He saw her and stopped. "Why, Emmy!"

It was Bar again and very welcome. She clutched at his arm. "Bar, I've had the most terrible scene with the Judge. I told him just what I thought of him and what he had done and—you can't imagine what he has done! Oh, Bar!"

"Steady now. He can't kill you, you know. He's sentenced many people to death—or at least life sentences or something—but not you. Where are you going?"

"Kate's house, of course, if I can find it."

"I'll take you there. Come on. Here—why, you are shaking with cold—"

"No, it's fury! Do you know what he did?"

"You were trying to tell me." His arm went around her and she was thankful for its warmth and steadiness.

She stopped shaking. "He got me fired! He did! He knows somebody high up at the network. The Judge knows everybody. All he had to do, I suppose, was say that I was his—in a way his ward as well as his niece—and he had other plans for me, so he resigned my job in my name. And wait a minute. That's not all. He has a murderer staying there! A man he sentenced, Homer Jones!"

"He— Why, is *that* the scrawny young man who is their guest? It can't be!"

"Yes! He is! Homer Jones! And that's not all. The Judge says I'm in great danger! Danger. That's what he said. And oh, Bar, that's not the worst of it!"

Three

They scrunched around a curve.

"It's bad enough," Bar said. "Here's Kate's house. I'll take you in and then I'll just whistle for her dog. She can't be out for romance this time, but we certainly don't want any more puppies. At least, I don't think Kate does. She has another bee in her bonnet, I hear." He led Emmy into the house and put her down rather forcefully in a chair. He lit a fire, which blazed up in a perfectly normal way.

Nothing else in the world was normal—except, of course, Bar and a fire and warmth.

Bar looked down at her soberly. So, she thought, still angry, he did believe her. However, she didn't quite believe herself. Yet the scene in the living room with the Judge was clear and hideously real.

Bar was wearing the sheepskin-lined coat, his hair ruffled by the wind. He disappeared for a moment or two and came back with a glass in his hand. "Here. Drink this."

"No. I think I've had too much already."

"Then a little more won't hurt you. Drink it." He actually held the glass to her lips. Her teeth seemed to chatter against it. Yet the stinging warmth was helpful.

"I've got to tell you!"

"All right. I want to hear. I'll just get Kate's dog back first. I promised to see to her." He went to open the door; an icy blast of wind swept through the room and made the flames dance. His whistle was shrill and almost at once productive, for an overly fat, indescribably raffish dog waddled into the room, gave Emmy an indifferent glance, gave Bar an equally indifferent lick on his hand and trotted out of sight down the hall. Bar disappeared and, apparently, opened a door, for all at once a tumult of barks burst out. The door banged and Bar came back, half grinning. "The fountain of nourishment returned. Although actually the pups have been weaned. They are getting too big to be called puppies. Now then —" He dropped his coat, pulled up a footstool and sat down. "Now then, let's have it. All."

"You won't believe me."

"I can try. But not all at once, *please.* Just begin at the beginning. You said he resigned you from your job. How could he do that?"

"He couldn't. At least—no, he can't. But he says he can. Because I'm not twenty-five, and he has my power of attorney and will control my affairs until I'm twenty-five, and he says my entire income is involved, so I can't touch a single penny without his consent. He's going to starve me out if I don't accede to his demand!" she cried furiously.

"Oh, I don't think he can go that far." Bar was again very serious. "First, tell me *why* he wants to get you out of your job. Why does he say it is dangerous?"

"Because of the research I'm doing, I guess. I'm never before a camera, of course. Never. I'm not that important. I'm just the smallest cog in the wheels. But I do research—oh, all kinds of research. And I have to be accurate about it, too.

"Oh," said Bar. "Well, now how about danger to you? And what does this—this Homer Jones have to do with it? Wasn't he convicted of murder?"

"He *was* a murderer, I mean *is.* You remember the case! Homer Jones was tried and convicted, and the Judge sentenced him and then, just lately, he saw to it that Jones was paroled to himself. I mean, the Judge. He said he had had to pronounce sentence because it was the jury's decision. But he never thought it was right, he told me. So before he retired—did you know he had retired?" she asked on a tangent.

Bar nodded once. "Sure. China made it a condition for marriage.

Listen, Emmy. Tell it all just as you remember it. Words, everything. *Accurately.*" He grinned with a spark of teasing. "I believe you are a good reporter. Now, take it easy. Word for word in sequence. It's fresh in your memory, I'm sure." There was the faintest little, but reassuringly normal, smile in his eyes.

It was indeed very fresh in her memory. It had begun, of course, during their before-dinner drinks when the Judge told her she must give up her absurd job. She hadn't taken his words seriously at first. It didn't seem possible that the Judge meant to control her actions to that extent; she simply, she told Bar half tearfully, put it aside as one of the Judge's casual remarks. But then—oh, then over coffee the Judge reminded her that he was her trustee until she was twenty-five and that she had agreed to a power of attorney for him.

"Of course I remember," she had told the Judge. "I don't understand why you—"

"Why I am so serious about it? You will." The Judge leaned back. He must have looked just like that when presiding in court. Very calm, very cautious, very determined. "The present subject is the Homer Jones murder. I understand there is to be a series concerning famous but fairly recent murders."

"Why, yes!"

"Shocking taste," said the Judge, twirling his glass of brandy but keeping a daggerlike gaze on Emmy. "I must make you see that you are in a very dangerous position engaging in this"—he shrugged—"they call it research."

"But it is research," Emmy had flashed.

"Granted," said the Judge coolly. "You do not appear yourself on the screen—"

Emmy interrupted again. "How could I! I'm not a star or a face that anybody knows or—you don't understand. I *am* a researcher."

"Only a researcher, yes. Too bad. I'm sure you were disappointed. Before we go further I ought to explain Mr. Jones here. Homer Jones."

Homer Jones! She stared at the pale, self-effacing young man. She was quite unable to believe her ears. She had done little in the past weeks but study the news accounts of the murder of his wife, Belle Jones. With a butcher knife! Horrible!

That young man? So that was why she thought she'd seen him somewhere before. He shuffled one foot and then the other and looked rather like a kind but guilty dog imploring forgiveness.

Before she could stop herself Emmy cried, "But you—he is supposed to be in the penitentiary! A life sentence—the judge—but —but you were the judge! You sentenced him. You!" she shouted at her uncle.

The Judge twirled his glass again. "I didn't wish to sentence him. I did not believe that the evidence presented was sufficient for the guilty verdict. The jury believed otherwise, so sentencing was mandatory. However, I will say that I have been instrumental in getting him paroled. He had to have a job, a condition of the parole. So he is now," the Judge stated coolly, "working for me. An excellent solution. He is helping me assemble material for my autobiography."

Emmy checked her recital to look at Bar. "I should have thought that Archie Callser would prefer to do that."

Bar went to the fire, took a brass poker and prodded at the flames absently. "Oh, Archie wouldn't mind. That is, I don't know if he's aware of the Judge's decision to write an autobiography. Let me tell you, by the way, that the Judge is going to have to concentrate on the most dramatic episodes of his career if he expects anybody to show interest in the autobiography of another retired judge. The lawmen indeed have been noted for their abysmal silence about anything that hinges on professional secrets. So—but never mind that. No, Archie won't mind. He's out here, you know."

"Out here! Oh, yes, you or Mac mentioned him. Why on earth?"

"Bought a nearby house. He knows the architect for Alpine Village. So do I, as a matter of fact. We were once in school together. That's why I was pleased when my mother decided to buy a place here. I'm sorry, really sorry, to sell it. But that's another matter. Archie would be the most logical person to help the Judge with his memoirs: After all, he was the Judge's main factotum while the Judge was in office. But I don't think Archie really wants to. He has gone out for himself lately. He's a junior member of a very fine architect's firm. No, it won't hurt his feelings to be left out of the tedious business of the Judge's memoirs. Probably very thankful if or when he hears about it. I suppose the Judge took on this—this Homer Jones as sort of proof that he believed him to be wrongly accused. Proof that the presiding judge himself thought him wrongly convicted, although he obviously could not dismiss the case. Really, when you think about it, it is good of the Judge. He's an honorable man, no doubt of that."

"He's a meddlesome busybody!"

"N-no. I'm not so sure. You see, Emmy"—he turned around, sat down on the footstool again and looked at her seriously—"surely you must see why he decided that since you are digging into all the details as a matter of research, it would be just possible that you might uncover a hint of the real murderer, as the Judge believes there is one. Only a remote chance but—yes, it could be dangerous for you."

Emmy was receiving too many shocks in too short a time. First, merely seeing Bar again, being with him even so briefly, hearing what he said about China (and noticing China's still proprietorial manner with him), all that had been, in its way, a deep but inner shock. She was sure that she had put the whole episode of Bar's defection aside, yet it had been a kind of jolt to see him again so unexpectedly.

The dinner, and all the wine, and the Judge's utterly unexpected, crushing declaration were another kind of shock.

She stared at Bar. "But I—I don't know anything like that! How could I? Only what was in the newspapers and . . ."

Bar waited. After a moment he said softly, "And what?"

Emmy was beginning to feel a kind of inward shakiness, not identifiable. It was rather as if she had unintentionally stepped into a small fringe of quicksand. If she went further, she might find herself drawn into the sucking depths of the whole.

"Now I'm being silly," she said aloud.

"You may be," Bar said equably. "But let me hear what has occurred to you."

"I can't be in danger, I mean danger from the real murderer, even if the Judge thinks there is a real murderer and he's afraid I'll bring—"

"Danger, sure. Remember, Emmy, the Judge is an honest and reasonable man. Isn't he?"

"Y-yes, well, he always has been that, I guess. But that man! At the dinner table! Staying there as a guest!"

Again Bar waited a moment. Then he said, "Did he hear all this conversation?"

"Yes. Oh, yes. He was right there."

"How did he take it?"

"He listened. At least, he was sitting near a wall, and honestly, I thought he was trying to get through it backwards." She said it drearily.

A spark of light came into Bar's eyes. "I take it he didn't succeed."

"Oh, don't make fun of me, Bar. My job—it's so very important to me. I'm just beginning to make a little headway. Everybody else is so much more experienced and quick and—" She flashed up in anger again. "I tried to tell the Judge how many people were involved in one single half-hour—or hour—of broadcasting. Why, he didn't even know what a crawl is."

"Thought it some obnoxious form of the insect world?"

"I couldn't make him see how many people work behind the scenes. Researchers, yes. The writers. The editors. But also the camera crews, on tap day and night. The foreign hookups. The telephones. The light men, working, working. The—oh, the typists, the scene shifters, the—he wouldn't listen. I explained that a lot of them don't even know my name. I'm too lowly—that is, no! I won't say lowly, because I do work very hard. I do indeed, Bar."

"I'm sure of it, Emmy." He looked thoughtfully at the red flames and said absently, "I see that Kate has managed to get some applewood. Or rather, I smell it. *Did* you find any evidence about the murder that struck you as—out of line? Not quite according to facts?"

"No! Oh, well . . ." She thought of what had seemed miles of microfilm, passing slowly as her hand cranked the viewing machine which the library had most obligingly arranged for research.

"What about it, Emmy? Any brain waves on your part?"

"No! Of course, it did strike me that the evidence, most of it, was circumstantial. Except, of course, for the butcher knife." She swallowed hard but looked straight at Bar. "That butcher knife, their own, seemed to be a very strong piece of evidence against Homer Jones. At least the jury thought so. Although, of course, anybody who had entered their apartment could have gotten into the kitchen and gotten out that horrible knife. Oh, Bar, it was really a massacre. I didn't even like to read about it. The knife argued against premeditation. It also was circumstantial."

She thought briefly back to the moment when the Judge, eying the roast beef, whetted his carving knife and tested its sharp edge with his thumb. Had Homer Jones so much as winced? No. He had merely looked hungry.

She said thoughtfully, "The Judge always says that most evidence *is* circumstantial."

"A trout in the milk?"

"Well, yes. He always said that if anybody is going to murder somebody, he doesn't invite people to watch him do it. That is, aside from some barroom brawl or widely shouted family quarrel. He does admit the trout in the milk as being convincing. But he always said that you rarely find a trout in the milk. People are too smart for that, he said. A drunken quarrel, a wild, possibly drug-induced quarrel ending with murder, yes. He always said this is different and probable."

"I take it you did not find even the famous trout."

"No." There must have been a faint uncertainty in her reply, for he turned around abruptly and caught her hand. "Out with it, Emmy. You thought of something or other that didn't square with the evidence presented in court. Is that it?"

"N-no. No."

"Come on now, Emmy. This is important, you know."

"Well, but—"

"The Judge just could be right, you know. If you did happen on some—call it notion, some item that didn't quite square with the accepted facts—then Emmy, my dear, the Judge could be right."

She swallowed hard. "You *can't* mean me! In danger!"

"I can. We'll have to see about that. Where are your notes? I take it you kept notes."

"Oh, yes. Loads of them."

"Where are they?"

"In my suitcase. Oh, no! I shoved them in my handbag just as I was leaving my apartment."

"You left it at China's?"

"Yes, I simply snatched my coat and ran! But honestly, Bar—"

"Were the notes typed? So anybody could read them. That is, provided your typing has improved recently."

She ignored the quite justifiable slur. Her typing was too quick, too faulty, too utterly stupid, she reflected dismally. "No. In shorthand."

"*Whose shorthand?* A recognized one, like Gregg's?"

"No. I tried to learn that but it seemed easier just to invent my own sort of—well, private shorthand. I mean—"

"You mean that you would know what some scribble of yours meant but nobody else would be likely to decipher it. That's what I thought. Oh, Emmy, you were not made to go on a witness stand. Never mind. I'll get the handbag. And your suitcase. Now."

"Oh, no, please. I'll borrow something from Kate."

He eyed her speculatively and rose. "Somehow I can't see you in the doubtlessly worthy and sensible night clothes which Kate would supply you with. Besides, I told you, Kate's waifs have the extra bedroom. I don't think you'd get much sleep."

"But Kate is expecting me. I can drive back to town tonight instead, of course."

"No, you can't. Emmy, you must believe me. The Judge could be right, and if he is, you are in—yes, I'm going to say it—danger. No, you cannot drive back to town tonight carrying with you what may be a loaded gun in the shape of those notes. You'll stay at my house."

"Oh, but Bar—"

"Nonsense. There's furniture, beds and linens and so on."

"I can't sleep in your house with you, Bar," she said wearily. "Thank you all the same. Kate—"

"I'm not asking you to sleep with me," Bar said patiently but with a small glint in his eyes. "I'm telling you you can use the extra bedroom in my mother's house. It's in order. I've had to keep the place in a state of gemlike cleanliness. Possible buyers are likely to arrive at any moment. Even the closets and basement are in perfect condition, neat and tidy." He was quoting a favorite phrase of Kate's. Emmy recognized it with a rather weak smile. "Now," Bar said soberly, "you said that the possible danger to you was not the worst of it."

"Oh!" She felt her cheeks flame with remembered anger. "You won't believe this! You see, my research isn't finished. There's the fact of Jones having been paroled recently. I didn't know that until the Judge told me. And he—the Judge . . ." She all but choked.

"He said that now I knew about it I would naturally add that fact to the account, the series, and bring the whole thing up and it would reflect on him, a well-known criminal judge, after all his efforts to keep it unreported and out of the media!"

Bar looked at her very seriously for a moment. Then he said, "And you would use that fact, wouldn't you?"

Emmy swallowed hard. But she was used to acknowledging any truth that her job required. "Yes. I would, Bar. I will! I have to! Don't I?"

Four

Bar thought for a moment. "I don't know. I'm not sure just how far—and I suppose the fact that the Judge is your uncle would probably be a complication."

"That's what he said! He said that if I used the information, I would be using him and his name to further my own name. My own career. He said I'd be a traitor to every fine instinct. He said —oh, Bar, he said that I was becoming unscrupulous. He said I wouldn't hesitate to put him in a bad light. He said he had made plenty of enemies in his life in court who would be happy about it. I'm sure he has many enemies. He wasn't an easy judge to come up against."

"I know."

"But all the same, facts are facts."

"*Wouldn't* it give you a certain cachet to use the parole as a recent postscript to the murder story?"

Emmy answered honestly, "Yes, I suppose it would—I mean, will add a kind of convincing news note—something that not everybody knows. He said that the powers that be have arranged it so hardly anyone is aware of it. Yes, it just might add to my standing. But that's not why I intend to use it. It's—it's professional! Isn't it?"

Bar considered. "Naturally, it could add a kind of 'I was there' note of personal experience and first-hand interest. I really don't think any writer or editor could pass up such a good climax. But, Emmy, doesn't it strike you that that might be a very cruel thing to do? Not so much for the Judge as for this man, Homer Jones?"

"I didn't even think of it until the Judge accused me. He said I would be feathering my own nest at his expense. Oh, Bar, I would never have thought he could be so—so cruel!"

"I'm not sure that is cruel," Bar said slowly. "Seems to me it wants thinking over. Meantime—"

She never heard what he meant to say, for at that instant the door was flung open. Kate entered.

It would be more appropriate to say that Kate Brace plunged into the room. Every move Kate made seemed to stir up some tangible commotion. The mother canine in the bedroom set up a vast clamor of welcome; her offspring contributed vigorously, quite as if practicing to be watchdogs. Icy winds blew in with Kate and ruffled up the rug. Even the flames in the fireplace shot up. Kate whirled around and banged the door shut. She never did anything quietly. When she turned back, a bundle of printed leaflets dropped from her gloved hands. "Oh, hello, Emmy! I forgot you were coming. China said you had arrived. She told me to bring your suitcase. Why didn't you bring it over yourself? My hands were full, so I didn't. The meeting tonight was simply superb. I could feel everybody with me. I tell you, Bar, they're going to vote for me. See if they don't."

She dropped a fur-lined coat and came forward, her solid country oxfords thumping along the floor. She kicked the rug into place and shouted "Shut up" to the dogs, who miraculously did quiet down. Perhaps not so miraculously, Emmy decided, although feeling rather guilty. Perhaps they had good reason to shut up when Kate spoke in just that voice.

Bar said in an aside to Emmy, "Your penmanship is better than your typing, I hope. All these leaflets undoubtedly must be addressed."

Kate was vigorously stirring the fire with a thrust of one of her rather large but certainly sturdy oxfords. "Get some more wood, will you, Bar? You know where it is. Now then, Emmy, what is all this about the Judge? China says you two had a disagreement.

She didn't know why. The Judge had just told her he wanted to talk seriously to you. She couldn't—at least she was in the kitchen and couldn't hear the quarrel. Probably," Kate added, "she tried to overhear."

Bar cast what could only be called a warning glance over his shoulder at Emmy. It meant, she knew: If you tell Kate, she'll tell you exactly what to do and she may be wrong. His lips even formed a word which she thought was "Quiet."

He disappeared toward, Emmy supposed, wherever Kate kept her stock of firewood. In the dining room, perhaps, or in her study, or anywhere else she found convenient. Kate lunged into a deep armchair. "Good meeting tonight! Extra good. I could feel the weight of public opinion behind me."

"What are you running for?" Emmy asked in a small voice. She never knew quite how Kate would react to even the merest polite inquiry.

Kate raised thick, emphatic eyebrows. "I should think even you would know that by now. I started campaigning last month."

Emmy felt the usual compulsion to defend herself. "I didn't know. I've been so busy . . ."

Kate gave her a suddenly purposeful look. "H'm, yes. Television. I would appreciate some assistance, Emmy. A notice—perhaps an interview with me . . ."

"Kate, I do not have anything at all to do with programing or editing. Or producing. There are entire staffs for all that and they make all the decisions. Besides"—she sought around for a reasonable argument—"besides, it is only when a contest for Congress becomes of national interest—"

"My dear, this is state politics," Kate said indignantly. "I'll have to get the constituency accustomed to me and my strong views before I am nominated on a national ticket. No, no, this is the State Legislature but important just the same, my dear. Important."

"I'm sure," Emmy said weakly.

Kate continued to eye her with a purpose. "You are still working for that television station, aren't you? Surely you can do something to influence them—"

"Kate, no! I'm a researcher and that's all. There is a big staff—"

"One person, one vote," said Kate rather obscurely but added indignantly, "Why do you keep at such a job? You say yourself that it is not important. No sense in continuing to do something that does not involve you—all of you!" Said Kate, sitting very straight, "Every nerve and muscle and—and—muscle," she ended, having apparently run out of suitable words. But it was a scarcely perceptible pause. "You don't need the money. Or do you?"

"No. That is, yes. Anyway, I like to have a job." It was all she could say, but it was true. She liked to earn money; no cheating herself about that. But she also liked the feeling that she worked for it. If she couldn't have what she wanted, she could at least work and work hard; it had been a mandatory rule she had adopted.

Kate shook her head. "How much do you get paid?"

"Now really, Kate—"

"I'll pay you more," Kate said astoundingly.

"What for?"

"To help manage my campaign, of course. That is, I have already half engaged Archie. He is joining a firm of architects, but he will have plenty of time I should think. However, I'm not sure he's the person for the job. Not inventive enough. Not forceful enough. No, you'd do better for me. Under my supervision, naturally."

Emmy forced herself to reply slowly. She must not lose her temper, although her clashes with Kate had gone on, it seemed to Emmy, practically since she was born. "Thank you, Kate," she made herself say. "But, you see, I am very content in my job. And it has more possibilities than I think you realize." She stopped, suddenly reminded of the plain fact that the Judge (rather like Kate really) had simply made a decision that was not his to make and told the top network brass that his niece was resigning. She'd have to summon up the courage to go to the head man herself and explain.

"But, my dear Emmy," Kate was beginning in a patient, long-suffering voice when Bar returned, his arms full of logs. He dropped them on the hearth and paid no attention to Kate's cry of "No, no, Bar, in the wood box."

"So you talked to China," he said to Kate.

She rose and went to snatch up the logs, one at a time, and place them very precisely in the iron-framed wood box. "Of course. That's how I knew that Emmy had come."

"But you were expecting her."

Kate shrugged. "I forgot. I believe she did phone the other day."

"Yesterday," said Emmy.

Kate nodded, as if it didn't matter. "But, you see, Emmy gets involved with this stupid job of hers and could phone at the last minute and say she can't come—or even may not phone at all."

"I never did that," Emmy protested indignantly.

"Well, anyway, I didn't really expect her to come. So I never explained about the puppies or my meeting tonight. You see," Kate said defensively, "I was busy writing my speech. So I didn't really pay much attention. Sorry, Emmy." She changed course. "China seemed to feel a little upset."

Nothing to the way I feel, Emmy thought.

Bar said, "I'll go and get your suitcase, Emmy. Where did you leave it, Kate?"

Kate adjusted another log. "China pushed it at me and I had to take it. She went inside and shut the door."

"Then where is it?"

"Oh, I dropped it somewhere—on the road, I think. Had to. Bar, where are you going?"

Bar was out the door, leaving it open. Icy drafts poured through the room. The open door let out a stream of light, past glossy but coldly shriveled rhododendrons, onto the blue-stoned road. Almost at once Bar reappeared, running, Emmy's suitcase in one hand. He ran in, shoved the door closed, brushed past Kate, dropped the suitcase and went to a table near the door. "You keep your gun here, don't you, Kate?" He opened the drawer.

Kate, never one to fly into panic, said coolly, "You know I do. I showed it to you sometime or other. But what are you going to do with my gun?"

Bar was opening the gun. "Loaded, huh?"

"Certainly," said Kate. "No use in having a gun around unless it is loaded."

"Right," Bar said. He jerked the door open again, ran out and closed it again with a bang behind him.

Emmy went to pull the door open, she didn't know why really, but Kate put a hand on her shoulder and dragged her, none too gently, back into the room. It was a hand which was remarkably strong; golf and swimming and tennis—and caring for pups, Emmy thought rather wildly.

"Stay here!" Kate was never slow on the uptake—especially, Emmy thought wildly again, if a fray of any kind was in prospect.

Kate listened and listened and said "Hush," with such a frightening hiss that Emmy automatically stifled her questions. After a moment Kate looked at her and condescended to explain, although tersely. "He wouldn't want a gun without a reason. I think I'd better phone Mac at the gate."

Before she could reach the telephone that stood on a table beside the door, Bar came back, still running, thrusting the door open and closing it rapidly. "He got away."

"Who got away?" Kate demanded.

"I don't know."

"I'll phone Mac, the guard."

"No," Bar said.

"But why not? We can't have crime here in Alpine Village . . ."

"There wasn't a crime." Bar got his breath. "At least, I don't know what it was or who it was."

"Why did you take my gun?"

"Saw a man. Or a shadow. No, of course, it was a man! Dodging around behind a boulder. Then before I could stop him he jumped into some of that thick shrubbery and—"

"Why take my gun?" Kate was not going to be put off by anything but plain facts.

Bar had the facts. "Because I didn't like the way he ran. If there's no crime in Alpine Village, why do all of you seem to have burglar alarms?"

"That is only to keep crime out. We are near cities and need security systems," Kate said loftily, then descended and swerved. "Why didn't you stop him?"

"Because he was gone. I couldn't find anybody or hear anything! Do you know anything about all the inhabitants of—well, of Alpine Village?"

"Not quite all," Kate said factually and very efficiently. "But quite a lot. I have a file . . ."

The canine population of the bedroom had belatedly awakened to the excitement, every single one of them, Emmy thought briefly.

Kate raised her voice. "*Shut up!*" she called again over her shoulder. The mother's voice stopped; the puppies' squeals continued. Bar said, "Come on, Emmy." He picked up her suitcase. "Emmy is going to stay at my house, Kate. I'll borrow the gun in case I see anything suspicious on the way. Good night!"

It was another almost-seismic shock for Emmy, in an already upsetting evening, when Kate failed to utter one word of protest. Instead, she said, brooding, "I don't know what the maintenance men are going to say about all the damp newspapers I keep putting in the trash basket! However, I have tipped them well. Oh, good night, Emmy!"

Kate was really an astonishing woman. Emmy felt curiously proud of her.

Bar, though, hustled her through the patches of light along the road, toward what had to be his own house, her suitcase in one hand, his other hand at her elbow thrusting her ahead and, possibly, she thought madly, the gun in his teeth.

It proved to be, however, not in his teeth but in his right-hand pocket. He pushed her up several steps and opened a door, which held an enormous brass knocker with an ancient coat of arms engraved on it, and led her into a small hall and a large living room. Here he touched a switch that brought lights everywhere, dropped her suitcase and took out the gun.

"If I can just remember how to set my mother's burglar-alarm security system," he said with the very slightest amusement. "There—I think that's it. Anyway, there's a red light where a red light should be. Now then, I'll light the fire."

"It's warmer here than in Kate's house."

"She keeps it cool for the dogs. My God, did you ever hear so many dogs! You didn't manage to identify the one you are slated for, did you?"

"I didn't see them. Only heard. Who was out there watching you?"

"I really don't know, Emmy. I can't make a guess. Although—maybe you'd better open your suitcase."

"Why—oh!" A moment later she said "Oh!" again, but in a very small and indeed a rather frightened voice.

The suitcase had been ransacked. Emmy was not as painfully

tidy as Kate had tried to teach her to be, but she was neat enough about packing, even the few things she had brought with her. It didn't need even her stunned little "Oh!" to tell Bar the truth.

"So it has been searched."

She nodded, trying automatically to straighten out the folds of night clothes, the small stock of lingerie, sweaters, jeans. Even her zippered case for toilet articles had been opened, and a toothbrush and aspirin bottle spilled out.

"Your notes about the Homer Jones case are gone?"

"No. No, they are in my handbag. I told you."

"Where is your handbag? Still at China's?"

"Yes. No. I don't know. I just ran—"

Bar touched some buttons on the small box which held the alarm. The red spot vanished and a green appeared. Bar opened the door again, looked out into the night, shrugged, closed the door, pressed the buttons again and came back. "Not much use trying to find it now. Probably China still has it in the house. But Emmy, I'm afraid the Judge was right. Somebody's searching your suitcase seems to prove it, doesn't it?"

"But I told you the notes—"

"Sure. In your handbag. It may still be in China's house but it may have gotten into other hands. I couldn't see anybody at all now. Not even a shadow. Could you remember your notes if you had to?"

"Yes. In a way."

"But you think nobody else could read them."

"I don't see how. No."

The flames were beginning to dance in the fireplace, sending flickers of rosy glints over his face. He understood her look of dismay, perhaps fright, for he smiled. "Never mind. That is, yes, mind a lot but don't worry. We'll get the—whoever did this. It's got to be somebody living here in Alpine Village. No," he contradicted himself. "It needn't be anyone living here, but it's certainly somebody who knew you were at the Judge's, who saw China give Kate your suitcase. Emmy, who knew that you had those notes in the first place?"

"Why—why, the Judge, of course. That man, Homer Jones. Perhaps China overheard all the fuss."

"Nobody else?"

"No. That is—oh yes, Mac! I mentioned them when I stopped to speak to him at the gate. But Mac wouldn't take my suitcase."

"I can't see why he would," Bar said after a moment. "Of course he might have told someone—not purposely, just gossiping. Mac always liked to talk but—" He sighed. "I do wish Kate hadn't dropped your bag—because she didn't want to be bothered."

"She couldn't have known."

"Well, no. But Kate is—oh, you know Kate."

"She didn't know and she can be very just and very kind." No use trying to escape a sisterly bond.

"I know! All those puppies down in The Barn."

Sometime, Emmy thought vaguely, but not now, she must ask Bar why the residents of Alpine Village said "The Barn" as if it were a very special kind of barn.

"Anybody could get into the Village. Couldn't they, Bar?"

"Not past Mac. He's fully empowered to make an arrest. There are a few but complicated other ways, however: some high fences, a scattering of old rock walls, even some hurricane fences. Of course anybody can get over a hurricane fence if he has sufficient reason and a long enough ladder. And the fences don't surround the entire Village. However, the woods and the boulders, and the brush and trees make an escape by any intruder very, very difficult. As for burglars—I think almost every house in the Village has its own alarm. Kate is right, though—it is better to prevent crime if one can than to allow it to occur. Oh, I'm talking on and on. The fact is, Emmy—"

"I know, I know. You think that proves the Judge is right. But, Bar, I *can't* be in danger. I don't really *know* anything."

"How about those notes of yours?"

"I told you nobody else could read them. Unless—oh, no, not fully enough to make any sense. Besides, honestly, Bar, I have no idea who murdered that poor woman if it wasn't her husband."

The fire was warming the whole long living room. Unexpectedly Emmy yawned.

Bar said abruptly, "All right. That's enough. Mother's room is this way. Want a nightcap first?"

"No, no. I've had plenty to drink already—"

He led the way along a hall, opened a door and turned on the lights.

It was a large room as he had promised. It was, however, sadly bare of such things as pictures, books, cushions and all the oddments that accumulate in a woman's bedroom. Or a man's bedroom, for that matter, Emmy thought, and turned to Bar. "You must have removed all your mother's—oh, personal things."

"Yes, I did. Couldn't bear to let them be sold, I suppose." He was bending over the bed, removing a handsome white silk cover, turning down smooth sheets, making a neat triangle of them as he did so, fluffing a little to make sure the blankets were in line. She smiled. "Thank you, Bar. I'll be very comfortable and warm."

"There's a kind of dressing room–bathroom over there. Soap still there. I'll get your suitcase." He went back to the living room.

Emmy sat down on a chaise longue. Too much had happened too suddenly. Suppose, just suppose the Judge was right. But danger? Danger to her?

Quite impossible, she told herself firmly, gripped the arm of the chaise longue and repeated it aloud to herself: Quite, quite impossible.

Five

Bar knocked lightly at the door. "Okay, Emmy?" He opened the door and grinned. "I expected to find you flat in bed—or on the floor. Too tired even to take off your shoes. Here's your suitcase." He drew a luggage rack from behind a curtain, opened it and put her suitcase on it so she could lift the top without swirling the entire suitcase around, and then went to examine the windows. He checked them very carefully. "Seem all right. But I'll put on the lock—oh, don't look scared. Merely a precaution. I'll leave this one open a little for air. Okay?" Try not to think about all this until tomorrow. Good night."

He went out, closing the door rather firmly, it occurred to her, but quietly.

She sorted out toothbrush, comb, hairbrush, creams, toothpaste. The small dressing room, the adjoining bathroom were, she was sure, as luxurious as those in the Judge's house. Certainly (her sleep-numbed thoughts went), whoever felt sorry for people who had bought condominiums were wrong. The Alpine Village condominiums, in spite of a patently but rather disarmingly false pretension to rusticity, were extremely elegant. There were, of course, just as fine city apartments. Her own was sensible and, for her, expensive but not luxurious.

She yawned so hugely, brushing her teeth, that she nearly choked. Once in bed, warmly snuggled down under fleecy blankets and a silk blanket cover, she reminded herself: Danger to me—danger? Quite impossible. Besides, Bar was there. It was a comforting if sleepy consolation.

Morning was cold, and it had snowed heavily during the night. Emmy awoke with a start and at once remembered the night before. She told herself, with a fair degree of truth, that she had been tired and too full of what the Judge sometimes called alcoholic nourishment to reason clearly. Too much wine, too much food, too much everything, especially shock.

But the long sleep had refreshed her. The bathroom bore out its promise of the night before; the water was hot, there were plenty of towels and soap. Clearly, Bar had not wished to present to any possible buyer the look of a vacant and consequently rather dreary house.

She had known and liked his mother, a tall woman with dark hair and gray-green eyes which seemed to see a great deal. She had always been very kind to Emmy and to Kate, though now that Emmy herself was older, it seemed to her that once in a while those gray-green eyes held a sparkle of laughter when Kate was on her high horse, which indeed was Kate's youthful way of settling any matter of dispute.

Probably it was still Kate's way. All the same, she did have her good points; her loyalty, for one thing, even if she might disapprove of Emmy and some of her ideas.

The fragrance of coffee began to penetrate not only Emmy's nose but all her senses. She hurried into sweater and slacks as seemed suited to country (and Alpine Village!) life and went out. Following the coffee scent, she came to a kitchen which was, in her eyes, simply and completely a marvel. There was everything she could have thought of to facilitate the cooking process and a good many things she had never thought of. Ovens set in between cupboards, a stove with a white top: glass? some special material? Bar was at the stove, turning over bacon. He waved a fork at her. "Ready for coffee? I'll get it."

"Ah . . ." She settled into a chair beside a table that seemed to have grown out of the wall but was in fact on hinges, supported by a single leg. There were neat linen place mats and folded napkins to match.

"How do you like your eggs?"

"Oh, Bar, I never have time for eggs!"

"You have here." He reached into what looked like a handsome brown cupboard but proved to be a refrigerator, took out two eggs, broke each neatly into a saucer and slid each into the bacon fat. He laughed over his shoulder. "What a lucky girl will marry me!"

"Where did you learn to cook?"

"I just picked it up as I went along. Learned a few simple things. But I'll bet I can follow any recipe book. If Kate can, and—oops! I must get the toast." Toast, just brown enough to be crisp, had popped up near him.

He'd been about to say "and China," Emmy was sure.

If so, however, he didn't go on but put a neatly filled plate down in front of Emmy, saying absently, "See, I still have my mother's silver. Got it out for this special occasion. To tell you the truth, I never had a lady guest before. Funny, Kate didn't have a fit last night when I told her that you were going to stay with me."

Emmy sipped steamy coffee. "Kate can be very sensible."

"When she wants to be," Bar said.

"You have to admit it was very kind of her to take on the care of all those puppies."

"Yes, I guess so. Otherwise they'd have gone—oh, Kate is fine. You needn't feel you have to defend her. She's quite capable of defending herself."

"I know but still—oh, Bar, this is wonderful food." She crunched on a piece of toast, tried to impale some bacon on a fork and then, happily, took a crisp slice in her fingers.

Bar was pleased. "I told you the girl that marries me will be lucky. More coffee? Here—" He poured the fragrant brew into her cup.

Then he sat down again. There was a very serious something or other which suddenly intruded into the pleasantly domestic atmosphere.

Emmy looked up. "What is it, Bar?"

"This Jones case, of course. Your notes. I don't know what to say. I think the wisest thing for you to do is to go straight to the Judge and tell him what happened."

"No!"

He waited a moment. "I thought that's what you'd say. Well, then—do you feel sufficiently restored to talk about it?"

Emmy put both elbows on the table and eyed him, probably for too long a pause. He looked just the same, just as she had remembered him, as she thought of him being lost to her forever because he was so head over heels in love with China. She determined to check any runaway emotion. Heart-throb Emmy, she told herself derisively.

Bar said, "What's the matter? You look as if I'm going to eat you."

"No. It's only—I'm so sick and tired of that Jones case, and honestly, Bar, the Judge has to be wrong. All the evidence pointed to Homer Jones."

Bar took a spoon and made little circles on the tablecloth with it. "I read the newspaper accounts at the time. It was really a devilish kind of thing. As that poor tragic woman's husband, he was bound to be a suspect, wasn't he?"

"Oh, yes. And he reported the murder. So the police arrested him."

"I know, but tell me, what was the evidence against him?"

She had all but lived with the tragic and indeed revolting case, it seemed, for weeks now. She didn't want to talk about it or even think of it again.

Bar said gently, "You'll have to report your findings to the editors of your TV station. By the way, how did the Judge happen to know you're working on the case?"

"Why, there are a hundred ways, Bar. First, the series was announced. In preparation, anyone would know. Then, the whole staff could find out who had what cases to research. Or at least make some very accurate guesses as to who would work on what."

Bar nodded. "Oh, I understand that, all right. But still, the Judge must have had some, say, stable information."

"Right from the horse's mouth? Let me see—oh, Bar, there are so many ways: the camera crew sent out to cover the surroundings of the Jones murder; the—well, of course, the top men, the heads; the Judge has friends. Nothing would have been simpler than for him to say to one of them, 'What is my niece doing in your employ?' Something like that."

Bar considered it and nodded rather slowly. "I can't help thinking there might have been something more definite to induce the Judge to get out his big guns."

"Oh!" said Emmy.

"Well, what—"

She could feel her face turn pink. "Why, China! Perhaps!"

"Go on. Why China? Do you still exchange girlish confidences over the phone?"

"We could if we wanted to," Emmy said crossly. "But—but two weeks or so ago China had to come to New York for some shopping, and we met and had a quick lunch. I"—she felt like a guilty child—"I did tell her that I couldn't make it a long lunch because I was working on a case that the Judge—"

Bar nodded. "I see—oh yes, I see. So China went home and told the Judge and he unlimbered every gun he had."

Emmy nodded miserably. "No matter who told him, he'd have found ways to discover who did the research and the work on writing the account and, of course, he would have finally got down to me."

"Yes, I'm sure he would have. Emmy"—Bar leaned over the table—"tell me everything about the case. I remember some of it, but not all. Just tell me the kind of thing you put in your—"

A door somewhere was flung open and a blast of cold air followed. "Hi, Bar. Who's the lady?"

"Archie," said Bar and then called out, "Come on in. It's Emmy Brace."

Archie, done up in a storm jacket and a once white woolly cap, stuck his head in the door, tugged off both cap and jacket and said, "Hi, Emmy. Glad to see you."

"Kindly do not sprinkle the place with snow," Bar said. "Put your coat in the washroom."

Archie gave Emmy what she couldn't help feeling was a rather inquisitive glance and disappeared. Bar groaned. "I'll bet he hasn't had a bit of breakfast. Now he'll eat everything in sight. Archie lives high among the hostesses of Alpine Village. "Well, Arch. How about some breakfast?"

Archie bounced cheerily into the kitchen. "Sure. Great. Wish I could cook. That smells divine. How are you, Emmy? Didn't know you were here. Thanks, Bar."

Bar had put down another cup of coffee. "You can cook your own eggs," he said. "That is, if you want any."

"But—" Archie yielded, as if seeing something adamant in Bar's eyes. "Oh, all right. I can but try. I'm on my way to the Village Market. I've been in the city for a couple of weeks. Out of food. I'd better put in a supply before the snow closes the roads. Do you know our Village Market, Emmy?"

He broke an egg over the stove instead of in the pan. It smoked as it burned fiercely. "Oh, I'm sorry! I'll wipe up." He pulled a hand towel off a rack.

Bar yelled, "No! No, you won't! It'll scorch and smell like—oh, all right. Let the spilled egg burn. Can't do anything about it until the stove top cools. Really, Archie!"

Archie subsided into a chair opposite Emmy's. "I'm no cook. Never pretended to be. But we do eat well here in Alpine Village, Emmy."

"You mean you contrive to eat well," Bar muttered, busy getting out another spoon.

Emmy had known Archie Callser since he was a rather fat little boy, cozily ensconced with an obliging godmother after his parents separated, divorced and then apparently lost all interest in him. This, however, never seemed to trouble Archie, for he went his blithe way, scrounging whatever he could from his godmother or anyone else from whom he could reap any benefit. He started out to be an architect, apparently ran out of money, and eventually, merely by the force of his own need, it had seemed to Emmy (that or the Judge's natural kindness of heart), had gone to work for the Judge. Along the way he had managed to learn the rudiments of secretarial work; he was always grateful to the Judge, as well he might be, and very loyal. (Unless, Emmy suspected, the Judge's well-being conflicted with Archie's. This was a mean, and as far as she knew, entirely undeserved reflection upon Archie's character.) Finally the obliging godmother had died and left him enough money to resume his studies and even now to enter a firm of architects.

He had always had rather thin, curly blond hair; there was now a bare fringe of it, long, probably to prove that he once had hair. He was plump, for he liked to eat. He always looked shiny, as if recently scrubbed, had a merry smile, a rather sharp nose and an air of warm friendliness which, to do him justice, she did not think was always assumed for his own purposes. He had been an excellent kind of general assistant for the Judge. He giggled a little now and replied to Bar.

"Bet I get more invitations to dinner than you do, old fellow. Have you eaten here, Emmy? Let me tell you, there's every delicacy you ever heard of at the Village Market."

Bar sat down. "She's never heard of the Village Market. You see, Emmy, it is really a great boon to all the newly born cooks around here—"

"Gourmet cooks to a man, or I should say, to a woman. Although some do pronounce it gormé."

Emmy laughed. "Like Mr. Peggotty."

Bar grunted; Archie laughed merrily. "Sure. Remember he said he'd be gormed if anybody ever thanked him for anything. No such verb but it meant something dangerous. Well, now, don't look so savage, Bar. I do want to tell Emmy about this modern kind of marketing. You see"—nothing could ever stop Archie when he got launched into speech; Emmy didn't try—"you see, a thriving grocer in White Plains—"

"Mount Kisco," Bar said crossly.

"Might be Ossining for all I care," Archie said pleasantly. "The point is, this splendid grocer decided to set up a branch out here, near Alpine Village, a branch carrying very special groceries, doubtless for what he felt, and accurately, would be a very extravagant clientele. Fruits out of season, peaches and pears and asparagus in winter. Caviar, black and red, and quantities of it. Sourdough bread—doesn't sound like a luxury item but proved to be. Oh, he's very smart, Mr. Grocer. Result: he's had a rip-roaring trade from Alpine Village. It's only a mile or so off the Thruway. You must have seen it, Emmy, when you arrived this morning."

"I didn't arrive this morning," Emmy said and saw a flicker in Bar's eyes which clearly meant "shut up."

But Archie stopped his flow of speech at once; his wide, pale blue eyes darted from her to Bar. "Dear me! Well, this *is* news. What does Kate have to say about this—"

This time Bar said it, but to Archie: "Shut up."

Archie's round face, his pink lips sagged in dismay. "But, Bar, I don't mean—that is, you and Emmy—that is, everybody does it nowadays—"

"Emmy," Bar snapped, "is not everybody. If I must explain—"

"No, no, don't bother. It's all perfectly clear. Good for you!"

"Wait!" There was such ferocity in Bar's voice that Emmy herself rather quailed. Bar went on more reasonably, "Emmy intended to stay at Kate's. She didn't know that Kate's house is full of puppies . . ."

"Tried to get me to take one of them," Archie muttered.

Bar went on, ". . . so she came here. Now, make anything you want out of that. Look here, Archie, you worked for the Judge all during that horrible Homer Jones case, didn't you?"

Archie's hail-fellow-well-met manner dropped away. He gave a very realistic shudder. "I did. Ghastly. Don't want to think about it."

"Well, Archie—you see, it's this way." Emmy could tell from Bar's look that he intended cutting as many corners as he could. "The television station Emmy works for has assigned her to research the case. It's already been announced as being in the works. It just occurred to me that you might have some details that didn't reach the press. Have you?"

Archie really did groan, slurped coffee and groaned again. "All I know is I decided I never wanted to have anything to do with a murder case again. Especially one like that! Ghastly," he repeated.

Emmy's hand on the table was unsteady; she put it out of sight on her lap.

Bar said too quietly, "Why? I mean, every murder is always ghastly."

"Not like this one." Archie slurped some more coffee. "Horrible. Pretty girl—this fellow's wife, this Homer Jones's wife. Dead with—" He swallowed. "Her throat cut and stab wounds and blood all over the place as if she'd fought—window curtains, sofa, everything in the room—a really hideous kind of battle for her life."

Bar stared at him. "How do you know all that—" he began.

Archie blushed and said, "I was there."

Six

"*You were there?*" Bar repeated, still staring.

Archie nodded. When he blushed, red came up into his face and covered his almost entirely bald head, then suddenly vanished, leaving only his eyelids still pink. Like a startled rabbit, Emmy thought deliriously, but Archie, despite his looks, was not a rabbit.

He coughed, looked back at Bar apparently as defiantly as he could and said, "I was with the police."

Bar took a long breath. "With the police? They let you in?"

"Well, yes. You see—" He swallowed some coffee and added, "I had a press card."

Bar blinked. "I didn't know you were working for a newspaper. I thought you were working for the Judge at that time."

"Oh, I was. I was. But you see . . . well"—his pink-eyed gaze went to his coffee—"there was a time before I went to work for the Judge when I was a stringer in a little town upstate. That was while I was studying to be an architect. I ran out of money and later got a job as a sort of handyman for the Judge. I'll tell you—"

"You kept your press card. How did you know—"

"That there was a murder? That was really"—he blushed and paled again—"accidental. I just happened to be passing near when I saw the police cars. So, naturally, I followed. Just plain old human curiosity." Suddenly his air of rather defiant explanation dropped. "I wished I hadn't when I saw all that."

"Better start at the beginning, Archie."

"Beginning is better than that frightful end. All right. The poor woman had been married to a man by the name of Homer Jones. You must know all this if you're doing the research, Emmy."

"Some of it."

"As I—as I remember it, he was a small-time broker, neither good nor bad. Barely enough income to keep what"—he shuddered again—"what was a quite pleasant apartment. In the East Eighties. Small but nice."

"Go on."

"That's all. The guy was arrested and the Judge knew there'd be a true bill against him and the case would come up before the Judge. So I knew just what it—the poor girl, the apartment . . ." Archie dragged a snowy handkerchief from some recess of his clothing and mopped his shiny forehead. "Really, I remember all of it vividly. I can see that poor pretty woman . . ."

"What happened after the murder?"

"Oh, Emmy must know all about that. The husband came home, found his wife, almost went out of his mind, he claimed, but had enough sense to phone the police. Then they took over. That's when I saw the police car and—well, in the end he was tried and convicted."

There was a long pause. Then Bar asked, "Do you think he was guilty?"

Archie shrugged. "The evidence pointed that way and the jury said he was guilty. It was done with a knife. Everybody said a kitchen knife, but that was never found. Any more coffee, Bar?"

Bar took the empty cup to the stove and said over his shoulder, "Did you tell the Judge you went in after the police?"

"Certainly not! He'd have accused me of trying to influence him."

"As if anyone could influence the Judge."

"China can," Archie said flatly.

"Why was the husband accused?"

"My God, Bar, you act like a lawyer."

"I *am* a lawyer, remember?" Bar said and deposited another cup of coffee at Archie's elbow.

"Then you know that the husband—or wife—is always the first

suspect. And, Bar, he hadn't a leg to stand on. He tried to show he had no motive. But there were one or two people, other tenants, who insisted they had heard the couple quarreling. Might have heard or might only have thought of it after it all happened. But mainly there just wasn't anybody else to accuse. Throat cut, stab wounds. No kitchen knife ever found. He'd had a chance to get rid of it."

"Where?"

Archie shrugged. "Who knows? Anywhere. So the grand jury sent him to trial and the jury convicted him. And the Judge pronounced his sentence."

Archie coughed and said glumly, "Her name was Belle. She was very pretty. There was a high school photograph of her in the apartment—also in the papers. Must have been—oh, very, very pretty. He had met and married her somewhere, I don't remember where. It was all in the papers, anyway; the entire gist of it is this. He claimed he had gotten home at his usual time, about five-thirty. The door to their apartment was open and he found Belle's body. He claimed that he sort of went out of his head for a moment—felt sick. I do believe that part of his testimony. I felt sick myself a long time afterward, just having seen the girl and the apartment. But then he said he realized that he must call the police, so he did. But—listen, Bar, this was almost an open-and-shut case, and I'll tell you why."

"Do tell me," Bar said quietly. Emmy clasped her hands together under the table.

"Why, because there wasn't anybody else, of course. Nobody even came forward and said they had seen her or knew her except a grocer over on Madison and he wasn't too sure. And the newsman at the corner; he only said that she bought her hometown papers from him. Nobody in the apartment house, no other tenant claimed to have more than the slightest notion of her identity. Of course when the case jumped into headlines some of them said yes, they were a very quiet couple. I told you, one or two insisted they had heard quarreling, but it didn't seem quite believable. It's all in the papers if you want to look it up. I don't."

"So that was the only motive the jury attributed to the husband?"

Archie sighed. "There wasn't anybody else they could accuse."

"A burglar?" Bar asked but rather tentatively.

"Nope. Door had been unlocked. The apartment house is small, no doorman. Nobody there could say when the poor girl was murdered. And so atrociously," Archie said with a quaver in his voice. He shook himself rather like a dog. "That's enough, Bar. I can't think of it now without getting sick. Let's change the subject. How long will you be here, Emmy?"

Bar replied, "Not decided. By the way, Archie, did you know that the Judge is collecting material for his memoirs?"

Archie's pale eyes popped. "Memoirs? My God! There's nothing to tell that hasn't already been told in the papers, over and over. What do you mean—"

"I mean," Bar said, steadily watching Archie, "that his—say—amanuensis is Homer Jones."

This time Archie's eyes nearly popped out. "What on earth do you mean? The Judge sent the guy to prison . . ."

"He's not there now. He has been paroled to the Judge and, in order to help with the memoirs, Jones is staying in the Judge's house."

This time Archie looked more than ever like the rabbit he wasn't; his mouth dropped open. "That can't be! Staying here!"

Bar simply nodded. Archie turned to Emmy as if in the hope of getting sense out of her. "But the Judge can't do that!"

"He can," Emmy said, "and has."

"I take it," Bar said, "that you haven't seen him, Archie."

"How could I have seen him? I told you I've been in town for a couple of weeks, sewing up my new job. Bar, this is dreadful! Dangerous, too. That man—"

"Wouldn't you recognize him?"

"I tell you, I've just got back here. Last night. Haven't seen anybody."

"You'd know him if you did see him?"

Archie rubbed a hand over his bald and shining head. "Why, sure. I guess so. Saw him at the trial a few times. The Judge kept me busy, so—but sure, I'd recognize him. Didn't look like much. However, I suppose if you are on trial for murder you wouldn't look like much. Good God, the Judge had better keep an eye on

China! She's even prettier than Jones's wife. My God, Bar! The Judge has gone out of his head!"

"I don't think so. At least," Bar said grimly, "not quite. You behaved a little oddly yourself, when you did not inform the Judge of your own presence so close to the time of the murder."

"Why, I—why, I—" Archie almost yelped. "I didn't know that girl! I knew nothing—"

"You seem to have seen a great deal."

"Well, but—mere curiosity . . ."

"You did pass yourself off as a member of the working press."

"But there I was! All this commotion—police cars racing up—I remembered that old card in my wallet. Couldn't help—impulse! Later I wished I hadn't," Archie said.

"But you never did tell the Judge anything about your—"

"Seeing the whole thing? So soon after it happened? You're out of your head. The Judge would have kicked me out so fast and hard I'd be sore yet. The Judge was great to work for, in a way. Knew just what he wanted and made no bones about telling you. But I must say that when he decided to retire I was relieved. Besides, it was about then that my godmother died and left me some money. I'm not rich, far from it, but have enough to live on. Even"—he smiled deprecatingly—"enough to indulge some of my—oh, my notions about living and all that. But believe me, I was relieved when the Judge made the decision to retire and I could get out from under gracefully. I really did feel under tremendous obligation to the Judge, but I have to admit he was what some people used to call a hard taskmaster. Personally, I'd call him just a man of granite. Can't see how he got himself so enamored with China. I suppose," Archie said thoughtfully, "it just shows what a pretty face and pretty ways can do to a man. Especially an old man. The Judge must be close to sixty."

"Fifty-five," said Emmy.

Both men looked a little startled, as if they had forgotten her presence.

Bar said, "Well, in any event, he's got this Jones staying in their house."

"I tell you, he mustn't! The Judge is no fool, certainly. When he makes up his mind, nobody can stop him. But he really cannot bring a convicted murderer to live in Alpine Village."

"Why not?" Bar asked with what Emmy took to be genuine curiosity.

Archie's pale eyes bulged again. "Why, because they won't have it!"

"Who won't?"

"Why, why—everybody! It's a kind of closed community, Bar. You ought to know that."

"But Jones has been paroled. To the Judge himself. Shows that the Judge believes Jones was wrongly convicted."

"Doesn't show he's innocent," Archie said. "I wouldn't trust him with a—" His bulging gaze fell upon a kitchen knife. He picked it up and flourished it. "With this! Not after what I saw."

"Now, Archie, be sensible. You all have alarm systems. There is a guard at the gate."

"I'm going to talk to Kate about this! She'll put the Judge in his place. I mean—well, nobody can exactly put the Judge in his place, but Kate can tell everybody who this Jones is and why the Judge has brought him here."

"No need for anybody to tell Kate. She probably knows already. And she'll take up arms—"

"That's what I want her to do!"

"—for Jones. Never against him."

Archie's face fell. "Oh! Sure. Kate. Like the puppies and—"

"Kate," Bar said gravely, "can never resist a sad cause."

This, of course, was true. Kate was a born crusader, and when she crusaded she did it with all her considerable force and energy.

"She always means well," Emmy said.

"Good intentions . . ." Archie began thoughtfully. "I can imagine Kate going on the warpath—for God's sake, going from door to door— What are we going to do?"

"Why, nothing that I can see," Bar said.

Archie rose. "I've got to be going. Come and see my cabin, Emmy."

"Cabin?" Emmy smiled, thinking of the luxury all about her.

"No, really a cabin. Logs, everything . . ."

Bar laughed. "Wood-pressed logs. Looks like an old-time cabin. Right in the woods."

"May be pressed wood, but it is a cabin and I like it and so will you. Let's just forget all this talk of the Jones murder and--now I'm off to the Village Market. I've got to stock up on food."

He gathered up his cap and jacket and left.

Bar looked thoughtfully out the window. "I ought to go to the Village Market too. Looks as if we might be in for quite a snowfall. Do you think Archie was really surprised to hear that Jones is here?"

"Why, yes!"

"Did his account of the Jones murder coincide with your notes on it?"

"I think so. I listened carefully, comparing what he said with what I had read of it. I think he didn't miss much. Of course, there were columns and columns of newsprint. Some handed over to me by the station. I also went back over the tapes of the television news account."

"Get anything from all that?"

Emmy sighed. "Oh, Bar, I don't know. I mean, I don't remember how much came from the papers and how much from the tapes. There were some photographs, too. They corresponded with—with what Archie said he saw."

Bar rose and started to clear up the remains of breakfast. Emmy, automatically, helped. She was pleasantly impressed with the handsome efficiency of the kitchen. Everything that was needed was there! She slid oranges into a kind of fruit bin. Bar wiped off the white, glasslike stove top where Archie had spilled an egg, whistling a little. It felt right, Emmy thought unexpectedly, right and comfortable to be doing odd kitchen chores with Bar. He said abruptly, "You mustn't forget that somebody around here may have taken your handbag and your notes."

The warm little feeling of comfort vanished. "No. I haven't forgotten."

"Can't you remember *any* of your notes?"

"Oh, yes. The main facts. But really, Bar, if only I had them, I might be able to recall something that—" She looked out at the flying snow for a long moment before she said flatly, "Something that might account for the Judge's belief that the wrong man was convicted."

He put the last glass in the dishwasher and it began a cozy murmur. "If we go to White Plains or Greenwich—well, each place has a remarkably good reference library. Could you bring yourself to—"

"Read all those columns of newsprint over again!"

"I know. It's asking too much, but, Emmy, I think it's important to find out why anybody around here would try—maybe has succeeded in stealing your notes. Reading all the accounts might remind you of—something that—well, something."

"You think the Judge was right. You think that the real murderer is afraid of something I may have discovered. You think—"

Bar said steadily, "I think we'd better do something about it."

"Well, yes. Certainly I don't like the idea of being in any sort of danger! But honestly, Bar, I can't think of a single thing that raised any real question in my mind."

"What do you mean, real questions"

"I mean—oh, Bar, I'm not sure that I mean anything! It just seems to me that—at some time reading all that and comparing every account and all the photographs and testimony—it just seems to me that there was something—" She hesitated and yielded. "All right. You make me say it. Just something—"

"Something out of kilter," Bar said. "Something not quite coinciding with some other statements. Something like that?"

"I don't know. I can't remember. So if it was anything, it must have been only something very unimportant, very small. Such an idea never even occurred to me until you asked me last night. No, there couldn't have been anything important at all. I'd remember. Wouldn't I?"

Bar sighed. He led the way to the living room. There was now no cheerfully sparkling fire. The hearth was as blank, she thought dully, as her own memory. Yet—yet hadn't she made a question mark in her notes? Well then, where and what about?

Bar said, "The Judge must have some specific reasons for getting Jones out. You must ask him to tell you precisely what they are."

Emmy considered it. She remembered all too well her flaming rage with the Judge and his cold, adamant response.

Bar knew what she was thinking. "Hard, isn't it? But I think it's got to be done. I can't imagine anyone but Jones being at all interested in your suitcase or your notes. Or your handbag. Don't forget that."

She nodded soberly. "The handbag is at China's, I'm sure. But it had to be Jones who searched my suitcase."

"Jones. Or the real murderer, if there is one. So if the Judge has the faintest idea about this real murderer, he'll have to explain who and why and—"

"No. If he knew anything like that, he'd have gone straight to the district attorney. Wouldn't he?"

"At least he'd have had to explain to the governor and—well, he's got to have some factual reason. So," Bar concluded sensibly, "first we'll get your handbag from China. Then we'll go to the Judge and ask him."

It was, of course, sensible, even necessary. On the other hand, she knew the Judge better than Bar knew him. He would never, never talk to her about anything he didn't choose to talk about. He would only tell her to mind her own business and stop thinking about the Jones case and . . .

She shook her head. "He wouldn't talk to me about it. Believe me, Bar."

"Oh, I think he will. I'll go with you. I'm a lawyer. Let me represent you. I don't care," Bar said as Emmy put up a protesting hand. "It doesn't matter if he does have your power of attorney. And why you didn't take that away when you got to be twenty-one, I can't understand. I really think that you are in your right mind and as a matter of fact an intelligent young woman."

"Not with the Judge," she said bleakly.

"He got you under his thumb when you were too young. We must put a stop to that. That is, you must put a stop to it. Only you can. I'll help if—there's Kate!"

So they didn't get a chance to try to make the Judge talk reasonably and frankly; they didn't make a trek through snowy roads to either White Plains or Greenwich. Kate stopped that without knowing it. She simply lunged through the door, a puffing and rather startling figure in boots, baggy jeans and a sheepskin-lined jacket. A red scarf bundled up her head and she carried an enormous basket with a firmly closed lid. She dropped it and caught her breath. "Heavy," she gasped.

Bar eyed the basket suspiciously but said, "I left your gun in that drawer—"

"Oh! Thanks."

"Do you always leave your door open while you're away? All I had to do was walk in."

Kate thought for a moment. "That must have been while I went to make sure the heat was turned on in The Barn. I was gone early this morning."

"That's when I returned your gun. What's the use of a security system if you pay no attention to locks?"

"I was only away for a moment or two." Kate was a stickler for the truth and amended it. "Perhaps ten minutes."

"*What's in that basket?*" Bar asked sternly.

He needn't have asked, for suddenly, protesting and indignant yelps came from it. There was either an odd sort of echo in the basket or more than one yelper.

Kate shrugged out of her heavy jacket, displaying a remarkable sweater, done by busy hands, probably for some fair, in a wildly geometric pattern of what looked like thistles and goldenrod. "Puppies, of course," she said.

"Two! No!" Bar's eyes were as steely as the Judge's could be.

Kate laughed. She had a very musical, low laugh; it was one of her attractions. Too bad, Emmy thought briefly, she doesn't know how engaging that is; she'd use it more often. "I'm not going to leave them here, although really I see no reason why you shouldn't be of help to small friendless animals and take both." She must have felt thunder in the air, for she amended it quickly. "Or perhaps only one. Your choice, of course."

"Kate," Bar said firmly, "they're not even housebroken!"

"Oh, they are almost housebroken. And all you would need is some old newspapers, milk and ground steak." Apparently she felt an impending storm again, for she added hurriedly, "Don't worry, I'm taking these to the Village Market."

Bar stared at her. "Not for sale!"

"Oh, heavens, no! The grocer's wife has promised to take two. I'll still have five to dispose of. Or perhaps only four. The Board really ought to let me keep at least one—"

"What Board?" Emmy asked, caught by this cryptic remark.

Kate flashed her an impatient glance. "The Board for Alpine Village, of course. Elected by the householders. Makes the rules. We have to abide by them. Matter of fact, I helped make the rules. I'm a member of the Board."

She would be a member of any available board, Emmy thought, and added to herself, reproachfully, and a good and reliable member, too.

"So now I'm fighting the rest of the Board," Kate said with a certain zest. "I think I may win, too."

Bar said dryly, "Nothing like a good fight. I hope you have newspapers in that basket?"

"Why, certainly. But I'll get rid of them before the grocer's wife quite—quite—"

"Understands the need for so many papers," Bar said, again dryly.

"Well, what of it?" Kate cried. "It'll be a good home for the poor little things."

"I'm sure. How much does your grocery order run? Must have cost you quite a lot to find this good home."

"Not at all. That is"—Kate's sometimes irritating habit of truth at any cost got the better of her—"that is—well, yes, I may have bought more this month than I do as a rule. But one should have a certain stock of food. Snow, winter. I must tell you, Emmy, the Judge came to call on me earlier today. You know, he really has a mean mind sometimes." She settled herself in a lounge chair. "He came to see you, of course. He was very, very upset when I told him that you were staying here with Bar. Said it was shocking—thought—well, we had a bit of a disagreement."

"About me?" Emmy said.

"About your staying with Bar, naturally! The Judge said he was appalled. He said that was what came of your living in New York and associating with dissolute characters. I told him off. Heavenly days! Even if you and Bar wanted to live in sin, it was no business of his. But I knew there was nothing to be shocked about. You and Bar!"

Bar said warmly, "Kate, you are a very nice woman."

Emmy said, "Thank you, Kate."

"Don't thank me! I know things about people. I knew that you and Bar weren't engaging in any nonsense. So I told the Judge—" She stopped, a pleased smile on her face.

Emmy said, "Kate, what did you tell him?"

"Why, I told him he was a dirty old man. I told him to mind his own business. He didn't like it," she added demurely.

Seven

"Kate," Emmy said, "I do think you are great!"

Kate's smile vanished. Her dark blue eyes grew sharp. "But the Judge is right about getting you off that job you have."

"But he had no right! It was inexcusable."

"No. He was perfectly right. He explained that this young man staying at his house—his name is Homer Jones"—Bar gave Emmy a helpless, I-knew-she'd-find-out look—"helping him with his memoirs had been wrongly convicted and I believe him. He said you might put yourself in danger from the real murderer if you kept on with this—this research," Kate said as if it were something unacceptable. "I'm sure he is quite right. So I came to say that you really must accept his decision and give up your job. I understand the Judge has already taken the step of resigning for you. You must not go against his very wise decision. Do you have any sherry, Bar?" she went on as if the matter were all settled.

Bar opened his mouth, shut it again and went into the dining room.

"You see," Kate said after accepting the glass from him and taking her first sip, "it's a bit of a drive to the Village Market and I may surprise Mrs. . . . Mrs. Grocer—can't think of her name—"

"Never mind that," Bar said. "But how do you plan to induce her to take two puppies?"

"How do you know she isn't expecting two? Don't worry, Emmy, I've saved the choice one for you."

Somehow the conversation got switched around by Kate into dog talk. Emmy could take one if not two puppies; they were paper-trained. Soggy newspapers, Emmy thought wildly, every night, when she came home from the office.

It gave her an argument. "I can't leave them alone all day, Kate!"

"That's why you should take two. One might be lonely, I agree. Oh dear, Emmy, you've got that stubborn look on your face. I almost wish I'd left the puppies in The Barn."

A nagging if small curiosity tweaked at Emmy. "What is this barn? I didn't think any of you had barns attached to your houses. You all seem to think—"

Kate interrupted. "It's The Barn, of course. You must have seen it when you came in past the guardhouse. The swimming pool is just behind it. Olympic length. A lifeguard all summer. The tennis courts—"

"The Barn?" Emmy persisted.

"Oh, well, it's the old red barn that belonged to the farm which once was Alpine Village."

Bar said quietly, "The developers of Alpine Village first bought the entire farm from an old-time family here. Simpsons, wasn't it, Kate?" Kate nodded. Bar went on, "The Barn is a sort of social center. It has been done over, washroom, kitchen, enormous fireplace, coatroom . . ."

"The Board meets there," Kate said. "I just may be chairman in another year. I don't think Mr. Manders is interested enough in Alpine Village affairs to run again in spite of the fact that he owns one of the houses and does live here most of the time. At least some of the time. I understand that he is quite a financier. Votes here, too," she said knowledgeably.

"Also saves him some taxes, I should imagine," Bar said dryly. "However, his presence does have a certain—" He hesitated.

Kate supplied the words. "Cachet. Money. Authority. But not authority for long. I'll replace him next year."

"But what does the Board do?" Emmy asked.

Kate was clearly appalled at her ignorance. "Really, Emmy, you can't imagine the problems that come up. Taxes, guard duties, swimming-pool rules, schedules for using the tennis courts, golf course, road clearing, maintenance. There'll be a Christmas party in ten days; the entire Village will attend. Christmas Eve. You must come back for that, Emmy. You'd enjoy it."

Suddenly that look of intense interest which Emmy knew so well flashed into Kate's handsome face. "That's where I found that poor stray bitch and her puppies. The Barn, I mean. The Board says a householder may have no more than two dogs and they must be pets. Dogs are rather discouraged around here. So," said Kate, at full blast now, "I'm having a real fight with the rest of the Board. I'll not let anyone simply pack any of them off to be destroyed. I won't have it!" said Kate, sticking out a good firm chin. "So," she finished with a certain pleasure, "I have them and I'll keep them until I can find homes. The mother—well, that's in the future. Now I've got to deliver the pups before the grocer closes. These short December days!"

She was on her feet, bundling the scarf over her head, shoving into her coat. The passengers in the basket had apparently gone to sleep; they awoke with quite mature barks of interest when Kate picked up the basket. She was lugging it out the door before Bar could reach it.

He stood in the doorway. "There she goes. Plowing right through the drifts. The boys won't be along to clear the roads until the snow is heavier. You'll probably hear the plows tonight."

"Kate will fight for what she feels is right. Human justice and kindness," Emmy said.

Bar closed the door. "And she does love a fight. This time, though, Kate is certainly right. No question of it. About your job, I mean."

Emmy barely kept her voice on an even tone. "Monday I'm going to the top men, those friends of the Judge's. I'm going to tell them—"

The door, barely closed, flung open again and China ran, stumbling, into the room and flung herself at Bar, who automatically put out his arms to support her. China was sobbing. "I've left him!" she sobbed. "I've left the Judge! I'm not going back! I'm never going back! Oh, Bar, I made such a mistake. How could you have let me marry him when—oh, Bar, you still love me, I know you do!"

She lifted her pretty face, cheeks flushed with cold, toward Bar's face. Her lovely reddish curls were touched with snow. She had a fur coat wrapped around her. In one hand she held a big handbag, which looked crushed and wet. Emmy gasped and ran to get it. China reached her arms up toward Bar. She said over her shoulder, "Oh, Emmy, this must be your handbag! It was out there along the road. In the snow. Open. Oh, Bar, never, never let me go back to the Judge!"

She dropped the handbag into Emmy's clutches and nestled against Bar. The bag fell open and disclosed a mass of wrinkled, damp papers which Emmy recognized as her sheaf of notes about the Jones case.

There it was, her own scratchy handwriting, decipherable only to herself. She scrambled the papers together. Bar saw her and said quickly, "That it?"

Emmy nodded. "Oh, yes. Yes—"

"Are they all there?"

"I think so. Yes."

"Good," said Bar.

China clung to him. "Bar, listen! I'll never go back to the Judge. It was such a mistake! I ought to have known. I ought to have married you then."

Bar took it, on the whole, with a certain self-possession. "Well, you can't exactly marry me now, China. Law's against it."

"Oh," China wailed. "But I'm going to divorce the Judge."

"Now, now!" Bar removed her coat—sable, Emmy thought absently. In the Judge's opinion, nothing was too good for China. She said, "What's the matter, China? What happened?"

China didn't look at her. Bar dropped the coat on a chair and China clung to him again and sobbed. "You'll never believe this. He's got a convicted murderer staying there. He's been there four —no, five days! Right in the house. And the Judge says he's going to let him stay as long as he pleases. The murderer, I mean—so, I—well, finally I left. I told him I was leaving. I told him, Bar, I had to come to you. My only friend, my only refuge. That is"—she turned her tear-streaked face, lovely even with tears, toward

Emmy—"that is, Emmy is my friend too. But I—oh, I'll never go back to the Judge. Not when he acts like this."

"Here, China." Bar neatly deposited her in the big chair Kate had recently left.

China leaned back and clasped her hands. The handsome ring the Judge had given her twinkled. It was set with a huge and lovely sapphire, flanked by two diamonds. "Blue-white Wesseltons," China had told Emmy proudly, pointing out the diamonds.

As far as Emmy was concerned, the stones could have been good glass; but the ring was truly stunning. Somewhere deep in her mind there was a kind of quiver, like a spark in a dark layer of memory. She couldn't understand exactly why. She must have seen the ring often on China's hand. Bar, of course, could never have bought such a lavish piece of jewelry for China. He could never have bought her a sable coat either.

Bar sensibly disappeared for a few seconds; he came back with another glass of sherry, which he gave to China. "Drink it," he said kindly.

China drank, indeed she almost gulped it. Bar leaned over, stacked logs in the fireplace and lit them. A thin red flame or two shot up, China's ring caught lights and again stirred a remote twinkle in Emmy's consciousness, not really associated with China. It was not important; what was important was that she had the notes and could now, perhaps, decipher them. But China and the Judge and Bar! She said firmly, "China, you must not talk like this about the Judge."

"Don't tell me what I can do!" China cried, sobbing loudly again.

"Now, now," Bar said. "Finish your drink. We'll talk about it."

"No need to talk. I'm going to stay right here. With you. That," said China with an air of confidence, "will give the Judge a reason to divorce me!"

"Wouldn't you prefer to divorce him?" Bar asked.

"I don't care!" China cried. "A man who brings in a murderer and doesn't tell me and insists upon keeping him—why, I'll never sleep a wink now that I know. I didn't like that man Jones when he first turned up. The Judge said only that he was someone who was having a hard time, couldn't get a job in New York and asked the Judge for help. I didn't know he had been convicted by the Judge and then—*then*"— China's voice rose—"then he came out here to stay, supposedly to help the Judge write his memoirs. The Judge never told me the whole truth until today. I couldn't hear what the Judge and Emmy were fighting about last night. The Judge had only told me that he wanted a private talk with Emmy, so I stayed in the kitchen. But I knew they were quarreling and that man Jones had something to do with it." Her eyes flashed with fury. "So I made the Judge explain. He says he must help Jones. He says a lame dog over a stile or something! He wouldn't listen to anything I had to say, so I'm simply leaving the Judge. That's settled."

"Where are you planning to go, China?"

China's eyes widened. "I'm going to stay right here with you."

"Can't," said Bar.

"Why—but why not?"

"Because I said so," Bar said gently but firmly.

"You can't desert me when I come to you for help. I had to come to you! Nobody else!"

"There's Kate," Bar said. "If you refuse to go home, perhaps Kate will let you stay there."

"I don't want to stay with Kate! I'm going to stay with you."

"We really must—that is, you must be sensible about this."

"Sensible!" China cried indignantly. "When the Judge—"

"Sensible," said Bar. "Stay with Kate if you refuse to go home tonight. You can be a great help to Kate. She is house-training—that is, paper-training—seven, no, five now, puppies. You can help with all the papers." Surely there was the slightest wicked little gleam in Bar's eyes. Emmy herself suppressed a sudden impulse to giggle, which would be fatal, in view of China's dramatic tears.

"But that—oh, Kate—puppies and—Bar, I have to stay here with you. My place is here. Surely you can't forget what we have meant—"

"I think there's somebody on the doorstep," Bar said and strode across to open the door. "Come in, Judge. We were speaking of you. China is here . . ."

The Judge stormed in and he was in a towering rage again. He threw off his coat and flung his dashing beret on the floor. "What do you think you're doing?" he shouted at China.

"I told you!" China shrank back but was defiant. "I've left you. You'd rather have a murderer than your own wife. I'm going to stay with Bar. I'm going to marry Bar."

"You'll have to get rid of me first." The Judge didn't so much as glance at Emmy. Instead his eyes, steely with anger, fastened on the sable coat on the chair. "You intend to stay here and—marry Bar, did you say? By the way, does he agree? Well, never mind. I see that your mind is made up, my dear. So I'll just take that coat. Set me back forty-five thousand. Plus sales tax," he interpolated dourly. "Perhaps I can sell it somewhere. Or give it to somebody who appreciates it. Oh, and that ring, if you please, China. I'll take that, too. Surely you'll not want it." He held out his hand to China, who shrank back further and stopped crying. The Judge looked at Bar. "I can recommend her cooking," he said. "She has become a really fine cook. You'll enjoy that. When you marry her—as she intends."

Rather unfortunately perhaps, Bar was suddenly seized with laughter. He tried to stop and, doubled up, sat down on the footstool and laughed and laughed.

After a moment, remarkably, the Judge joined in. Both men simply laughed with the heartiest shared merriment. China stared, her pretty eyes wide.

Emmy clutched her notes and wondered what, if anything, she could do and decided there was nothing. She almost hated China; she was jealous, no question of it. Yet at the same time, paradoxically, she wanted to slap both men.

China's tears had gone. Her face was pink with anger. She looked at the coat. The Judge stopped laughing.

"I can't go out in the snow without a coat!" China cried.

"Oh, yes, you can! You didn't return that ring either. That cost me a pretty penny too."

"I'll do no such thing!" China snatched the coat and flung it around her as she eyed the Judge. "You've got to get rid of that murderer!"

The Judge had turned serious, although a look of amusement was still in his eyes. He touched his neat mustache and said, "I explained to you, China. He is not a murderer. This was merely a case of justice. He tried to get a job in New York—or anywhere. He tried and couldn't, not with his record. So he came to me and

—what could I do? I know he was wrongly convicted. I had to try to undo what I had most reluctantly been obliged to do. In plain humanity I've got to help an injured man." The Judge meant that. His voice was low and sober.

Bar, too, had sobered. He rose now. "Judge, I can't help wondering why you're so convinced that this man, Jones, is innocent. You *did* sentence him."

"Certainly. I had to. The jury had so decided."

"But won't you tell us why you are so certain of his innocence?"

The Judge got out his imposing spectacles, twirled them on a finger, thought and replied. "I believe the jury so decided because there was simply nobody else. Bar, you're a lawyer. You must realize that during the investigation every shred available about the past lives of both the dead woman, Belle something—"

"Caraway," Emmy said.

The Judge flashed a reproving look at her. "Oh, yes. Our Emmy is well up on all the information she could possibly gather. Well," he went on, turning back to Bar, "she was born and lived in a little town upstate—actually, its name was . . ." He paused and Emmy, almost in spite of herself, supplied it: "Knoterville."

"Yes, I believe you are right. She was apparently a very pretty girl. Went to high school there. Met this poor Homer Jones while he was selling something or other . . ." This time he gave Emmy a demanding glance and again she supplied the words: "Farming implements."

"Yes. Anyway, he fell in love with her; they were married. He thought he'd do better in New York. Somehow he got a job in a broker's office. She worked too. Wanted to help with money—"

"A model for ladies' underwear," Emmy said, feeling like a prompter but also wanting to get the entire record as accurate as she could.

"Yes. Yes, as I remember, that was it. She was a good little housekeeper. None of the goings-on one seems to associate with successful models. Not that she was overly successful. However, she did work."

Bar said abruptly, "But then, if the husband didn't kill her, who *would* want to get rid of her?"

"Why should her husband want to get rid of her?" the Judge

snapped. "My God, Bar! She was a lovely-looking young woman. She was helping with the money. As far as we know, she was a loyal wife and homemaker. A real boon to a young fellow trying to work his way up in a difficult and risky business. No reason for murder. No motive at all. Yet the jury said yes, he was guilty. Mainly because he was her husband. He *could* have got that kitchen knife. No proof that he did. It was never found. But Jones himself told the police they had had one. It was gone."

China said, "I'll *not* have him in my home. Knives and—no! I won't stay there—"

"Stay anywhere you want," the Judge said almost pleasantly. "But give me that ring. And that coat. Then you can do as you like."

Bar had risen. "Wait a minute, Judge. There's something serious—"

The Judge smiled and lifted his sleek black eyebrows skeptically. "You can't mean China's anger—"

"I mean about this man, Jones. You'd better know—" He glanced at Emmy, who understood and nodded. "Last night China gave Kate Emmy's suitcase—"

"Of course I did," China flashed. "And her handbag today. Kate must have dropped the handbag. It was under a shrub and some snow and—"

"The point is, Judge," Bar said firmly, "somebody got that suitcase of Emmy's and searched it. Somebody got her handbag and searched it and—and probably looked at Emmy's notes about the Jones case. Who was it?"

"But, Bar—now, really—" The Judge's formidable eyebrows lowered. "How should I know?"

"Was Jones in your house all night? Did he go out at any time?"

"H'mm," said the Judge, coming back and settling himself with one leather-patched elbow on the mantel. "H'mm! I see! You think that after he heard the—the little conversation I had with Emmy and which I'm sorry to say she took rather badly—you are suggesting that, following that, he dashed out, got the suitcase and the handbag, searched both and then got back into my house without my knowledge." He shook his head. "He didn't. I am perfectly sure of that."

"But suppose you were asleep and didn't hear . . ."

"I'd have heard," the Judge said simply. "I have a most horrible, shrieking burglar alarm."

"But couldn't he have turned it off, gone out, returned and turned it on again?"

The Judge considered. "Highly unlikely! Possible, perhaps, but not probable. The alarm panel is beside the door. Like yours. But I don't see how he could have known how to turn it off. Unless he's watched me. Each alarm has its own set code of numbers. Suppose he *could* have watched me sometime, but I can't believe he did without my knowledge. And if he tried to get out of the house without turning off the alarm, the whole Village would have heard it. Police would have raced from Appledown. I have excellent hearing, Bar. Believe me, I'd have known if he left the house. However, this *is* extraordinary. Was anything taken, Emmy?"

"Nothing," Emmy said. "But my notes—look at them—" She brandished the damp wad of papers. "Still here, but somebody had them."

"Too bad whoever looked at them didn't destroy them," the Judge said sourly, but added more sincerely, "Just might have saved your life, Emmy. You must pay attention to what I told you. That man Jones did not kill his wife. Therefore, somebody else did. A murder case is never closed. There must be something that was not fully developed at the trial. So the real murderer of that poor girl is scared. Just believe me. I've seen much more of the seamy side of life than you have."

"But I'm still going to keep my job," Emmy said, albeit impressed by the Judge's air of authority.

"And you also intend to finish your account by broadcasting to the world why *I—your uncle—*was instrumental in getting a convicted murderer paroled." He turned to Bar. "She is stubborn about that. Certainly I can see that such a finish would add greatly to Emmy's own position as a researcher."

"All right!" Emmy didn't yell but wanted to. "How can I possibly help telling the whole story and the way you got him out of prison?"

"I'll tell you how," the Judge said. "Because you don't have a job anymore. That's how."

"But see here, Judge," Bar intervened smoothly, "other people had to know of this parole."

The Judge shrugged. "Certainly. But no big news of it. We," he added smugly, "all saw to that."

"All?" Bar asked quietly again.

The Judge flashed a daggerlike look at him. "All," he said. "And I mean all the people concerned with Jones's release."

"But, sir, it does seem to me that your reason for getting this man Jones paroled is not based upon very solid evidence."

The Judge fixed his spectacles on his nose and looked at Bar for a long moment. Bar did not wilt, which, Emmy suspected, rather annoyed the Judge. However, he said, with an even increased air of authority, "I *know* he did not kill that girl. I have staked my whole professional life upon that. You must realize that I've seen much of the world. I know people—rather more accurately than sometimes I like. But I must trust my own experienced judgment. That young man is not a murderer."

"I certainly grant you judgment and experience, but somebody killed her . . ."

"Certainly. And it is my feeling that there is a real murderer very interested in Emmy's research. So interested that he searched her suitcase, he searched her handbag—I don't understand why he didn't take the notes—but the fact remains, there has got to be a real murderer—and he is somewhere. Very close to us."

Eight

China squealed like one of Kate's waifs. "Here! In Alpine Village! Jones, that's who!"

"No." The Judge thought for a moment and then added gravely, "I'll speak to Mac at the gate tonight. I'll consider all this. Any more questions, Bar?"

"Quite a number of questions, Judge. Are you *perfectly* certain Jones could not have got out of your house last night? Out a window—anything?"

"Everything around that house is what they call bugged. Even a strip before the silver drawer in the dining room. Below my Utrillo. On the stairs. There is simply no way he could have got out unless he turned off the alarm. I can't be certain that he didn't look over my shoulder as I set or turned off the alarm, but I find it hard to believe that he discovered my own code number."

China nodded. "Oh dear, I felt so safe here. Until you brought that man, Judge . . ."

"I'm going home." The Judge took his coat. "Think you can manage two guests, Bar? Emmy is staying here with you too. Well, a chaperone I suppose—"

"Emmy is *not* staying here!" China cried. "There's only one extra bedroom and I—"

The Judge grinned wickedly. "Why, my dear, I thought you

were going to oblige me to sue you for a really shocking lack of good manners."

"You mean Bar? Well, I'm staying here."

"Here's your coat, China," said Bar pleasantly. He dropped the sable over her pretty shoulders. China smoothed the fur around her chin.

The Judge chuckled. "How long do you plan to stay with Bar, Emmy? Until Kate gets rid of those puppies? Dear Kate! How like her to take pity on waifs! And how she enjoys her fight with the rest of the Board over them. Too bad she never married. Marriage just might have channeled all that energy—on the other hand, she'd have made life hell for a husband with no backbone. By the way, Emmy—"He came across and reached for the notes in Emmy's hand. She clutched at them, but he moved so suddenly that he opened them and was smoothing out the sheets of yellow paper. He adjusted his glasses with one hand, stared down at the scribbled notes and finally turned, almost savagely, to Emmy. "Do you mean to say these are supposed to be notes?"

"Yes. And they're mine. Give them back!"

"But can you read these—these? I suppose they are meant to be words?"

"Yes. I think so." He caught the doubt in her voice.

"Dear me. And you had such an expensive education. Why didn't you learn to write legibly?"

"But that's my way of—"

"Shorthand. Emmy's version," Bar said briefly. He quite clearly agreed with the Judge.

The Judge shook his head, turned the notes one way and another and upside down. He shook his head again. "All right. If you say you can read these—Bah!" said the Judge as savagely as any Scrooge. "All right. You work on them. Get them in some legible order. Then I'll come in tonight and you can read them to me."

"Why?" Bar said too pleasantly.

The Judge shot a furious look at him. "Because I say so. It is barely possible that she has managed to dig out something that didn't come out fully at the trial. I can tell if she has. I remember every bit of the trial—that trial," the Judge said, "and a few others. But this one is very clear in my mind. So, I'll go now. I'll be back tonight. After dinner. Then, Emmy, I'll expect you to make some sense of this—this pack of scrawls. By the way, Kate agrees with me. You must not try to get your job back again."

"But of course I'll get it back! Or—or—" Do something, she told herself.

The Judge shook his head. "No. If you are planning to go to the top about this, it's simply no use. See you tonight."

He started for the door. China gave an indecisive glance around her, snuggled into her sables, said in a small voice, "I'll get your dinner before I leave you," and started after the Judge.

The Judge chuckled again, gave Bar a look of masculine conspiracy and swept the door open. China's fleeting voice came back, repeating that the least she could do was fix his dinner before she left him. A blast of icy air sent wisps of snow into the room before Bar closed the door. He, too, chuckled. "Well, that's fine. Now then, can you make anything at all of your notes?"

"I haven't had time. I've got to think and remember . . ."

"May I see them?"

He took the sheaf of papers and studied them under the light for a few moments. His face took on a curious expression of frustration but also a kind of indulgence.

"Really, Emmy, sometimes the Judge is right. However, you *may* remember what—what you *meant* to say by"—he frowned at the paper—" 'Bl. O. Ev.' " He sighed.

"I'm not sure now. I'll remember . . ." She was not altogether positive of that either. "I'll look at them."

It had darkened early; the black windowpanes winked at them. Bar went to them and drew deep red curtains across each window. The room took on a warm and safe look. Safe, Emmy thought. What a word to use, even in her thoughts!

Bar came to her, lifted her chin and looked down at her soberly. "No. You are looking too—too white and tired. No more of your hieroglyphics for now. We are going out to dinner. We are going to a very fine restaurant. Change if you want to. But you are really all right just as you are."

She wasn't all right; she glanced down at her jeans and sweater and hurried into the room she had used, and her suitcase. After all, she told herself, it was mere feminine vanity to wish to do Bar proud—that is, as proud as she could. In that mood she shook out a thin red wool dress, made, as a matter of fact, by a famous designer who had been interviewed on the program and expressed her gratitude for Emmy's careful research by handing out the dress. Emmy had not the slightest qualm in accepting it; it was humanly impossible to refuse. She heard Bar's voice in the next room; he was using the telephone. When she emerged, he gave her, she was pleased to note, a distinctly approving glance and reached for her matching red coat. "I phoned to ask about the roads. All right as far as Mount Kisco. I phoned for a reservation at the restaurant. And I phoned to tell the Judge we are going out. My car is this way."

Another spotless, large, efficient garage yielded Bar's rather battered car.

Emmy was pleased with herself and her dress. The snow made glimmering curtains in the headlights of Bar's car. No one was in the lighted guardhouse. She had a glimpse of a chair, a shelf, a telephone, an electric plate and a stack of magazines. Bar slowed down. "That's unusual," he said. "Old Mac is always very prompt, very efficient." He glanced at his wristwatch. "Five thirty-five. Mac is supposed to be here by now. It's not like him to be late."

The snow made moving, bewildering veils around and ahead of them. Emmy could barely see the big boulders and clumps of darkly outlined firs beside the country road which twisted on ahead, out of Alpine Village, toward the main highway. From a distance there was the throbbing sound of a motorcycle, two motorcycles, revving up as they approached some unseen hill, then diminishing in sound. Bar said shortly, "Blasted kids! Make the night hideous sometimes. But then, we can't hear the racket from our little cul-de-sac. Mac has a little apartment in Appledown. He likes to walk to work. Says it gives him exercise. Must have been delayed by the snowy road or probably caught by somebody who wanted to talk to him. I'm sure he's all right."

They went on. Bar was, however, still puzzled and, indeed, rather annoyed. "Not like Mac," he said again as they passed the humped-up shadows of whitened boulders and snow-laden firs, all black and white in the lights from his car. He turned into the main road. Here were scattered lights. A snowplow surged up a nearby hill, shoving a fan of light ahead of it. Bar went a little faster and finally turned off the main highway into a country road, almost a lane, which climbed sharply and was unnervingly slippery but passable.

The restaurant was cheerfully lighted. They left the car to a young man in uniform, climbed some steps and entered an inviting and, Bar told her, rather famous restaurant. Perched high on the hill, it had once been, obviously, a private home. There were many rather narrow rooms, all filled with tables, lights and, surprisingly on that snowy night, people.

There were shaded, rosy lamps on the tables, there was a delicious odor of cooking and an almost equally delicious, soft sound of voices and laughter. The maître d' came, beaming, to greet Bar. "Ah, Monsieur Slocumb," he said, showing a fine set of white teeth. He bowed low to Bar and Emmy, so low that he scarcely had looked at her as he said, warmly, "And Madame again. How very nice! And on this bad night. So glad you could come. Your favorite table—" When he raised his head, his black mustache drooped and his bright black eyes widened upon Emmy. "Oh, oh—sorry . . ."

"This is Miss Brace," Bar said coolly. "Glad you could save that table near the windows. Thank you."

So, Emmy thought, so! Madame, huh!

They sat down, the maître d' forestalling Bar's gesture toward pulling out her chair. The maître d' was almost purple with embarrassment. He handed the menu to Bar as if he proffered a burnt offering to his gods.

Bar took that coolly, too; he ordered, consulting Emmy politely, advising her as to what he considered particularly good dishes. The waiter came swiftly at a short hiss from the maître d'. Another waiter, a sommelier, done up with great keys on a great chain, approached, bowing too, and greeting Bar but letting himself eye Emmy intently if politely. Bar ordered wine. Emmy, whose own command of French was barely sufficient to cope with a simple menu, couldn't help admiring Bar's smooth orders. Yet she couldn't help loathing, detesting, despising Bar! So he had brought China here, had he? She knew perfectly well who Madame was.

Once their cocktails were put down, Bar thanked the waiter and nodded at Emmy. "Cheers," he said. There was a kind of twinkle in his eyes which added to her wrath. She sipped her cocktail and said, quietly but icily, "So you bring China here."

Bar nodded. "Sure. Sometimes."

She had to go on probing, although it hurt and knowing what a fool she was making of herself. "Often, I take it."

"Our host has an eye for pretty ladies. He almost glitters if he thinks he scents a romance in the offing. Especially," Bar said dryly, "if those bright eyes of his detect a wedding ring on Madame's finger. Appeals to his sense of romance."

"Illicit romance, you mean." Emmy couldn't help an unsteadiness in her voice.

Bar put down his glass and put his hand over her own. "Come on, Emmy. China's marriage is a happy one, I mean it."

"But you bring her here. Oh well, I have no right whatever to seem to—to—"

"Accuse me of breaking up her marriage? But I don't. I mean, I'm not. I mean—oh, for God's sake, Emmy, of course I see China when I can. She's a charming companion. The Judge is often out of town on business, something about the Bar Association, so—"

"So you rally around," Emmy said. She had got a measure of control over her voice, but she would not meet his eyes.

"Well, yes, I suppose I do when I'm here. As I've been here quite a lot recently. All this business about my mother's house."

Monkey business, Emmy thought meanly but didn't say it. Bar guessed.

"Now, Emmy, surely you understood all that—that scene this afternoon. China," he added, "China is like a child. Really she is."

A child who knows which side her bread is buttered on, Emmy thought, meanly again.

Bar said, "You saw all of it. You heard—why, we both laughed. The Judge and I. Little China—she really is so childish, so helpless in a pretty, feminine way."

Helpless like a rattlesnake, Emmy thought resentfully, and did not reproach herself at all. "She's no different than she ever was!" Emmy twirled her glass around.

Bar said thoughtfully, "Well, no. No, I can't say she is much different. Just about the same as when I fell so hard in love with her. I must have made a spectacle of myself," he added ruefully.

"You didn't exactly conceal it."

At last she looked up and met Bar's eyes. He was not laughing but almost.

He put a firm hand over Emmy's. "Let's forget it, Emmy. All that is in the past. Surely you could see that. The Judge knows it. In her heart, dear little China knows it. She's only upset and mad at the Judge now and—but she didn't really mean a word of all that talk of leaving the Judge and—and coming to me."

Emmy thought for a moment. "Let's talk about something else," she said stiffly.

Bar smiled exasperatingly but said, as stiffly as she had spoken, "Now don't go all haughty on me. I'm Bar, remember. And as a matter of fact, I am also your host and I expect a certain amount of politeness from a guest. And how do you like that?" He finished with an abrupt return to his usual manner.

She wasn't going to meet him on their old-time terms of friendliness and also, for a memorable time, something definitely more than friendliness. That, however, had to have been actually on Emmy's side and a product of her imagination. Bar had met China and fallen in love with her; in spite of what he said he still, in a way, was in love with her. That afternoon he and the Judge had both laughed at China's spirited defiance; yet in his heart Bar had to have been touched and, perhaps, quite definitely moved to the point of wondering just how far and how fast China's declaration might lead them both.

No; Emmy hardened her own determination. No more being in love with Bar; not again! She had conquered that once. She would not let it start up and thrive again. Like a weed that might be lovely but couldn't be allowed, she would simply pull out any possible romance about Bar—"root and branch" she said to herself savagely.

Bar took a slice of pâté on toast and said, rather neatly, considering his mouth was full, "I always thought that you and China were such good friends." He didn't look at Emmy at all.

She felt her cheeks grow hot. After a moment she said as firmly as she could, "But we are friends. Have been for years."

Bar crunched steadily. "You didn't sound much like it."

No answer to that at all; it was quite true and obvious to Bar.

She attacked her own pâté. Presently Bar said in a remote voice, "There's quite a view from these windows. You can almost see the river on a good day."

China was not mentioned again. Bar seemed to give his wholehearted attention to the dinner, which indeed required anybody's complete attention and pleasure. But Emmy couldn't help thinking how well Bar knew the wine and the menu the tiny, charming restaurant offered. He had to have been there many times with China. Madame!

China might seem childish and certainly was feminine, but she was by no means helpless.

Snow struck the black windowpanes near them with a gentle but persistent swishing sound.

There was little more conversation. Bar seemed to have lapsed into a kind of troubled yet remote mood. When their coffee came he said, glancing at the steady flakes of snow outside the windows, "I suppose we'd better get along before the roads are worse." He looked quite seriously at Emmy. "You are so silent and—you're thinking about that Jones murder, I suppose. Brace up. It is really nothing that affects you. Or me." He paid the check, and Emmy could not help noting what she considered a shocking price. But it wasn't the Jones murder that had kept her sober and depressed.

They slid a little more than was quite comfortable going downhill. The main road was completely cleared. When they turned into the Alpine Village road Bar stared ahead, leaned forward as if to see better through the snow and suddenly put on the brakes.

There was still a light in the guardhouse, but again, Mac was not there. A gleaming white ambulance was drawn up beside another ambulance near a big, fully lit building which loomed up behind a cluster of automobiles. Bar said something under his breath, started up again and swerved his car into a kind of paved, large parking place. He happened to come to stop near the car with the blackened windows which Emmy had seen the previous evening. "I'll just see what—" Bar began when Archie came springing out of the snow and glimmering lights. "That you, Bar? Thank God—"

"What's wrong?"

"Mac—our good old Mac and that man, that chauffeur, secretary or whatever of Manders. Both of them killed."

"*You can't—*" Bar began and Archie cried, "Yes. I do mean it. It's true. Everybody is here. Just look! The ambulances. Police. Everybody from Alpine Village. Whole place. My God! Mac!"

"But, Archie! What happened? When—"

"Nobody knows. Somebody found that Mac was not in the guardhouse and then Mr. Manders couldn't find this man who works for him. Name is Guy something . . ."

"Go on." Bar's voice was like ice. "Where did it happen? Why? Who knows?"

Archie burst in, "Who knows anything! They were just simply found. Way out in that clump of pines and boulders, just where the turn from the main road leads to the Village. Both of them shot . . ." Archie gulped. "Through—that is, through the head. Old Mac—"

"I can't believe . . . No, I do believe you, but what are they doing?"

A long white ambulance came smoothly along the pavement, passed them and went on, turning into the Alpine Village road. Almost at once another white and ghostly ambulance came after the first, as if pursuing it.

Archie said, "There they go! Both dead. I heard. I saw. Bar, it's terrible! Old Mac! Why should anybody shoot him?"

"Who is in The Barn?"

"Everybody! I told you. Police. A couple of doctors. Every single resident of the Village. Oh, I've got to go—" He yanked the woolly cap from his pocket, pulled it over his bald head so only the fringe of blond hair showed below it and started off, his snow boots thudding.

"Wait! Where are you going?" Bar shouted.

Archie shouted back, "Kate sent me to see to those damned pups. I'll be back."

Bar took a long breath and turned to Emmy. He was clearly trying to steady himself. He put an arm around Emmy. "Don't cry. We've got to—to see—well, come on. Kate must be in The Barn. Look out for these steps!"

He kept her in his steadying grasp. The path was paved, but rather irregularly, in flagstones. Low lights on standards outlined it. A wide door was opened and she could see The Barn, but only through the blur of tears. Mac? No, no—not Mac! She must have said it aloud, for Bar, looking strangely white and stony said, "Don't, Emmy, don't. You can cry later. Right now we've got to hear—" They entered The Barn.

It was her introduction to The Barn and also to some of the residents of the Village. This included Mr. Manders, who appeared to be the spokesman and acknowledged head of affairs. He was seated in an armchair, a mammoth fireplace behind him; this was heaped up with huge logs, all of them flaming briskly.

There was a haphazard circle of chairs before him, all of them occupied; beyond there was a table, crosswise in the wide room, so other people were seated there. Emmy had only a fleeting impression of pale faces, intent eyes and country winter clothing—boots, heavy tweeds, down coats, sheepskin-lined jackets. Hovering around were several policemen in blue uniform. Kate wasn't sitting in the outlying circle. Not Kate. She sat firmly, very near Mr. Manders, and contrived to look very authoritative, although her eyes were red. The Judge sat farther back among the other residents, his face quite inscrutable but his spectacles perched on his nose. China was beside him, huddled in her furs, white and scared. Not all the permanent residents of the Village were present; Emmy learned later that many had gone South, were on cruises or were using any means of getting away during the winter months.

Somehow Bar had got her into a kind of light folding chair. She was thankful for his steadying presence. Mac, good, reliable, kind, always there when he was needed! Murder! Two murders, in the short space of time while she and Bar had driven away and up a hill, eaten dinner, driven back again.

She was going to cry and couldn't stop it; she heard herself give a muffled kind of gasp, and Kate must have heard it too, for she lifted her chin, firmed a rather unsteady mouth and gave Emmy a look that meant "Don't cry in public." It reminded Emmy sharply of her handsome young father who, in the event of some childhood disaster, would say sternly, "Ladies never cry in public" —he would pat her head—"not even little ladies."

She understood Kate, gave her a slight nod and steadied herself as best she could, but it was not possible to put aside, even for an instant, the brutal fact of murder. Mac, who had never hurt anybody, who had been a mainstay of her childhood, a constant and devoted servant—no, not servant, that was the wrong word, although she had heard him use it, but with pride, referring with sturdy determination to himself! Such an ugly and undeserved death was not possible, yet it had happened. She gripped her hands together in her lap. Bar whispered, "Easy, easy, Emmy. Try to listen . . ."

So she listened, fighting back outraged questions, saddened tears.

Holding her head up, trying to be as steady as Bar and Kate expected her to be, she glanced around The Barn; there were open doors showing glimpses of kitchen cupboards and sinks, and others revealing a wash basin and hooks for coats. Back in one corner, fantastically out of place, stood an enormous Christmas tree, waiting silently for glittering ornaments and Christmas carols and all the warm beauty of Christmas. Its presence seemed a sad rebuke. When she turned back, Mr. Manders had the floor; his accustomed place, Emmy felt sure.

It also struck her in a dim, tangential way that he really ought not to use an automobile with black, impenetrable windows, for he was an extraordinarily handsome man, slender, with darkly gleaming hair which looked as if it had been plastered into a cap, dark eyes, a finely featured face with tight lips and strong chin. He was dressed like a dandy in an expensive tailor's idea of country clothes; his tweeds and leather jacket were a thought too perfectly designed. At another time it would not have surprised Emmy to see him launch into a tango, a highly stylized tango.

A uniformed policeman stepped back from him, as if they had concluded some quiet conference. "I have been told to make a statement to you all. I'll do my best," Mr. Manders announced. "I found the two murdered men." His eyes caught ruby lights as he glanced around the room, as if ensuring attention on the part of his audience. He needn't have checked. Every eye was on him expectantly.

Nine

Mr. Manders looked at nothing for a moment, probably marshaling his account. Then his dark eyes traveled around the big room. "I found them myself. I had sent my secretary, Guy Wilkins, to speak to MacLane about a trivial matter at the guardhouse. Guy did not return. After some time I became—not alarmed exactly," said Mr. Manders smoothly, "although I did think it possible that perhaps he had slipped on the icy walks." This time he looked directly at Kate. "Our Board has not yet instructed the maintenance men as to their duties as precisely as one would like. They really must be made to clear the roads and walks."

Kate, being Kate, bristled, gave her eyes a swipe and rose. "I did speak to the head of the maintenance crew. He promised . . ."

"I'm sure he did, Miss Kate," said Mr. Manders. "Allow me to continue, if you please."

Kate sat down but with obvious reluctance. Mr. Manders said, "As you may know, Guy was my right hand." His right hand was raised a little and it was a very white manicured hand. "I did not find MacLane in the guardhouse where he was supposed to be," he went on. "I was rather upset about this. His duties are clearly defined. He is—was to be on duty at five-thirty. From then to one-thirty. We keep rational hours here in the Village. No need for all-night guards. I walked down the road, thinking to meet him and explain that he must be in the guardhouse during that period. He was not there. I went on expecting to meet him somewhere near. I had got to the—" He stopped there, cleared his throat and faltered for just a second. "I got to the clump of pines and that outcrop of boulders at the turn from the main road to Alpine Village. It was quite a walk in the snow but I—at least at the time—I rather enjoyed the exercise. But—" Again he coughed a little. The silence in the room was almost palpable. Probably, Emmy thought numbly, nobody breathed. Mr. Manders said, "I saw something dark showing under the pines and—I went to look and—you all know what I found. I came back hurriedly, through the snow, after first ascertaining that both men had been—" This time actually he stopped to swallow. "Both men had been shot. I came back and stopped at the first house." His dark eyes went to a rather plump, white-haired, pink-faced man leaning against the table and looking rather sick. "Mr. Clements' house. He permitted me to use the telephone. Now, as I'm sure you all know, Alpine Village is in Appledown Township. It is, as advertised, a country residential community. The nearest town, Appledown, is of course not very big. It maintains only a small fire department and a small police force. Alpine Village is under the jurisdiction of Appledown and also of the state police. Therefore, the Appledown police chief instantly phoned the state police barracks near Mount Kisco. They sent men at once. In addition, the Appledown chief and his two men as well as the Mount Kisco and White Plains police came. Both White Plains and Mount Kisco sent ambulances. MacLane was just now taken to Appledown, where he lived. Guy Wilkins is to be sent to New York, where proper services will be arranged. You understand that we must all give whatever information we can or"—he smiled rather thinly—"aid and assistance to the police. I believe there is a close mutual-assistance understanding between all the—the police. I myself have given them as full a report as possible. That's all," he ended abruptly.

There was a long moment of utter silence. Emmy was, oddly then, subtly conscious of the fact that the building had, indeed, once been a barn; there were hand-hewn beams supporting its lofty roof. Underneath it all there was the smell of old wood and a lingering barn smell. The walls were plastered, however, and decorated with brightly colored posters. All of the residents, some in those consciously chosen country clothes, seemed, just for a second, to have been posing as country people but were now, in the face of an authentic tragedy, obliged to shed all pretense. They were, simply, people of the present, not of the time when The Barn must have been built, and built so solidly that it had resisted age and change.

Finally the Judge got up, took off his spectacles and said decisively, in his courtroom voice, "I don't think that is all, Mr. Manders."

Surely there were again flashing ruby glints in Mr. Manders's eyes. "I'm afraid that's all I know."

The Judge said, "What time did you start down to the guardhouse, Mr. Manders?"

"Why, I'm not sure exactly."

"You meant to speak to MacLane. So it must have been after half past five."

Mr. Manders replied smoothly that he supposed it was. "But if you'll remember, it was a very early dusk. The snow and all. Still what really sent me on toward the main road was the notion that I must speak to MacLane about his being late at the guardhouse. So, yes, you may be right, Judge. It must have been after five-thirty."

The Judge was not at all checked. "I believe there were two doctors here. The doctor from Appledown—" He glanced sharply around. "Oh, yes. I thought you were still here, Dr. Selling. What time would you say MacLane was shot?"

Dr. Selling proved to be young, bespectacled, thin and nervous. He replied, however, in a startlingly robust, loud voice, that he couldn't tell. "Snow—cold—but there'll be post-mortems, you know, Judge. On both men."

The Judge adjusted his own glasses and eyed the young doctor. "Do you think the medical examiners will be able to state precisely the time of the murder?"

The young doctor held his ground. "I'm not sure, sir. It may be difficult, as I say, because of the snow and cold. I can only assure you that they will try."

"Thank you," said the Judge crisply and the young doctor sat down suddenly, almost as if he'd been pushed. The Judge resumed, "Then, Mr. Manders, you were alone at home for some time before you decided to find out where Mr.—Guy Wilkins had gone?"

"Certainly. Except for Mrs. Clark, who, as they say, does for me. She was in the kitchen, however. She may not have been aware—"

A female voice piped up from the last row of spectators. A small wiry-looking woman came up too, like a jack-in-the-box. "Oh, I knew. Mr. Manders was smoking. In his library," she said belligerently, as if daring anybody to question her. "He has a perfectly vile pipe. I could smell it. You see, Judge, I do know Mr. Manders was in the house at the time these dreadful murders must have occurred. So," she added rather too aptly for the Judge's dignity, "put that in your own pipe, Judge, and smoke it."

The Judge, Emmy was sure, restrained a sudden half-grin; however, he said firmly and magisterially, "Thank you, Mrs. Clark. It does seem too bad"—he now addressed the intent circle around The Barn—"it does seem too bad that concerning this shocking affair, everyone of us really must come up with some kind of alibi. Doesn't it?"

Kate surged up, eyes blazing, and sat down again.

"I might say, for myself," the Judge went on, "my wife and I were at Kate's—I mean Miss Brace's house at about the time in question. So the three of us have alibis. Not that my wife wouldn't give me an alibi if I asked her to, and I would certainly be inclined to give her one. But as it is, no one, I think, will doubt Miss Kate's word." He sat back, took off his spectacles and looked around composedly.

Mr. Manders rubbed a white hand over his glossy hair and turned to a man near him who had been watching and listening with close interest, very keen eyes and, Emmy was sure, sharp ears. He took Mr. Manders' glance as a signal and said firmly, "Now then, ladies and gentlemen, we'll have to go about this in an orderly way. I really think it might be best for you to return home for the time being. I believe that the police, that is, certainly with the welcome counsel of these men who have come to the state police's assistance—all of us may wish to have some time to work over this and—" He shrugged. "Thank you all, very much. I have each person's name, phone number, address." He turned abruptly to a young man in blue uniform. "Haven't we, Stone?"

"Oh, yes, Chief. Yes, sir." Young Stone patted a uniform pocket. "There's a dictaphone in the car, sir, as you know. And our new computer . . ." he added with pride.

The chief smiled briefly. "I'm not sure we'll need either at the moment. I'm afraid plain old horse sense is sufficient just now. However, thank you—"

"Just a minute." To Emmy's horror China was scrambling to her feet, clutching at her furs. "Just a minute, please, Chief. You see—"

She was going to tell them about Homer Jones. The Judge knew it too. He quite simply stood beside her but put what Emmy was certain was a very firm arm around her. "I have a guest. He was on his way to see you, Kate. We met him as we left your house. He has nothing to do with any of this, I'm sure."

Kate, of course, was instantly sure too. "Why, he"—she began, getting to her feet, her voice wavering only a little—"he was at my house. He came a few minutes after the Judge and his wife left. When you phoned me, Mr. Manders, the Judge's guest was in my house."

There was another silence. Then the door burst open; Archie and gusts of snow came surging into The Barn. He dashed off his woolly cap, brushed snow out of his eyes and gasped loudly, "Did I miss anything?"

"No," said the Judge firmly. "Good night, Manders. Good night, good night . . . this is an excellent idea of the police. They can't do much at night and in this snow and—Good night . . ." He was all but elbowing his way toward the door. But then, as if by magic, everyone (everyone but the police, Emmy noted), like sheep, started for the door too. Nobody talked much; they seemed entirely bent upon resuming their quiet and safely hedged-in lives. Safe, up to now, Emmy thought grimly.

Archie had caught Kate by the arm. "Kate, that man—that man, Homer Jones, was there! In your house! That man—"

"Yes, I know," Kate said crisply. "He offered to stay with the pups. Feed them."

"So you sent me to check up on him," Archie all but squealed.

"Not at all," Kate said. "I was afraid you were going to cry. I wanted you out of the way until you got hold of yourself."

"But Kate—that man, that murderer—"

"He was in my house, certainly. What about it?"

"But he—but he's a murderer!"

"The Judge says he isn't. Do compose yourself, Archie."

Bar said, "Did you recognize him, Archie?"

Archie blinked. "Why, yes. Once I got a good look at him."

"Did he recognize you?"

"How should I know! We kind of talked—not much. He said he was supposed to feed those damned dogs."

Kate resumed command. "Of course. I told him to do that. When Hazel Clements phoned and told me what had happened, I just thought it better to keep Jones out of all this. I was afraid—"

Archie did not help. "You were afraid he had shot those two men!"

"Nothing of the kind," Kate said icily. "I was only afraid everybody would blame him."

The Judge heard it all for he had paused to listen when he reached the door. He said shortly, "All right. All of you go home—Kate, Emmy, Bar, Archie—come along—"

Such was the force of the Judge's personality that even the fleeing sheep gave way, as he strode back from the door to fix the police chief with his adamant, courtroom gaze. "I'm sure that you did not find the gun. With the snow and darkness and—"

The police chief replied politely, but also rather respectfully. "No, Judge. In the dark and all those snowy boulders and shrubs—no, we could not then give more than a quick search for the gun. I can say, however, that it was certainly not in the near vicinity of the—bodies."

"I thought not. Any idea what kind of gun it was?"

The chief blinked but answered. "Not a shotgun or rifle," he said as if yielding only to politeness.

Only because Kate had a gun and had lent it to Bar the previous night, Emmy flicked a glance at Kate and discovered that her sister had gone perfectly white. As Emmy watched, Kate's chin set itself and she returned Emmy's look with a piercingly distinct "Keep your mouth shut" message.

"Thought not," said the Judge. "A revolver then? You'll have to make a search for it in the morning. Not only," the Judge added as the police captain seemed to nod agreeably, "not only around those damned useless boulders and shrubs. They ought to have been removed long ago. All you Board members seem to like anything you feel gives the authentic country touch to Alpine Village—"

Kate interrupted. "Really, Judge! They've been here long before we were. Along with those stone walls . . ."

"Oh, yes," the Judge said. "Old stone walls, put together by the original farmers, straggling inconveniently all over the place. You wouldn't touch one of them, would you, Kate! It's not *my* taste. The point is," he resumed, fixing that magisterial gaze upon the police chief, "that revolver could be anywhere. If I may suggest it, there might be some inquiry as to which residents here have permits to carry a revolver. Not that that would help much."

The police chief sighed. "That will be attended to, Judge. As a matter of routine," he added, showing the merest trifle of impatience.

The Judge nodded, took China's arm and marched steadily out the door. By now, all the well-dressed sheep, everyone, had gone, except of course Manders himself, Kate, Archie, Emmy, Bar and the police.

Several of the policemen began to drift, muttering a little to one another, toward the door. Manders rose and adjusted his handsome turtleneck sweater as if it felt rather tight around his throat. "Then—then you'll keep in touch, Chief. Thank you."

He had, now that the necessity for formal speech was past, a musical voice, deep and resonant.

He gestured toward Bar and Emmy, nodded in a friendly but reserved way to Kate, ignored Archie and went to the door. His movements were graceful and superbly coordinated; Emmy thought briefly, he'd be splendid on the stage; perhaps, in a way, he was on a stage.

That, however, was an errant notion; it had nothing to do with —well, with murder.

Kate gathered up her sensible, down-filled coat. "I hope Jones didn't give the puppies too much milk," she said to Archie.

Archie smoothed his bald head. "Oh, no, I'm sure he didn't."

"I really must find homes for them soon."

Archie looked frightened. "Now, look here, Kate, I don't want one."

Kate eyed him with red-rimmed but stern blue eyes; her black eyebrows came down a little. She said peaceably enough, however, "You'll change your mind when you get acquainted with them!"

"Lord forbid! I asked you, What happened while I was not here?"

Bar replied, "Nothing. Come on, Emmy. Kate, do you have your car?"

"Certainly not. I walked. But just the same I'll take a ride back. The snow makes it hard walking."

Archie said, "I'll come too. I really want to hear all about everything. Good old Mac. Good and kind and reliable and—" His voice roughened. "He deserved a long and peaceful old age."

Bar's face was stony.

Kate said, "Oh, Bar, I am sorry . . ."

Bar nodded. "I know. He was, well, he was my greatest friend when I was a boy. Taught me to fish, taught me to hunt—oh, you know all that. Taught me to go easy with my mother's little whims. Taught me to tell the truth, too."

The Barn seemed to echo his words as if it, also, knew something of days past and remembered them. Archie gave Bar a troubled yet sympathetic glance and patted his arm. "I'm sorry, Bar. I liked him too. Everybody in our old neighborhood respected and liked him."

"Yes," Bar said. His face was white and hard in the lights from the walls. "Come on, Kate."

Archie trotted after them. Perhaps all of them were aware of the cluster of men, still talking in low but businesslike voices, there before the immense fireplace.

Kate said, "Let's go home and have a drink."

As they went out into the snow and darkness and cold, Archie said, "Just look! Everybody has disappeared already. Scared to death. I'll bet every one of them heads straight for a strong drink as soon as they get home. See here, though, Bar—" He was panting, trying to keep up with them. Kate strode ahead. Bar held Emmy's arm and she remembered the unevenness of the walk to the parking lot and was careful not to stumble.

Archie panted, "Hey, you're going too fast. I ask you, Bar—" He caught up with them. "Doesn't it strike you as peculiar that these murders occurred just after the Judge got that man, that Jones man, to stay with him?"

Kate heard and called back, "Not at all! There could be no possible connection."

Archie ran a little to keep up. "But no murder happened before. And now—why, that Jones has been at the Judge's—it can't be more than a few days. And no matter what the Judge says, he was a convicted murderer."

Kate found Bar's car and jumped in. "Do hurry up. I'm freezing. I've got to get some kind of better heating system for The Barn. Of course, everybody will squawk their heads off at the idea of spending more money on it. But it's got to be done if we intend to use The Barn at all in the winter! Our last Board meeting was so cold we were all shivering and I couldn't get anywhere with my arguments for keeping those puppies in my house until—but then I think the Board must have been cold and bored anyway—they shut up about the rule of having no more than two dogs—and those must be household pets—in the house—and—for goodness' sake, Emmy, get in."

Archie said, from the snowy veils around them, "I'll follow you."

Bar started the engine with a jerk; he drove swiftly, yet absently along twisting roads which Emmy couldn't identify until he came to a kind of curve which she recognized. Hadn't someone called their houses an enclave; the Judge's and China's, Kate's, Bar's, Archie's? All long-time friends.

Long-time friends, yes. She had known Bar and Archie since childhood; they had lived in a little town in Connecticut which she still remembered with nostalgic affection. As she remembered Mac.

Ten

The Slocumb place had been near the Brace home. Mac had seemed to her, as a child, practically on the verge of the grave with his shock of thick gray hair. Probably he had been then a fairly young and loyal gardener, also, it developed, a general caretaker for almost the entire neighborhood, especially the children.

He had taken a patient and almost proprietorial interest in all the neighborhood affairs, especially those of Bar's mother after she had been left with a son to educate and not much money. Emmy had been thankful and pleased to discover that when Bar's mother had felt obliged to get rid of that sprawling, expensive house, she had refused to part with Mac.

Her own parents had loved junketing around the world, now here, now there; Mac had known of it and had taken special pains to watch out for Emmy herself. Kate was then almost grown-up and could, and did, map out her own course and follow it, willy-nilly. Nobody could do much with Kate. Emmy didn't remember where her parents were when she went away to school; she vaguely remembered hearing of their sudden and fatal illnesses after daringly bathing in icy water somewhere. The Judge had taken over, kindly and sympathetically.

Bar eventually had disappeared into university and then law school. Archie, living in the same little neighborhood, had to give up his hope of becoming an architect. Eventually the Judge gave him work. She even knew, and thought of it with a half smile, Bar's full name, Hezekial Barselious Slocumb. He was mortally embarrassed by the first name and further embarrassed when some boys in preparatory school had discovered his middle name. Up to then he had preferred just initials. But after the discovery of Barselious and the resultant merriment of his school, he forced them to change it simply to Bar. Better than Hezekial any day, he had said once, grumbling, to Emmy.

And then—and then China became one of them. Emmy herself had brought her home. Bar met her, took one look and apparently went out of his head about China. China, Emmy was sure, most discreetly and sweetly encouraged Bar's devotion, of which certainly he made no secret. But he stopped seeing Emmy. Indeed, she did not see him at all during his infatuation, or real love or whatever it was, for China.

At that time she saw China, but only occasionally. China might have had a slight attack of conscience; she must at least have guessed of Emmy's feelings for Bar. Still, China was not apologetic; indeed, she rather flaunted Bar's attentions. Perhaps Emmy herself gradually cut off their former close friendship; certainly she had been deeply hurt.

But then—luckily, Emmy told herself—China, on one of her rare visits to Emmy, encountered thc Judge. He had made one of his admonitory visits to see Emmy, who by then had pulled herself together as thoroughly as she could, and got herself a job and a small apartment in New York.

The Judge, as Bar before him, fell almost instantly in love with China. For China, it seemed the choice was clear. So the Judge and China married. Bar disappeared.

All in the past, Emmy now told herself. The snow was falling faster. Archie came up beside them, hooting to pass. Bar paid no attention but drove steadily to Kate's little house.

Homer Jones opened the door and stood waiting for them. The lights behind him outlined his slight, if neatly tailored, figure and his rather disheveled hair. He said, "There you are. I lit the fire . . ." His voice came rather feebly through the snow and the thump of the cars' engines. Archie drew up behind them and crawled out.

Snow instantly began to crown the absurd knitted cap he wore. His face was tremulous, and so was his voice. He had apparently not seen Jones because he called shrilly, "Listen! I mean it! We had nothing like this before that man was brought here and—"

"*Archie!*" Kate descended from the car with such force that she fell against Archie, who automatically put out an arm to steady her. "*Archie,*" Kate cried in a voice that brooked no argument, "you are *not* to say that. Especially when he can hear you. He's had enough problems in his life, poor man. He didn't murder anybody. The Judge is never wrong."

Archie shoved back his cap but whispered piercingly, "The jury—"

"Juries can be wrong and often have been. Now then—" Kate marched toward the door and said pleasantly, her own voice very decisive, "How kind of you to see to the puppies, Mr. Jones. I've been thinking it over and I believe I can arrange to rent a room to you. That is—" Bar got out of his car, and Emmy, too, slid down from it into snow. She could hear Kate. "That is, by the rules of the Alpine Village Board I can't exactly rent a room to you. But if you help me with—oh, anything in compensation . . . Of course, I'll have to get rid of the puppies, but," said Kate, entering the house, "you will be a welcome guest. Nobody can quarrel with that. And," she ended triumphantly as Bar came up the steps, "I can tell the police so, or anybody else who wants to know!"

Kate gave Bar a look that ought to have pierced him but didn't, and then swerved her flashing blue gaze to Archie. "If anybody is talking about alibis, I can certainly give one to Mr. Jones. He was right here, talking to me about renting a room when those—those —when Mac—well, I mean when they were shot. Archie, you know where the liquor is! I think we can all do with a spot."

"But, Miss Kate," Homer Jones said hesitantly. "I wasn't here *all* evening, you know."

Kate never dodged any issue. "No. That's right. And they don't know just when the murders occurred. It must have been before you left."

Bar came through the snow. "Now wait a minute, Kate. Didn't the Judge say that he and China were here at the time the murders must have happened?"

"Why, I—do come in, Archie—everybody. Come in! Now let me see." She removed her bright scarf and shook her black curls. "Oh, yes. They were here. China wanted to look at the puppies. But the Judge didn't, so they left. Better put your coats down."

"How long were they here?" Bar asked, dropping his coat in the heap on a chair.

"Oh, how do *I* know!" Kate said impatiently. "Minutes—some time, anyway. And they went straight back to their house. I saw them go, and then—then Mr. Jones came. So—yes, all three of them have alibis, you see, Bar?"

"Doesn't that depend on what time Mac—and this other man—were shot?" Bar asked in a very quiet way.

Kate flashed a glance at him. "And you tell me, since you're so smart, how anybody is going to determine just when either man was shot. Snow—cold—everything . . ."

"Oh, I think there'll be some idea," Bar replied quietly again. "Certainly it must have been close to five-thirty."

"You don't know how long it took Mac to walk here from Appledown in the snow."

"I don't know anything," Bar said flatly.

Kate went on, "At least the police and Manders seem to have established it as fact that nobody heard the shots. Not that there has been much time to establish anything," she interpolated dourly. "But just the same, I don't think anybody would have heard the shots that far away and with the snow and those cars that keep plowing along, making all sorts of noise down the main road."

A rather wild chorus of yelps diverted her. "Just see to them, will you, Mr. Jones! I want to get out of this stifling coat."

Bar sank down in a chair and looked very grim. "I want the police to find that gun and trace it and—"

Kate went into the dining room; there was a clatter of glasses but she shouted, "No revenge, now, Bar! We can't have more—more murders. The way you look, that's what you are thinking of. Here—" She came back with a laden tray. "You must not even *think* of revenge. Besides, it's quite obvious that some motorist—some thug . . ." Her handsome face brightened. "Of course! It was somebody on one of those devilish motorcycles. They make such a racket. The sounds of the shots would have been drowned. I wonder if the police searched Mac's pockets or—I mean, both men's. Drink this, Bar. And get that black look off your face."

Bar's face was not black at all; it was still stony white.

Kate put one hand on his shoulder in an unusual gesture of affection. She glanced around the room. "Anyone else? Mr. Jones?"

During Emmy's heated conversation with the Judge the previous night she had paid little attention to the young man who had proved to be Homer Jones. Now she looked at him sharply but, she thought coldly, didn't see much. Certainly nothing more than she had seen before: a youngish man, in his thirties probably; thin, pale-faced, with wispy hair, and a little mustache, rather as if he hadn't the heart to shave. She guessed now that the newness and smartness of his clothes were accounted for by the fact that they had been purchased on his release from prison. Probably that stay in prison also accounted for his pallor; his face was hollow under the cheekbones; he had a high, shiny forehead; his eyes were light, gray or blue, but just now looked bright and troubled. She suspected there were rather narrow shoulders underneath his padded jacket, and certainly he didn't have what one would call a look of much outdoor exercise. But then, when does a stockbroker have time for much exercise? Perhaps—yes, he must have had exercise in prison. But mainly he seemed only shy and desirous not to intrude. She took a stinging sip of her whiskey.

Homer Jones shoved back straggling hair and said diffidently, "I think I'd better go. I know you want to talk without a stranger—that is," he ended lamely, "I'm sure the Judge and Mrs. Doane will wait up for me. Yes, I'd better go."

"Why?" said Kate. "You stay right here! That is, if you like."

Jones hesitated; he twisted boneless-looking hands together. "But, Miss Brace—you see—well, the fact is . . ." He looked at Archie, and Kate said, "Archie. Archibald Callser. Everybody calls him Archie."

"Yes, I know. He came here this evening. But until he told me about the murders I didn't—I mean, I didn't know . . ."

"We'll have to wait until the post-mortems are done," Kate said, nailing down facts as usual. She fixed Bar and Archie with a steely look. "Until then we can't do much. I know that Mr. Jones was here during the late afternoon. After the Judge and China went home. It was dark; must have been sometime after five. He wanted to know if there was any chance of renting a room from me during the time the Judge would be working on his memoirs. He felt that he was not quite—that is, not entirely welcome at the Judge's house."

"Mrs. Doane," Jones muttered, looking down at his hands.

And how right he was, Emmy thought in an oddly detached observation. Nothing just then seemed quite real.

"Probably China didn't like it," Kate said on a brisk note.

No, she didn't; but in view of Jones's limp and discouraged attitude, Emmy could not bring herself to say it. There were some squeals from the extra bedroom.

"*When* will you get rid of those puppies, Kate?" Bar asked.

"As soon as possible! They are growing rapidly."

"As soon as you can find some suckers to take them," Archie said unkindly.

Kate flashed up angrily. "I can't shove them out in this snow, can I? I couldn't just leave the little things there in The Barn! Manders had already heard of them and was about to have Mac take them to the nearest kennel—or," Kate said darkly, "just dispose of them, no matter how."

"Mac wouldn't have done that, Kate," Bar said soberly.

"No, not dear old Mac. But I couldn't trust Manders. Or the rest of the Board for that matter—always willing to fight me about having more than one dog in my house. Or two," she added, for the sake of accuracy. "However, as soon as I can find good homes for them, Mr. Jones—may I say Homer?" She turned to Jones, who looked up, surprised, and then nodded, so his lank hair fell over his high forehead. "Then there'll be a room for you. You can help me with, oh, all sorts of things. Gardening . . ." It seemed to Emmy, but still remotely, that Jones looked a little doubtful. "Driving?" Jones nodded, but rather uncertainly, too. He said painfully, as if wrenching out the words, "You're very kind, Miss Brace—that is, all of you, but you must see my position. I'm the only stranger here in Alpine Village, and now a few days after I came here—two murders!"

Bar looked stonily at the floor. Archie puffed out his pink lower lip and rubbed a hand over his bald head. Kate, however, was never at a loss. "See here," she said firmly. "You've had a bad experience. You've lost confidence in yourself and, I should guess, in people. You've got to get over that. You've got to stand up and face everybody."

It demanded some sort of reply. Jones knotted his hands together, looked beseechingly at Kate and murmured, "It's not so easy you know."

"You've got to do it," Kate said, and taking a deep breath, faced another problem. "Now then, Bar, I have to ask, do you really intend for Mac to be sent to a strange cemetery?"

Bar, too, took a deep breath; he, too, could face facts. "Certainly not. He goes to our family plot. He belongs there."

Kate's resolute face softened. "That's fine. Good. Now, we'll have to make some arrangements."

"I'll take care of that!" Bar said shortly.

"Of course," Archie said, rubbing his bald head again. "All that has got to wait until after the post-mortems and I suppose an inquest or—certainly considerable inquiry. I didn't like the looks of all those policemen." He all but squirmed. "Made me wonder if my driver's license is in order. If I've forgotten and passed up a date . . ."

"Oh, Archie!" Kate permitted herself a tense smile. "You are so fussy. Let's get down to brass tacks. Who could have murdered those two men? We knew Mac. He hadn't an enemy in the world."

"He was shot, though," Emmy said suddenly.

Kate swerved around and looked at her as if she had forgotten that Emmy was there; it was one of Kate's less flattering ways of dealing with a rebellious younger sister; if Kate couldn't rule Emmy, she was quite capable of simply ignoring her.

And she's not going to rule me, Emmy thought, not about anything!

Bar said, his face stony again, "We're getting nowhere. You are coming home with me, Emmy. Good night, Kate." He nodded at Jones, who rose, wavered and sat down again as Kate motioned him back to his chair. Archie debated and twisted his woolly cap. "I'll stay and talk to Kate a little," he mumbled.

At the door, picking up Emmy's bright red coat, Bar said to

Kate, "You did have that gun this morning. Are you sure it's safe?"

Archie leaped up from his chair. "What gun? Has Kate got a gun?"

Kate took it with her usual aplomb. "Certainly I have a gun. A permit for its use too. Bar borrowed it last night. He returned it this morning. I assure you I didn't use it to shoot anybody. Although I must say that man of Manders' looked rather as if he needed shooting. Perhaps I'm wrong. But our dear Mac—never."

"Where is your gun?" Archie cried.

Kate eyed him. "Where I always keep it, of course! Nobody's business. Good night, Bar."

But Bar rose and went to the table near the door. He jerked open a drawer. "I left it here, Kate, but it's not here now. What did you do with it?"

Kate hurried to look in the drawer. "But, Bar, you must be mistaken!"

"I am not mistaken. I put the thing in that drawer while you were out this morning. Where did you put it? Think, Kate."

"But I—no, no, Bar—" Kate clasped her hands together. "Bar, I didn't touch that gun!"

Bar stood for a moment, meeting Kate's gaze. Then he shrugged. "Guns don't walk. Who has been in your house, Kate? How often do you leave the door open?"

"Why, why . . ." Kate tried and failed to rally. She said weakly, "All the time. That is, not quite all the time. I lock the door and put on the alarm at night. But during the daytime—Bar, this has been such a peaceful place, so—so free of crime . . ." She faltered.

Nobody can say it is free of crime any longer. It is steeped in crime, Emmy thought suddenly, with ugly force. She put her glass down with a thump that broke an extremely strained silence.

Bar said, "All right, Kate. I walked in here this morning while you were out. Who else has been here today that you know of? That is, besides China and the Judge and Mr. Jones, here. I mean, say, during the morning. Or early afternoon, or whenever you were out—think now."

Kate, for once distraught and showing it, sank down into a chair, shoved her hands up over her face and mumbled, "Anybody. Everybody. No, not everybody! I mean, anybody *could* have come in, but—" She turned to Bar. "Don't look at me like that! It couldn't have been my gun that shot them. It couldn't have been!"

"I hope not," Bar said shortly. "But I think we'll have to tell the police about it."

"Oh," Kate wailed. "Oh, no, Bar! It couldn't have been one of my friends. Anybody who would have come into my house and—and known where I keep the gun? Or even have known that I have a gun? Bar, you can't mean that my gun—*my gun*—was used to kill—"

"I don't know. I hope not, Kate. You'd better take a look all through the house. You may have moved the gun yourself, put it somewhere . . ."

Kate was shaking her head in denial when the telephone rang. Automatically she went to answer it. Oddly, however, almost at once her voice and her shocked and dismayed face seemed to change. Emmy, all of them, listened, as if frozen in position. "Why, yes," Kate said into the telephone. A very strange expression, not quite smug, yet rather pleased came into her face and even carried over into her voice. She didn't coo, but almost. "Why, yes, Hazel . . . Of course, but you should have two. Company for each other, you know . . . Yes, certainly—" She did become just a little hesitant; Emmy guessed she wanted to lie but couldn't bring herself to do so. "Well, you see, Hazel, they are very young . . ."

"My God," said Archie.

"Oh, yes," Kate went on. "They—they make a noise, all right . . . Well, not to—to chew on a bone yet, no. But they lap milk and eat chopped meat and bark and very soon . . . Yes, early tomorrow morning . . . Leashes—well, no—I haven't—that is, not yet. You might bring a heavy string. Or a ribbon or something," she said, but cautiously. She hung up and turned to them with a light of triumph in her eyes. "You see? Two more of the puppies gone. Hazel Clements—"

"*Kate!*" said Bar. "Can you possibly mean that Hazel Clements wants two of those squealing pups for *watchdogs*?"

Kate bit her lips.

Archie said again, "My God! Of course, Hazel Clements hasn't got very good sense, but still—watchdogs, forsooth . . ."

"They *will* be watchdogs. They are watchdogs. Didn't you hear them when we came in?" Kate said with authority, "Just give them a little chance and"—she finished with a flourish—"this is the very best time for them to adjust to a home. And to their owners. Really quite the best time. I wonder now which ones I should send her."

"Emmy," Bar said, "I'm going home. Are you coming?"

"Yes. Oh, yes." Emmy rose. "But do find that gun, Kate. We've got to know if—if somebody here in Alpine Village shot them."

"All right," Kate said. "All right. I know perfectly well I'll find it. Oh, are you going too, Archie? Mr. Jones?"

"Thank you," Jones replied politely and pulled on a light city overcoat. Archie shrugged into his sheepskin-lined jacket, his fringe of blond hair tousled and his bald head shining.

Kate stood in the doorway as the four of them went down the path. They had scarcely reached the road when they all heard Kate shut the door with a bang. Archie said, "She's putting on the alarm. Locking the barn door—"

"Oh, no," Bar said wearily. "It's quite possible that Kate got interested in something else, took the gun out of that drawer and put it somewhere else. Forget about it. Something else got her attention. No. I expect she'll find the gun."

"Hah," said Archie from the depths of his jacket.

Jones paused and said hesitantly, "You know, I—I really am imposing upon the Doanes. I am deeply indebted to the Judge. I can't just walk out and leave him. He is paying me for helping him with his memoirs. I'm not bad at—oh, data, you know. Facts. I was a broker," he added a bit stiffly.

The night was very still and dark, except for the continuing white drifts of snow. Emmy saw, however, the way Jones wrung his hands. "Oh, I really—I don't *know* what to do!"

Bar said rather dryly, "Don't do anything. Actually you can't leave the Village just now. The police would not take kindly to that."

"Oh," Jones said, "no, I suppose not. Well—well, good night."

There were still lights in the Judge's house. Emmy wondered whether or not China would permit Jones to enter. Probably she would. At least the Judge would.

Archie trudged along with them toward Bar's house. Bar, properly, Emmy thought, had locked the door. He opened it and said to Archie, not unkindly but wearily, "If you must come in, do. But I think—"

"All right," Archie said quickly. "Tell you the truth, I don't favor that dark road over toward my cabin. Too many boulders, too many trees, too many shrubs. All right on a fine day, but *tonight*!"

"Come in, then. But you can't stay here all night, you know."

Archie ambled comfortably into the living room. "Kate and those damned pups. I'll bet she gets rid of every single one of them. She wouldn't say how old they were; she's too smart for that. But she didn't discourage Hazel Clements either. That Kate!" Archie shook his head admiringly. "Calls a spade a spade, but she can tinker with the truth when it's convenient."

"Oh, sit down, Archie." Bar went to the fireplace, put on more logs, stirred them briskly into darting red flames and said almost nonchalantly over his shoulder, "How long had you known Belle Jones?"

Eleven

Archie stared. He took his cap in his hands and savagely rolled it, still staring at Bar. One of his curiously painful blushes swept up over his face and head and swept away again, leaving only pink eyelids, which now blinked nervously. His face happened to be turned in profile to Emmy and she seemed to see it for the first time. In his youth Archie had always been a roly-poly, agreeable child. Now, in profile, his face had a snouty look, nose projecting sharply above a small, pursed-in mouth and chin. He felt her gaze and turned toward her and at the same time turned into Archie again. Emmy told herself she was having illusions and she was too tired and too drained emotionally even to listen. But she listened.

Archie swallowed and stuttered and finally said, "How did you know?"

Bar straightened up from the now crackling fire, turned and leaned his elbow on the mantel. "Oh, Archie! You gave it away with almost every word you said this morning. How could I fail to wonder?"

"But, Bar, what did I say?" Archie's voice squeaked up, reminding Emmy of the puppies.

"Never mind. Just tell me. How did you happen to know her?"

"You mean," Archie said, still squeaking, "how did I happen upon the—the Jones murder. Don't you?"

"Why, yes, I suppose so. It wasn't like you, Archie. Venturing in with the police like that. Passing yourself off as a reporter. Now, I don't say you lied about the press card. I'm sure you didn't. But you did know Belle Jones."

"You've got to tell me how you knew. I mean, guessed—"

Bar sighed. "I know what you mean. When you saw where the police car was going, you must have followed. You must have recognized the address when it stopped. You had to be in the neighborhood. I don't say that you were or had been calling on Belle—"

"Oh, no! I wasn't. I didn't intend to. No, no. But—oh, well, Bar. Yes. I knew her. I mean, had known her. A little."

"How did that happen?"

"I don't see why you—"

"I'm a lawyer, so I'm interested in this kind of thing," Bar said. "Go on. Where did you meet her? When?"

Archie fumbled with his cap. "In a bar," he said in a low voice. "It was a—a singles bar. And she sat there alone. She was very pretty, you know." He shot one glance at Bar and went on, "I was alone too, you see. Brooding about nothing. Feeling a little—oh, lonely. And there she was, and before I knew it I had slid over to sit next to her and then somehow we got into conversation. And then it was about nine o'clock, and if she was waiting for somebody, he didn't turn up, and so—all right!" He said with a burst, "I took her home! But I didn't stay, Bar. Truly I didn't stay."

"Did you stay with her at other times?" Bar asked in a remote, disinterested voice.

"I wanted to, Bar. Yes. I wanted to."

"So you kept on seeing her."

"For a while. Not long."

"How long?"

"Listen, Bar, you have no right to question me like this."

"How long?"

"Oh, not long. A few months. Perhaps."

"Then what happened? Did Jones get onto your—call it friendship?"

"No! She—Belle just decided not to see me anymore. We didn't quarrel, Bar. Never a word of a quarrel. The fact is, I thought she was right. I—" Archie said simply, "All right, I'll say it before you do. Suddenly I was afraid I was getting in too deep. I only knew what she told me about herself—or her husband. That wasn't much. I do admit I was astonished to hear from you that he was out of prison and here. To actually meet him tonight at Kate's house. I was surprised—"

"Surprised?" There was the faintest edge in Bar's voice.

"All right. Astounded. Made me very nervous, really. I have no idea how much he knew of my friendship with that poor girl. Oh, Bar!" He shivered; even his heavily booted feet seemed to quiver as if he wanted to draw himself up protectively. "That little acquaintance with Belle was nothing! Just a—a nothing. But when I happened—honestly, Bar, after she had been murdered, I only happened to be passing the corner near her—their apartment when I saw the police car and, of course, I had to follow—see where they were going and why, and when they went into the apartment house, that's when I remembered the press card in my wallet and—oh, God," Archie said, mopping his face with the woolly cap, "I wished I hadn't. I'll never forget . . ."

Bar watched him incuriously for a moment. At last he said, "No. You'll never forget. I understand that. But are you absolutely sure that Jones never knew of you and your—friendship with his wife?"

"Yes. That is"—there was the smallest doubt in Archie's reply—"she told me she had never mentioned me to him. At Kate's tonight we really met for the first time. He was simply polite, that's all. Bar, you must believe me. There was no life-and-death affair with Belle—oh Lord, why did I say that! But I mean, there was just no"—he seemed to hunt for a word—"no entanglement. Nothing. Really, you're trying to make me say there was a love affair, or something. There wasn't. After I met her we made sort of—well, dates. A movie several times. Usually just drinks, and if she didn't expect her husband home that night, sometimes we had dinner. Seems he was out of town occasionally. The girl was lonely and—Bar, she was so damn pretty! To see her like that—" He put his hand, still clutching the cap, up over his face.

Emmy believed him. She didn't think that Bar entirely accepted Archie's story, though. He said, "It's late. You'd better go home,

Archie. I promise you nobody is going to leap out of the trees and take a shot at you, even if there is a murderer in Alpine Village. No one has a reason for that. Not even this poor Jones guy. If he knew nothing of your—friendship," said Bar, again with the barest, slightest emphasis on the word, "then he has no reason to shoot at you. Oh, hell, Archie, we can't settle anything tonight. Go home."

"All right. But see here, Bar. There's no need to tell anybody that I actually knew poor Belle Jones. It didn't come out at the trial or in any of the evidence. I don't mind admitting that I was scared half out of my wits. You know the Judge. He'd have raised hell, fired me, anything that occurred to him. Even make me get up there and testify to the jury about my knowing her."

He came to a full stop. Bar nodded. "All right, Archie. Take it easy. I won't say anything unless I have to, and just now I can't see why anybody would have to know. Go on, Archie."

Archie scrambled, fumbled, blundered his way out, closing the door behind him cautiously, as if he might waken somebody.

"Bar, I can't believe it! Archie! But he didn't kill that woman, Bar. He couldn't—"

"I find it hard to consider," Bar said slowly. "But he didn't just happen to be near her apartment when the police cars dashed along, going in that direction."

"But he may have been."

"Not likely, Emmy. It was one of those narrow cross streets, going nowhere in particular unless to neighborhood shops. No, he was on his way to her apartment. To make peace with her, perhaps. Just to see her—" Bar paused there, and as if for something to do, poked up the fire again.

"But, Bar, we've known him forever. We grew up together."

"Emmy, did it ever occur to you that always, with murder, there are people who say so-and-so couldn't have done it because he's known him all his life and wouldn't hurt a fly?"

"But all the same! Archie!"

Bar replied as if she had asked a question. "I can't see that Belle Jones's murder has any connection at all with this tonight. Yet, as Kate says, Alpine Village had no crime until now, after a paroled murderer has come to stay here! Not," Bar added more naturally, "that he'll stay at the Judge's much longer. Not if China has anything to say about it."

Emmy felt tears coming, not about China, or Jones, not about anybody but good, dear old Mac. Bar knew it. He crossed to her, stood above her for a moment and said, "Emmy, don't. It does no good now. Please don't."

"I can't help it. It's so wrong. He deserved something so much better, and—"

"There, now, Emmy." His voice was harsh and commanding. "Stop it!"

"All right. But it's so terrible. While we were sitting in the restaurant, enjoying the dinner and the wine—why, we must have passed that place where he was shot very near to the time he died. He'd have been at the guardhouse by five-thirty. You know Mac. Always dependable. He—oh, Bar, he must have been lying out there in the snow, and if we had stopped and looked and—"

"We had no reason to stop and hunt through the trees and shrubs. No reason at all." Bar's voice was harsh again. He, too, was blaming himself.

Emmy said, "But we couldn't have dreamed that anything like that could have happened. Let's not reproach ourselves."

"I do. You do. We can't help that. But no, I didn't have the slightest notion there was anything wrong."

"You said it was strange that Mac wasn't on time at the guardhouse."

"Sure. I did think that. But, Emmy, I do wish we had looked for him. Yet would we have searched around right there?"

"No. No, I guess not. I'm just so tired."

He stood perfectly still, looking down at her. Why didn't he take her in his arms and try to comfort her? Only a friendly gesture, she thought vaguely, it needn't be anything else.

She stood up. "Oh, Bar—" and he put his arms around her.

"Emmy." His face was warm on her cheek. "Dear Emmy . . ."

His arms were strong and comforting and in a second she knew that she loved him all over again. More, really, oh, much, much more than she had ever loved him.

Once, long ago, she had recognized her feeling, and she'd been foolishly—not shy, but certainly not very forthcoming. But then she certainly had not intended to throw herself at him.

She was throwing herself at him now. It was the thing to do, clearly indicated. All her strength and—dear me, she thought vaguely, all my heart is going into this. She moved to turn her face toward his lips when the door opened, and cold air and snow hurled in. The door banged shut and China cried, "What on earth are you two doing?"

Bar continued to hold Emmy. She was grateful for that. He said, almost laughing, yet sharply too, "What do you *think* we are doing?"

China didn't laugh. She said, in her lovely, flutelike but just then piercing voice, "So the Judge was right! That's why Emmy insists on staying here with you. And everybody around here knowing both of you. Really, Bar! How can you let Emmy do this to you?" Unexpectedly, in a burst, China began to sob. "I told you! I'll never go back as long as that man Jones is there. Emmy can go to Kate's. I am going to stay with you, Bar. For always. I know that your feelings have never changed. You knew I preferred the Judge, and you still—Why, Bar," she wailed, "this time I even left my fur coat at home."

Emmy had moved a little away from Bar. But at this statement of China's she could not repress at least one comment. Her face was still wet with tears; her voice was unsteady, but strong enough. She heard herself say, "But you brought your ring with you, China."

"Oh!" China's heavy lashes drooped over her pink cheeks. "Oh! I never thought of it," she sobbed, feebly enough to please some little feminine instinct in Emmy. Once before, she reminded herself, she had not fought for Bar. She had simply stood aside and suffered and watched China capture him with her charm. Never again, she told herself, never again!

Bar stood quite still. Surely there was a slight twinkle in his eyes. Two women fighting over him!

Emmy decided to dry her face, groped for, but found no handkerchief, and wiped her sleeve across her eyes.

Bar gave her, she thought, a rather approving look.

China stopped sobbing. "Remember, Bar, all this time whenever you were here at Alpine Village and—of course, only when the Judge was gone—you took me to dinner, you helped me when I was lonely, we had the most wonderful dinners at that enchanting restaurant. We drank and looked out the windows toward the river and talked and—Bar, I knew all the time, I *knew* that you had never changed. I told you this afternoon. You were—you are still in love with me."

"But you changed your mind about that only this afternoon."

"This afternoon! Those two dreadful murders hadn't happened then!" China flashed.

That was incontrovertible.

"You can't blame the Judge for that."

"I blame him for letting Jones come into our house and saying, at first, that he was only a new secretary to help him with his memoirs and then, when I found out who Jones really is, the Judge—" China mopped at her eyes and said plaintively, "You heard the Judge! Somehow he got me to go back to him but now —now," she cried angrily, "*never!*"

Bar said very quietly, "What has the Judge done now, China?"

"Knowing Kate, perhaps you can guess!" China sobbed again.

"You don't mean—surely the Judge has not told Kate he'd take a puppy! She said he didn't want one."

China touched her eyes lightly; lightly so as not to disturb any make-up, Emmy thought, still in a cat-scratching mood. At any other time, she could have thought up a number of crushing remarks. Somehow, just then, nothing seemed quite important enough to say.

China cried, "Not only one puppy! He changed his mind and Kate talked him into taking two of them! For watchdogs, she said. Now, you know, Bar—and you too, Emmy—those are puppies! Not watchdogs . . ."

"They're aging rapidly. Like me," Bar said dryly.

"And not only that, he expects me to feed them. Even the Judge says I'm a good cook, but I'm not a dogs' chef!"

Bar started for the telephone. "Are you now quite determined not to go home tonight, China?"

"How can I! After those murders! It proves that man Jones is dangerous and—Bar! He murdered those two men!"

"Why do you say that, China? What proof have you?"

"Nobody needs proof. It's—it's obvious. Nothing horrible like what happened before Jones came here. Listen, Bar, you may say there's no connection between Jones and killing that old servant of yours—"

"Not servant," Emmy said, not quite shouting. "He called himself that, but in fact he was like a—a—"

"Surrogate parent?" Bar suggested in a low voice, but watching China, and still not taking up the telephone.

"But he wasn't a relative, or anything. Oh, I know you and Emmy and Kate and even Archie were all foolishly fond of him. But even so—"

"Don't, China! If you are quite determined this time, I'll call Kate and tell her to make some space for you. She has a sofa—" Bar picked up the phone.

China's pretty lips set over her small white teeth. "No."

Bar sighed. "China, you must listen. Jones's arrival did, in a way, coincide with what happened tonight, but what does the Judge think about it?"

China pouted but replied, "He says there's always coincidence. He is wrong!"

Bar seemed to debate. Coincidence did happen, yet rarely that kind of coincidence: a murderer once convicted, turning up, paroled, and in just a few days not one but two murders. Emmy said, "Mac could have had no possible connection with Jones. Or his wife—"

But Archie had had such a connection with Jones, or by way of Jones, with murder.

The doorbell rang melodiously, yet somehow almost apologetically, twice. Emmy was not at all surprised when Bar opened the door and Jones, almost cringing and apologetic, stood on the threshold. His eyes went diffidently around to find China. "Mrs. Doane," he said in a small voice, quite as if he expected China to haul off and lash out at him with one pretty hand. "The Judge, your husband—I mean, he sent me to tell you that you still have your ring."

"Oh!" China cried. Anger came up like a pink tide into her face. "Tell him—tell him—" She looked down at her hand, already

stretched out as if in truth she wanted to slap Jones. Her gaze fixed itself for an instant or two. Bar didn't smile. Nobody smiled. Emmy, though, said too gently, "It's a beautiful ring, China. Must have cost the Judge—almost as much as your sable."

"Oh," said Jones, almost wincing. "That reminds me. Your husband also said, don't worry about the fur coat. He has plans for it."

Emmy could not resist another comment inspired by the green monster. "I wonder who," she said. "Kate? He has always admired Kate. You did say he had talked to her about my job, and the puppies and—Kate is a beauty, of course."

"Kate!" China's wide eyes flashed. "Not Kate!"

"Of course, she wouldn't like giving up her hopes for a political career. But then, I'm sure the Judge admires her for that, too,"

China hesitated scarcely a second. She snatched up the old tweed coat she had worn since she and Emmy were in school together and flung it around her shoulders. "I'll be back, Bar. This is only—I'll be back, darling." She added the word with a sharp glance at Emmy, which obscurely—perhaps not so obscurely—pleased Emmy. Bar said agreeably, "I'm sure that's sensible, China."

"For now," China turned back to snuggle her head against Bar's shoulder. "Dear Bar! You must believe me. I was so wrong . . ."

"If you please, Mrs. Doane," Jones said in a low voice, "the Judge told me not to wait—"

"Oh, all right." China, lifting her head swiftly, gave Bar a kiss, whirled around and went out.

Not surprisingly, there was a moment of silence in the room. Bar stood, simply looking at the closed door. Emmy waited, listening for something, she didn't know what. When China said she would be back, she meant it. China was remarkably adept at getting her way, and even in her school days had never given up anything her small hands had succeeded in grasping.

Bar said soberly, "I can't quite believe in coincidence. But I can't see any possible connection between Jones and dear old Mac. Unless Mac just—just got in the way."

"What can we do?"

Bar gave the most disappointing reply a man can give a woman.

"I don't know. I really don't know. First, though, Emmy, go to bed." His eyes had been far away, now he looked fully at her. "Try to sleep." He turned and lifted the pad of her notes out of a table drawer.

"Why, those! I haven't even thought of those."

Twelve

He glanced at her. "Dear Emmy, don't you remember that the Judge said you were in danger?"

"Oh, yes! Yes."

"But you forgot, tonight. Actually, so did I. Yet somehow I keep thinking that there just might be some sort of link between this Belle Jones murder and tonight."

"But Mac—"

"No. Not Mac. It occurs to me that we know very little of that man who worked for Manders. That's all, Emmy. So far, what we know is so little. It's like two approaches to a bridge, if you can put it that way. I mean, the middle span, if there is one, is not here."

"I know . . ."

"A main connection is not available. If there is one. I may be, probably am, all wrong. But look here—on one side is the Judge's seeing to a parole for Jones, the Judge's warning to you, Jones's presence here. On the other end are two murders. Nothing between."

"You forget Archie and Belle."

"I don't forget Archie and his little love affair. Yet I don't think —no, I can't find a connection there. At least—oh, go to bed, Emmy."

"What are you going to do with those notes of mine?"

"Try to read them, of course." He gave her a brief smile. But then he came to her, tilted her face up and kissed her, but on the cheek in a merely friendly way, which gave Emmy a pang. She made reluctant, yet very weary progress to the bedroom door. She turned back there, half hoping for something, she wouldn't let herself think just what, but Bar had already settled down near a table lamp with the wadded-up, still damp papers.

She watched him for a moment, then closed the door.

She was tired to her very bones, emotionally, completely wrung out, not even a trace of vigor. Behave sensibly in emergency! Somebody had drilled that into her at an early age; it must have been Kate, who was always sensible and stern with a young sister.

At another time she might have felt at least a quiver of amusement over Kate's adroit managing of the puppies. By morning, she rather thought, Kate would have neatly palmed off every one of them on the frightened residents of Alpine Village. Their reactions, on discovering that they had taken in untrained puppies to care for would never trouble Kate. Nobody, oh, nobody, would be able to summon up the sheer courage it would take to face down Kate and force her to take back a single pup.

At another time she might also have admired the adroit way the Judge had got China to return. At another time she might have thought it surprising that China, threatened by the loss of her various luxuries—and the implied loss of them to another woman—had gone swiftly away in the care of a man she regarded as a murderer, in spite of her husband's judgment to the contrary.

China had not even hesitated to grasp Jones's arm on the slippery step. Emmy had noticed that.

She looked at the bed and was thankful that, impressed by the neatness and shiny cleanliness of the house, she had carefully made her bed, folding back the eiderdown. All she wanted just then was to crawl into bed and—but of course she would never be able to sleep.

She was wrong about that. In the midst of a warm bath, she found herself sliding down and down and suddenly roused, half-frightened. She got safely out and into bed as quickly as she could, but of course she would not sleep. There were too many things to think of, too many questions. So she slept.

It was an intensely quiet night, for the snow continued remorselessly and became heavier and heavier. The wind rose and piled up drifts. Storm warnings, blizzard warnings came out over the air for all listeners. It seemed still dark in the room when Emmy struggled out of an almost drugged sleep and was aware of the fragrance of coffee and a little sound very close to her ear. She awakened sufficiently to know that something small, cold and moist was shoving at her cheek.

She managed to open her eyes and a warm body knew it and nuzzled again at her cheek. So, she thought dazedly, one of Kate's puppies had managed to get here.

It was indeed a puppy, rather large, white—or whitish—with black beguiling eyes, a black nose and a pink tongue.

"Oh," Emmy cried. "Oh, no! I won't even look at you."

"Emmy," Bar said from the doorway. "Here's some juice and coffee to help you wake up." He brought a tray and put it on the bedside table. "I couldn't manage both pup and tray, so I—oh, I see you've found him. You were so sound asleep. Emmy, don't push your hair back like that. It looked very"—he paused, set down the tray and said remotely—"very pretty. Here . . ."

He reached for her dressing gown, which lay on a chair, thrust it at her, considerately went to open window curtains while she adjusted the robe around her shoulders—and indeed around the pup who snuggled shamelessly and refused to be dislodged.

Emmy looked at the pup, who looked back at her in a completely beguiling but also determined way. "Oh, no," she wailed again. "Not one of Kate's."

"Oh, yes." Bar came back from the window. The gray light of day poured into the room. He poured coffee for her. "You'll feel better when you've had coffee."

"But, Bar! I told her! I told you. *No pup.* It isn't fair! I can't have a dog! You said, no pup!"

"I changed my mind."

He eyed her, half smiling, for a moment as she adjusted the puppy's warm weight within one arm. Then he said softly, "Why, Emmy, you are lost already."

"I'm not! I tell you I can't—"

"Kate brought it this morning early. She says he is the runt of the litter, although he's really big for a runt. She says the others hassle him only because he has such a sweet nature that he won't fight back. May be true, too." There was the faintest little twinkle in his eyes.

"*No!*" She couldn't help feeling an unwelcome kind of warmth as the puppy eyed her thoughtfully and then, as if satisfied, wriggled closer. "I can't," she said again feebly.

"All right," Bar said agreeably. "You can board him with me. Until I sell this house. And"—his voice hardened—"that may not be soon. After last night."

Last night! The memory of the previous night fell upon her. Bar said, "Kate says he's to be given milk and I think she said ground steak. And she meant steak."

"Might as well have said caviar," Emmy said crossly. "Does she expect me to take out a bank loan to feed this"—her voice softened in spite of herself—"this creature?"

The creature was nosing at the cup she held and not liking the scent of coffee. But he liked snuggling down beside Emmy and stretched out enormous paws contentedly.

"If he grows into his paws," Bar said absently, "he'll be quite a dog. I wonder what his ancestry is."

"That doesn't matter," Emmy began hotly before she realized that he was again amused. He said, more seriously, "It's a good thing Kate is so rich."

"Oh, she's not rich! Neither am I. That is, even when I get my share of my father's estate."

"How about the Judge? Is he very wealthy?" Bar asked slowly.

"Why, I—why, I don't know! Yes, he must be."

"Where did his money come from?"

"Good heavens, you're not suggesting that he has mismanaged my inheritance!"

"No, no! He wouldn't—that is, he couldn't safely do that. Too many stiff laws about trustees. No, I'm not suggesting that. But I can't help wondering—that is, as long as I've known the Judge, it's only just lately that I realized that he must have quite a lot of money."

She sipped her coffee gratefully but thinking hard. "It's easily explained. He didn't earn it all himself, if that's what you mean. It was this way. You know that he is my father's younger stepbrother."

"Why, yes. Yes, I must have known that always."

"Well then, his mother was my—my grandfather's second wife. She was a widow with one boy. The Judge—well, he wasn't a Judge then—but she was very rich. Big rich, Bar."

"Very canny of your grandfather. And she left her money to her own boy. Is that it?"

"Yes. Oh, it didn't make any difference to my father. He was a kind of—I didn't know him very well, of course. He was away so much, he liked doing things like—oh, skiing and driving fast cars, too fast . . ." She remembered the puzzled day when she was informed that she now had no father and mother but that her uncle would do his best to take their place. She said soberly, "The Judge was very good to Kate and me. Always."

"I take it that he wasn't content with simply enjoying the money his mother left him."

"Oh, no. He was determined to become a lawyer and he worked very hard, he really did. And then he got to be a Judge, but you know all this."

"Not quite all," Bar said soberly. "I think he had been a Judge for some time when he met China. I can't remember."

A flick of anger roused her. She took a sip of coffee and eyed him above the cup. "You know perfectly well when the Judge met China. You had been head over heels in love with her for months. And then she met the Judge and—"

Bar laughed unexpectedly. "Naturally I remember that. I was ready to kill the Judge—not quite kill him, just push him off a cliff somewhere."

"You didn't."

"Thought better of it," Bar said coolly. "Have you decided to follow the Judge's mandate about giving up your job?"

Emmy sat up so abruptly the puppy rolled off the bed and gave a cry of protest.

"Certainly not!"

"I thought you'd say that." He scooped up the puppy. "It's time for you to go back to the kitchen, pup. Newspapers on the floor there. See you later, Emmy."

"What are you going to do?"

"Take this creature to the kitchen first. Then—" He sobered. "Yes, then I'll go to The Barn. Kate says the police have taken it over as a kind of office. I'll find out what's going on there. Besides, I understand—Kate again of course—that they are questioning everybody here in Alpine Village. Then, I think, Emmy, I'm going to beard our tycoon. Nobody that I know of so far knows anything about this Guy Wilkins. Manders, of course, employed him. He can fill in any details, all his background, I should think. I have a feeling that Manders wouldn't miss much of an employee's background and ability before he hired him. The police have already checked with him, I'm sure. But I want to talk to Manders myself and—" He held the pup closer as the animal gave an impatient wriggle. "Tomorrow if I can I want to go to the city. One or two errands . . . small—"

"You mean you found something in my notes! You intend to investigate, explore—what?"

"I'm not sure. Oh, I contrived to translate some of it—I'll check with you later. 'Bl.O.Ev.'—must mean 'Blood over everything.' You were very accurate if that is what you meant. In view, that is, of what Archie told us. I have to see some of the newsprint myself."

"There must be snowdrifts . . ."

"So the weather report says. Fix yourself a real breakfast unless you are above cooking. You should model yourself upon China." He grinned a little. "I'll get to The Barn. See you when—when I can. All right, old fellow," he addressed the wriggling bundle. "Just hold everything for a minute. What are you going to name him, Emmy?"

"I'm not going to name him anything. He goes back to Kate."

"What'll you bet," Bar said and disappeared.

She had scrambled into jeans and a sweater when Bar knocked at the door and, at her word, opened it. He was vigorously drying his hands on a towel. "Only a suggestion. But you might name him Mopup. Seems suitable."

"I'm not going to name him anything! Bar, did Kate ever find her gun? Did she say?"

"She said no, she hadn't found it. Oh, she searched, all right. Kate is very thorough. But no gun. All right, Emmy. I'm off. Don't go out or if you do, look out for drifts. See you."

A few minutes later the outside door closed heavily. A small wail of loneliness arose from the kitchen.

In the neatly shining kitchen she made herself breakfast. A small package on a table turned out to be finely chopped steak. The puppy lifted his head and sniffed hungrily.

But I'm not lost, Emmy told herself; I can't keep him. She wished he didn't remind her of the succession of dogs of her childhood.

She put the chopped meat in a saucer and the puppy devoured it, gulping as if he had learned quickly to defeat any encroacher. He made funny little growls as he did so—probably, in a lively imagination, fighting off other puppies.

She restored the kitchen to shining order. She telephoned Kate and got no answer. Kate was probably in the thick of whatever was going on in The Barn. Emmy was beginning to capitalize The Barn in her thoughts as other people did in their speech. She made her bed; she aired the room but did so very quickly, for icy drafts came in, although only the barest slice of window was open. Bar had already neatly made his bed. His was a big room, sparsely furnished.

Snowdrifts were so heavy that they rose against the windows and darkened the day. By the time she looked out the front door the marks of Bar's footsteps had disappeared under the merciless, flying curtains of snow. Kate must have had to wade out to bring the puppy and go to The Barn.

Her notes were lying on a table below a big lamp. She looked them over carefully. Bar had dried them, or they had simply dried out themselves. Bar had obligingly made penciled notes above curtailed words and, as far as she could tell, had made surprisingly accurate guesses. If she could once get back to newsprint, she might be able to fill in those words, not very sensibly shortened to merely symbols, but surely she would be able to recognize her own hasty scrawlings.

In her apartment in the city she had a thick sheaf of newspaper and magazine clippings, offered her obligingly by the top editor of the television channel where she was employed—still employed, she determined, still employed. As soon as she could see those, surely she could interpret every little abbreviation she had made.

The snow stealthily drifted down without stopping, a steady, unrelenting whiteness. She turned on the lamp beside what seemed to be Bar's reading chair and studied all her jottings. There were the names, Belle Jones, Homer Jones, the dates of the murder, arrest, arraignment, trial. Only one trial; it had not been appealed. Probably, Jones's attorney had believed that an appeal was not worthwhile. There was the address of the Jones apartment; there was a rough drawing, which she had hurriedly made, showing the layout of the four rooms. No indication there of any intruder; there was no back door and no nearby fire escape. The murderer had had to enter by the front door. There was her own translated version of the hideous condition of the room where Belle's body had been found. Yes, "Bl.O.Ev." meant "blood everywhere," so Belle had put up a fight for her life. "No. W." That was easy: "no weapon found." "No K.," easy, too: "no knife." Time of Jones's report to the police; time of his questioning and first report and the fact that he had been taken, as "mat. wit—!" "Material witness." Only later did it appear as "M. sus": "Murder suspect."

One or two scribbles of her own shorthand baffled her. "No Rg." could mean anything—no, what? She thought over words beginning with "r" and including a "g." There was a faint scribbled question mark here. She went through the alphabet. There were many—rag, rang, rig, rug; at last it occurred to her that she must have meant that the rug had been ruffled up, indicating a struggle.

In the main, from what she could read, she believed with sufficient accuracy that her notes followed the newspapers' and Archie's accounts of the murder—poor old Archie, dragged into the terrible business of murder by his own curiosity and his interest in pretty, young Belle Jones!

It had grown rather dark as she worked over the dried but wrinkled papers. The darkness was due as much to the snowdrifts against the windows as it was to the natural shortness of a December day. Eventually the puppy got tired of being alone in the kitchen and, with rather a qualm, Emmy let him into the living room where he bounced over to her chair and as soon as she resumed her seat, made a scrambling, pawing but successful climb into her lap. "I'm not going to keep you," she said to him, ruffling his ears.

Inevitably, half-dreaming, her thoughts went back to the days of her childhood and teens. A thin and awkward child, hadn't she been? Working hard at school because she'd been urged on relentlessly by Kate, who naturally, had always been a brilliant and obedient scholar. There had been Bar. Older than Emmy, not as old as Kate, but brave, he had often stood between Kate and Emmy, always ready to help Emmy solve any problem. Bar had taught her to skate. Bar had not taken her to her first dance; by that time he was old enough to look (with probably a rather indulgent eye) upon teen-age dances. But suddenly, then, Emmy was almost grown-up; Emmy *was* grown-up and Bar began to see her not more often but with a different attitude. She had been all but overcome by the increasing warmth of his affection; she couldn't, she thought now, have been entirely mistaken about that.

She had known that she was in love with him; she told herself that the time would soon come when Bar told her that she was the only girl for him—and then China had come to visit. Bar had taken one look at China and China had taken, Emmy had to admit, more than one look at Bar. China was always irresistible; Bar hadn't, as far as Emmy knew, even tried to resist.

As a result, Emmy and Bar drifted apart. Even after China met and married the Judge, Bar did not come back to Emmy. So she had taken herself to New York to find a job and to put Bar completely out of her mind. Since she couldn't have what she wanted, she had to take what she could get and stick to it with all her will.

That, she told herself, watching the snow, is all in the past; nothing in the past could be altered. Somebody had once said to her, a relationship between a man and a woman never stands still; it changes one way or another.

It was true; her relationship with Bar had not so much changed as reverted to her childhood and his teen-age years when he took upon himself the part of protector, guide, constant ally.

That was something valuable, however, she told herself firmly and forced herself to stop remembering long-ago days.

She wished she knew what was going on in The Barn. She wished she knew what Kate was doing, why Bar did not return, what, if anything, of interest he could succeed in digging out of Manders, who—in Emmy's opinion—would not be an easy man to interview very minutely. She wondered about Archie and thought over his sad, faltering yet, she felt, truthful account of his interest in Belle Jones. From the snow-blocked windows, Alpine Village was a dead village, merely a vaguely seen cluster of houses, each standing well apart from another, no visible smoke from fireplaces, even in the direction of The Barn. But then, the strong wind and the flying snow would hide every evidence of human activity.

She went back to her notes, but search as she might she could still find nothing which would suggest to Bar that a trip to the city might enable him to discover what he had said was needed: a link between Belle Jones's murder and the murder—yes, she thought dismally—the murder of two men the previous night. Nothing!

She hadn't thought of lunch. She did realize that it was quickly darkening. She hunted for and found a clock in Bar's room. Four-thirty. It couldn't be! She also found a radio and turned it on. "Four-thirty-two, Accu-weather report," said a voice in her ear. The snow had assumed blizzard conditions, roads were blocked. Advice about not driving followed: "—cars stuck in snow along the road—"

So they were marooned right here in Alpine Village until—well, Emmy thought, until. It was close to five and midnight dark when Bar returned. He shook snow from his sheepskin-lined coat and brushed back his hair. "Everything all right?"

"What has happened?"

"Not much really. Police got here but had to leave for emergencies somewhere. Roads are all but blocked everywhere, I suppose."

"Did you see Manders?"

"Oh, yes." He sat down to pull off his heavy snow boots. "He was very cagey. He said there could be no possible connection between his secretary—that's what he called this Guy Wilkins—and the Jones murder." He dropped one boot. "I didn't believe him."

"Why not?"

He frowned. "I don't really know. That is, in a way I can guess.

I do not think that a man like Manders would employ anyone, especially in what seems to have been a more or less confidential capacity, without knowing a great deal about him. He'd have searched out every single item of Wilkins' past."

"Well, then—"

"Yes, I know." Bar settled down in a deep chair, stretched out his long legs and sighed vastly. "It's no fun navigating those drifts. Actually this snow is blocking the police inquiry. So many cars in trouble, so many people phoning in for help. The whole thing must delay their inquiry. Luckily, our own snow plows are out." He grinned a little. "Kate has been delivering her pups. Seems everybody in Alpine Village wants a watchdog. Speaking of dogs, how's Snoopy here?"

"What a name! I won't call him Snoopy!"

"Seems to me rather a good name. If you don't like Mopup." The pup had found a corner of a magazine and was dragging it happily across to Emmy.

"Anyway," Emmy made her voice as steely as she could, "I'm not keeping him.

At this point the puppy started his awkward scramble to her lap. Emmy looked helplessly at him and couldn't help laughing as he reached his goal and stretched up a cold, black nose to her chin.

Bar was kind enough not to grin openly. "I think I'll mix a drink. Want one, Emmy?"

"Sure, anything. This blizzard has really confused things, hasn't it?"

"Bitched, is the word one uses. Not polite but—there." He brought a glass to her. The pup snooped at it and retreated, his nose wrinkling distastefully. "A white-ribbon boy." Bar sat down and sipped and thought. "Now Guy Wilkins, I gathered from Manders' very neat statements, was a wonder boy. Taught himself bookkeeping, shorthand—" He shot a glance at Emmy. "Seems to have succeeded better than you did, my friend. However, the point is, he progressed. Manders said that for at least three years Guy has been acting as chauffeur and secretary, a really confidential secretary, I gathered. I can't help wondering if that also means a man who can accomplish any of Manders' possible dirty work without a qualm. Doesn't sound very nice but that was my impression. Not that Manders even hinted as much. I don't know how or where I got that notion, but I did. One odd thing. Manders took me into his study, complete with books, desk, all the usual, plus"—Bar sipped again— "a glassed-in case of knives."

Thirteen

Emmy sat up. "Knives!"

Bar nodded. "Sure. Odd, isn't it? I've heard of people collecting all sorts of things, paper weights, guns even, but never knives. Some nasty-looking ones, too."

"But"— Emmy did not need to examine the path her thoughts took— "both men were shot."

"Sure." He looked white and tired again. "But somehow I just didn't like the looks of all those knives. Odd ones, of course, all sorts of shapes and I imagine points of origin. There was the Bowie knife. He pointed that out to me. He was a little amused, I think, when he showed them to me. However, I can't believe that he would be such a fool as to ever employ one of those knives."

Her mind gave a leap. "Belle!"

He shook his head. "I don't really think so. First place, nothing to connect him to Belle Jones. At least nothing that anybody knows about. But also, he's not such a fool. He wouldn't use one of his own knives on anybody. A dead give-away. But I can't see his using a knife from the kitchen in Belle's apartment either. That seems to have been the knife somebody used on her. At least, according to Jones's testimony. It was never found. Of course, the fact that a knife right there in Belle's apartment was used does indicate a lack of premeditation. So, if it was Manders, he simply might not have had time to get one of his own knives—but also he'd be a great fool to use a weapon so easily identified, and Manders is no fool." He paused, brooding.

Emmy said, "Suppose he, too, picked up Belle in some bar. And then wanted to get rid of her."

Bar sighed. "No proof of that. But I'll tell you this. I wouldn't trust him around me if I happened to displease him very much and the knives were handy. All in all it's been a frustrating day. I talked to several people who were out shoveling their sidewalks. Hoping for the snow plows to come along. The roads are wildly drifted." He took a long drink. "You realize, Emmy, that these houses are completely dependent upon electricity. If the storm downs some wires, here we are."

"All the amenities of home," Emmy said rather crossly.

"See here! You and I both have known blizzards and downed phone and electric lines before now. Besides, Miss Smarty, my mother saw to it that there is a plentiful supply of candles and also," he said triumphantly, "one of those little stoves that unfolds and food can be heated over a can of something—"

"What things? Soup? Oh, I *am* mean! I'll not give you a dinner such as your dear China would, but I'll fix something."

Bar never kept a cross mood very long. "We'll both work on it. There are things in the cupboards. And if the electricity does go off, I am told that with electric refrigeration, hours may pass before frozen foods are, so to speak, unfrozen. Kate told me."

"Kate would know. Haven't the police done *anything?*"

"They wouldn't tell me if they had. That is, yes, they were trying to question people when I got to The Barn. But then the phone began to ring. And they began to look harried. Finally I heard that a truck was stalled on the main highway with a string of snow-laden cars stalled behind it and—I think at that point they sort of said, 'to be continued as soon as we can,' and left."

A thunderous knock at the door was followed by Kate's tumultuous entrance, snow flew everywhere from her heavy cape. She shoved off a rather peculiar arrangement of a red scarf around her hair, shook out her handsome head of short dark curls and noticed the pup. "Ha, I knew you'd take to him, Emmy. Isn't he a sweetheart! The other pups did rather harass him because he just naturally has a very sweet nature."

"You'll have to take him home with you," Emmy said sternly.

Bar's lips twitched a little.

Kate saw his drink. "May I help myself, Bar? No, don't move. I know where—"

Kate always had such a healthy command of herself and circumstances that it was no surprise to see her go straight to the dining room buffet and come back with a full glass. She sat down. "What a day! But anyway all the pups—"

"What did you tell people, Kate?" Bar said. "They want watchdogs, but these puppies—"

"Oh, naturally, there was a little surprise now and then. Old Mr. Lowe almost reneged. But then I talked to him, reasoned with him. He saw the advantage of the early training of watchdogs."

Bar sat up. "Do you mean to say he took it? That crusty old guy!"

"Not crusty at all," Kate said indignantly. "Not if you talk to him a little."

Bar sat back. "You've gotten rid of the pups, Kate, but I'm afraid you've lost some votes."

A second's regret crossed Kate's face. However, she said briskly, "What's going on about the inquiry?"

Emmy listened. Bar said that he knew nothing. One fact did emerge; he had arranged by telephone for Mac's body to be sent when possible to his hometown cemetery and later placed in the Slocumb plot.

Kate nodded. "Good. Now this Guy Wilkins. You know, I never trusted that man. Too smarmy if you know what I mean. Oily. Wanted to please everybody but really—yes, really I should say—very secretive somehow. I'm afraid it occurred to me that probably he did some things for Manders which might not have been quite admirable," said Kate, moderately.

"You mean quite legal?"

"I don't know. I can only say that it wouldn't surprise me. But to be fair, I just don't like Mr. Manders. Can't help it. No special reason."

Bar watched her over his glass. "Woman's intuition," he hazarded. He didn't duck, although Kate's hand shot out toward a book on the table.

Kate resisted her obvious desire but a flush was in her cheeks.

"Not at all! I wouldn't trust woman's intuition that far. By the way, have you seen China or the Judge today?"

"No," Bar said flatly.

"Oh, dear!" Kate sighed. "I do hope she's not filling up those pups with some of her fancy foods."

"Kate," Bar said, "can't you get your mind off those dogs for just a few minutes?"

"Of course I can and do." Kate's blue eyes gave him a sharp glance. "I've been trying to find out who shot those men. Not much help from the police but I expect they're busy right now rescuing stranded people—cars or houses or—Emmy," she said sharply, "have you given any thought to the Judge's advice to you?"

"Certainly, Kate. I decided that, immediately. I don't intend to follow it. If this snow ever ends, I'll go back to town and straighten everything out."

"The snow will end." Kate spoke definitely, as though she controlled the weather. "My point is the Judge thinks your research may prove dangerous to you. Surely, it has occurred to you that he is right."

"Sometimes, yes! Not about this!"

Bar intervened rather hurriedly. "She knows absolutely nothing that would endanger the real Jones' murderer. Believe me, Kate. I've seen her notes."

"Besides, Kate, my notes were made not only from my own search through newsprint, but also that of the editorial department of the studio, which gave me tear sheets of the entire case. I still have them in my apartment. These—these notes that somebody" Emmy's defiance did falter a little there— "somebody took such an interest in are merely notes which I intended—I mean, I intend —to flesh out later—here, this weekend, as a matter of fact. There is simply nothing new in them."

Kate considered it and found the weak spot. "But you *may* have happened upon something, some line of inquiry which—well, which nobody else noticed. I suppose that does occur sometimes. An amateur, as you certainly are, Emmy, may occasionally see something that experience just does not see. I hope I'm making myself clear. What's a tear sheet?"

"A page torn out from a magazine or newspaper. Sometimes just a clipping, not the entire page. But always of value for information on some particular subject." Emmy was a little proud of her small professionalism.

Kate, however, snorted into her drink. "Then if you have all these precious tear sheets, surely you could go over them again—no!" She caught herself. "That you must not do! Really, you must pay attention to the Judge."

"I'll do as I think best." She did say it with reasonable calm. However, she felt an old fury bubbling up within her at Kate's authoritative manner.

"Let her alone, Kate," Bar said wearily. "You'd better be getting home to the rest of your pups before the paths are completely impassable. How many do you have left?"

"One." Kate was visibly triumphant.

"You're mistaken," Emmy said firmly. "You have this one." She put her hand upon the pup's back but most inappropriately he snuggled down against her.

"What's the pedigree of that one?" Bar asked in a disinterested way. However, it had its effect upon Kate.

"How can I tell? The mother was a stray, no tag, nothing. I suppose some of the summer people had taken her to the country for the summer and then when they went back to town, just dropped her somewhere. They do that. No stopping it. I'd like to catch somebody doing that," she added, implying dark deeds and, actually, Emmy was sure, probably meaning the darker the better to apply to anybody cruel enough to simply drop off any animal of which they had tired.

"I found her in The Barn," Kate said thoughtfully. "Nobody knows exactly how she got here and brought her pups along with her. Possibly when the Christmas tree was delivered. We ordered it very early. We put water in the stand so it will keep fresh and green. Christmas!" said Kate, looking sadly at the fire.

"Anybody can skip Christmas once in a while," Bar said tentatively.

Kate fired up. "Never!" She did not quite say it through her teeth, which would be difficult, but with determination. "We'll decorate it and have our Christmas party in spite of everything. Anyway, when that Christmas tree was delivered somebody might have left the door open. Some scraps of sandwiches from a board meeting were left in the kitchen. The sink there drips. So the poor thing had a kind of food and some water. I really don't know exactly how old the pups are," she added, daring either of them to deny her.

"But you think they are very young. Still are—" Emmy began.

Kate went blithely on. "I had to do something about it. And what a row I caused." Her cheeks flushed again. Kate dearly loved a fight, especially if she won; she didn't like losing. Who did? Emmy thought, and Bar said, "How is your campaign coming along, Kate?" He wasn't really interested, Emmy knew that; he had a faraway, very thoughtful look in his eyes.

Kate sighed and for almost the first time in her life, Emmy guessed, her spirits and shoulders sagged. "Not coming along at all. There'll have to be a quick and final settlement of those terrible murders before anybody will truly trust a single soul living here in Alpine Village. Most discouraging publicity. What's the matter with Archie?" The question came, as so often with Kate, unexpectedly but with urgency.

"Archie?" Bar looked so blank that Kate ought to have suspected him of knowing something about Archie.

Kate, however, was staring fixedly at Emmy. "What are *you* upset about, Emmy? What has Archie been doing? Don't look so innocent. You know something or other. You may as well tell me."

Emmy tried to fight back, as she had done really all her life. "What makes you think anything is the matter with Archie?"

"I could tell. I know Archie."

Bar said, as if idly, "When did you see him?"

"Today. About noon. He was struggling along the road. That was before the snow plows came so he stopped to give me a hand through a drift and then he turned that funny color, you know, red and then white and asked me if you had told me. Come on, now. What did he tell you and didn't want to tell me?"

"Oh, Kate, don't start imagining things—"

Kate eyed him for a moment. Then she turned to Emmy. "Something, I should say, about the Jones murder. Am I right?" She waited but nobody replied. She said, "I see that I'm right. What does he know? He told you, so what was it?"

Bar took over. "All right, Kate. He did confide something to me and to Emmy. But whatever it was, if you'll forgive me, is none of your business. None of our business either."

"Then it *was* something about the Jones murder!"

"Shut up about that, Kate," Bar said and again did not even duck.

Kate only gave a kind of shocked exclamation and Emmy might have adored Bar if she hadn't known that he didn't want or invite adoration.

Bar rose. "If you are going to stay, Kate, you can help with dinner."

"No thank you," said Kate rather hurriedly. "I must go before the drifts are even worse. I'll tell Archie to tell me everything he knows about the Jones murder." She wrapped up her head in the heavy red scarf.

"Kate, it is really nothing to you—" Emmy began.

"Are you sure of that?" Kate asked shortly.

"How can you get him to talk if he doesn't want to?" Emmy asked, inadvisedly.

Kate lifted her dark eyebrows in surprise. "Oh, I'll find a way!" she said with the greatest aplomb and plunged out.

Bar sighed. "I love Kate. I really love her, but she exhausts me. The man who marries her will have to be an athlete of great strength. And no nerves. Let's have another drink and see what there is for dinner."

There was, as it happened, a large supply of frozen food to choose from. Bar slapped down several packages on the table. Emmy read the directions; Bar turned on a gleaming oven. There wasn't much to say; Bar brought out a bottle of what proved to be a very good wine. That and the puppy helped to break into the heavy, thoughtful silence between the two, frozen, Emmy thought, like the food. After dinner she bundled up some damp newspapers and put them in a trash basket near the door. Kate did have some sensible ideas; so did Bar; possibly the name Mopup was peculiarly suitable to any puppy.

Bar, having been apparently not frozen exactly but lost in thought, told Emmy that it was time to go to bed and he'd take her notes again if she didn't mind. There was an absent, troubled frown on his face when he gave her a kind of frustrated push toward the bedroom, not in the least like the smallest and friendliest caress.

All right, she thought dismally. All right, I know when I'm licked.

The house was very still.

The murders would certainly be a minus when it came to Bar's selling the house. Yet this was a very comfortable and indeed peaceful and pleasant house. Bar was rather silly, come to think of it, to sell; he could easily use it for a weekend home.

He had said, however, that he needed money.

She wondered briefly just how the Judge expected her to get along without her job. Keeping it was, with Emmy, not altogether a matter of pride; it had become a thorough and engrossing interest in her life. It was also a means of providing herself with some small luxuries which she couldn't have afforded out of the income from her inheritance which the Judge considered adequate for a young woman's needs.

She'd like to see China getting along on that income, Emmy thought crossly. China wouldn't. Not if she could help it.

True, Emmy wasn't going to starve; however, she suspected that the Judge calculated what money would buy on a scale of, say, twenty years ago. He probably had little notion of what the average person had to pay for rent, or clothing (except for China's; he must have shut his eyes and signed checks when China wanted anything at all) and even for food.

There was not a sound from Bar's room. He had had the baffling wad of papers under his arm as he went into his room. Good luck to him, she thought sleepily, and told the puppy to stay on the floor.

The puppy had already proved himself to be a quick thinker and a quick mover. He had got into Emmy's room just a second ahead of her and settled down after scrambling and clawing up on the bed.

He was at her ear, making a peculiar little sound sometime later when she awoke. The sound, she realized, was in fact his tiny but ferocious growl.

She sat up and reached for the bed-table light. The pup growled again. He fell rather than jumped off the bed and as she fumbled for the lamp she knew he had trotted to the door and was snuffling and growling at the crack between door and sill.

"Oh, shut up," she said sleepily, but instantly decided this was something that just might need investigating. Although probably Bar had merely gone out to the living room.

She found the lamp and turned the switch, but nothing happened.

So the wires were down. Everything in the house, Bar had warned her, depended upon electricity.

She didn't have a flashlight. In the country one always should have a flashlight handy and with active batteries.

The pup unnervingly gave an amazingly mature version of a warning bark.

She groped in the darkness, found a dressing gown but couldn't locate her slippers, and felt her way to the door. She opened it and the pup shot out, barking wildly.

It occurred to Emmy that the burglar alarm—the security system Kate had loftily called it—was turned on by electricity.

Where was Bar? She got to the windows, drew open a curtain and looked out at complete darkness. There were no lights anywhere, so it had happened: no electricity.

As her eyes adjusted themselves to the night and the still-falling snow, she could barely make out the huge snowdrifts. One of them was very near the door.

Bar didn't appear. He evidently didn't hear anything. There was no movement from his room.

But there was some movement from the snowdrift near the front door.

It couldn't have moved. But it had, quietly, stealthily. It was nearer the door. Snowdrifts don't move by themselves.

Someone had only looked like a snowdrift, a crouching humpbacked kind of drift, stealthily but surely moving.

"Bar," she cried. *"Bar!"*

Bar did not answer. This is a nightmare, Emmy thought.

It was no nightmare. She dropped the curtain and began to fumble through the darkness toward Bar's room.

There was the smallest kind of shuffle and creak from the door leading out to the snowbound, frightening world. She got to Bar's room; her hand shook so she could barely grasp the doorknob but after seconds which seemed very long, she did find it, turn it and open the door upon blackness. "Bar? Bar!" She knew that she had shrieked his name.

The lights came on. As suddenly, a loud, eerie kind of scream rose from somewhere, everywhere. It screamed and screeched and the pup yelped ferociously.

The pup was still at the outside door, which seemed to be ajar, but he looked discouraged, tail and nose down, as if his quarry had gotten away from him. With the light from the lamps in the living room, and in the two bedrooms, some of Emmy's courage came back. She ran, stumbling, to the door, closed it hard and the piercing noise stopped. Then she made herself pull back the window curtains again and peer out. It was a changed world. The humps of snow drifts were still there, but a few lights had sprung up over the Village. It seemed to her that another eerie scream was coming from somewhere in the Village. So their vaunted burglar alarm system did work with remarkable efficiency it turned out, as long as the electrical wiring was all right.

There was no dark, crouching figure anywhere near the door. However, the door had been opened, only a little, setting off the alarm, while she was groping her way to Bar's room. On the rug before the door lay something shining, slender, ugly. It was a well-polished, wicked-looking knife.

Fourteen

She could not believe it but there it was, flat on the rug.

She was leaning against a chair, staring at the knife as if hypnotized when the door itself flung open. The alarm shrieked again and she screamed, too. Bar leaped to a small panel beside the door, poked some buttons and again the alarm stopped.

"Emmy! What happened? Emmy—"

She pointed at the knife.

"That—"

"It was there! It *is* there! Somebody was here. The pup—you were gone, I couldn't—then the lights came on—" She was making no sense.

Bar, however, seemed to make some kind of logic out of whatever it was she had said.

He leaned over the knife, started to pick it up, then stopped. "No fingerprints, only smears. Who was here?"

"I don't know! Only a—a snowdrift, but it wasn't a snowdrift and it kept moving toward the door and the pup yelled and I got to your room and you were gone and—and then the lights came on. The person at the door was gone."

"How did this knife get into the house?"

"I don't know. It was just there."

"I forgot about the alarm when I left. This door must have been opened. Whoever it was—yes, he was scared away the minute I got the light wires fixed."

"You—"

"Sure." He stepped carefully around the knife, towards the telephone. "I'll have to tell the Appledown police that the alarm—" He dialed, a voice answered at once; he said briefly, "Sorry. It was a mistake. All right. Thanks." He explained to Emmy. "The alarm connects with the police. No use in getting them here now. I don't think anybody could get here tonight anyway, at least not very fast. Now then—" He looked in a red-bound loose-leaf book, obviously found a number and called that. "Hello. Mr. Manders?"

Manders? Oh, yes, the knife.

"This is Bar Slocumb . . . Yes, I know it is late . . . Yes, I know the electricity was out, but I found where the wires had been cut and fixed them . . . Yes, I said they had been cut. Mr. Manders, I think you'd better come over here. To my house. I think it may be very important . . . All right, if you don't want to, I'll see the police tomorrow . . . It's not very good walking but I managed to get from here to The Barn and back . . . Yes, all right. You know my house . . . Right. I'll have an outside light turned on."

He put down the telephone.

"He's coming," Emmy said. "Is that thing one of his knives?"

Bar glanced at her. "Yes. I think I recognize it."

"He didn't want to come here?"

"He's coming, though," He shuddered out of his heavy coat and snowy jeans that revealed wrinkled pajamas underneath. "I'll fix up the fire. You must be freezing. Get into some clothes. Hurry now—"

"Why would anybody cut the wires?"

"To shut off our alarms, of course."

"But that means all of the alarms?"

"Sure. They all work by electricity and the main lead comes in from the highway to The Barn."

"How did you know it was cut?"

"I didn't at first. I just knew the lights had gone. I was trying to make sense of your notes and bingo, no light, no anything. Naturally the only remedy I could think of just then was the possibility that something had gone wrong with the circuit. So I got myself to The Barn. I took mending tape with me and—oh, get dressed for God's sake, Emmy! You look awful!"

"So would you look awful if you—and you don't look so wonderful yourself!"

"I'm cold. And I must say I was never fond of these pajamas."

He vanished into his bedroom. The pup gave a little murmur.

Emmy said, "You're a watchdog. You're a very fine watchdog! You belong to me and nobody can take you away." She gathered up the pup who snuggled down and touched her cheek with a rasping tongue.

She had gotten into warm jeans and a sweater; the fire was blazing when the doorbell rang imperatively. She could imagine Mr. Manders' fine white hand—it would undoubtedly be a warmly-gloved hand that night—pushing at the doorbell.

Bar came running from the kitchen and flung open the door. It was an angry, impatient, demanding Manders who strode in. "Now, what's all this, Slocumb?"

Emmy realized that the knife had disappeared from the rug before the door.

Bar had evidently been busy while Emmy was dressing because he went over to a table, opened a drawer and took out an object wrapped, Emmy noted with dismay, in a fine napkin. He didn't hand it to Manders but merely unwrapped it and showed it to him.

Manders didn't stare; probably he never stared no matter what he saw. However, he slid off a glove and put out a white hand, its nails rosily shining, toward the linen-wrapped knife. Bar held it away from him. "Your knife, I believe. Isn't it?"

Manders paused for a moment. Then he deliberately slid out of his fur coat—mink, Emmy noted with disbelief, but then, to be fair, why shouldn't he wear a fur coat if he so desired? He dropped the coat on a chair and emerged, a slender, athletic-looking figure in navy blue sweater and slacks; he wore high leather boots which were dropping small chunks of snow on the rug. The pup advanced rather cautiously and sniffed at his boots. Manders looked down and a foot twitched, but he didn't kick the pup, instead he gave Emmy a smiling but rather unpleasant glance. "So you have one of Miss Kate's puppies?"

"Your knife, isn't it?" Bar was not to be distracted by any chitchat.

Manders smiled, again unpleasantly. "I can't tell. You aren't holding it close enough to me."

"I might as well say that I recognize it. Remember, you showed me your collection. I'm sure this is one of your knives. As I recall, there was a label below it, suggesting that it was the knife which Charlotte Corday used when she stabbed Marat in his bath. But from the looks of the knife, the steel—"

Manders nodded. "Of course! Very little to attest to such a claim. Not much authenticity about it."

"But then—"

"Why? Because some people get a thrill out of seeing the label and looking at the knife and, indeed, I did pay more than such a fake deserved. Although I knew it was a fake and the seller knew it was a fake, nevertheless it is an attractive addition to my collection. Don't you think so?"

Bar eyed the shining, sharp steel in his hand. The blade was slightly curved, very sharp looking; it was clearly old. The handle was handsomely carved, ivory, Emmy supposed. There was certainly an antique look about it.

Manders laughed lightly as he continued. "Come now, my dear fellow. All collectors take a few liberties with fact. That is, we are probably far too likely to believe or even invent some historical or interesting claim to the items in our collections. Occasionally some of it is true. Usually one rather doubts present owners' claims, but for the sake of amenities accepts them. But to as discerning an eye as yours! My dear fellow!" He shrugged.

Bar's face hardened. "The point is, how did it get here?"

"Here! Impossible!"

"Here. Inside my door."

Manders was either astonished or gave a fine show of it. "But, my dear fellow, it can't have been—no, no, I don't doubt your word for a moment, but I have not the faintest idea how it *could* have gotten here!" He glanced around the room and shook his head.

Bar said, "Your alarm was working tonight, wasn't it?"

"Except for the time the electricity was cut off. All at once the lights came on again and my alarm began to shriek but I couldn't find anything wrong. I phoned the proper number and explained that it was a mistake—"

"It was a mistake, all right. You do recognize this knife?"

Manders' eyes had the ruby glow. "Certainly, now that I see it more clearly."

"Then how did it get here?"

"You do stick to your questions, don't you, Slocumb! Just like a lawyer."

Bar sighed and said, as he had said to Archie, "I *am* a lawyer. This knife traveled from your fine case of knives here to my house. Who took it—that is, if you didn't?"

Manders' face did not move, yet it seemed to take on a very stony look just the same. "That is a dangerous implication, Slocumb."

"I asked a question. If you know anything about it, I think you would do well to answer."

All at once Manders became easy again, adopting a kind of man of the world manner. "My dear Slocumb! I don't know! Believe me, I simply do not know."

"You must have known if someone came into your house—"

Manders shook his head. "No. You're quite wrong. Oh, I have that burglar alarm, as I believe does everyone in the Village—or most of the people at any rate. But I have lived much of my life in cities where crime is too well-known. Consequently, all the doors of my house, including the one to my bedroom, for instance, have special locks. I had the very best kind of lock I could find installed. I always lock my bedroom door at night. Merely," he said, "custom."

Bar thought for a moment. "You mean to say that after the alarm system had gone, due to electric failure, anybody could have entered your home, taken this knife and gotten away without your knowledge?"

"I mean that. Once the electricity was restored the alarm went off. By the way, might I have a drink? Only a small one, I am not much of a drinker, but it was a cold trudge over here—"

Bar almost laughed. "You are very calm, Mr. Manders. Your knife turns up in my house and you know nothing about it. What would you like?"

"Brandy, perhaps—oh, anything. I'm not fussy."

Bar went to the dining room still carrying the knife very carefully. That, Emmy knew, was in the slim hope there would be some fingerprints upon it.

Manders looked her up and down and smiled again. "Nice to see you, Miss Brace," he said. "Sorry if you have had any—any kind of fright. And this weather! Too bad. I had understood that you came to the Village to visit with the Judge and his wife. Or your sister. Or both. I see you are Mr. Slocumb's," he paused and said "guest."

Under that smiling bright gaze, Emmy felt obliged to defend, if not herself, then what her grandmother would have called her honor. Actually it was just as well to make the situation clear. "My sister—as I believe you know—has undertaken the care of a number of young dogs. There was no room in her house for me. So Bar made a place for me here. We are very old friends."

Manders lifted a shining black eyebrow politely but skeptically. Emmy said hotly, "Very old friends. Back to our childhood days. And Mac—dear old Mac really helped bring us up." Tears came into her eyes. She blinked them away in order to look steadily and probably angrily at Manders.

He nodded, his smooth black head shining. "I see, yes. Mac, our guard, was once in the employ of Slocumb's mother, wasn't he? I seem to remember that."

Bar came back into the room. He had done something or other with the knife, undoubtedly put it someplace he considered safe. He carried instead a neat little silver tray with three glasses on it. "Brandy?" He offered the tray first to Emmy, who took a glass gratefully, then to Manders, who made kind of a courteous bow as he also took a glass.

"Now, this is better," he said. "As neighbors should be. Since I am here, Slocumb, what do you think of the Judge's foolishness—oh, excuse me, Miss Brace, I believe he is your guardian—"

"Uncle," said Emmy.

"Oh, yes, uncle. But what *do* you think of his not only getting that man paroled and released from prison—and I'm afraid, from what I have heard, a richly deserved imprisonment—however, your uncle got him paroled and now he appears to be a guest in your uncle's house. I mean Miss Brace's uncle—but—"

"Oh, we understand," Bar said. "I'm not sure just what you

think about it, Mr. Manders, but I think that's the Judge's business."

Manders sipped rather cautiously, it seemed to Emmy, from his glass. She wondered fleetingly if there were, by any chance, good reasons for Manders to sip cautiously from any glass which was proffered to him.

If this was his custom, it argued a rather shadowy experience of life. Impossible, though, to think of the polished, suave Mr. Manders in connection with what was called the underworld.

Still, that was just speculation, but he did have that ugly collection of knives. It suggested some peculiar affection for what could be called lethal weapons, or else a need to defend himself at any time. A gun would more likely be such a weapon. The murders had been done by a gun.

Manders eyed nothing over his glass and said mildly, "I suppose we now have a new night guard. Do you know, Slocumb?"

Bar looked a little abashed for a second but only for a second. He said airily, "Oh, Kate—I mean Kate Brace has seen to that, I'm sure."

"I rather think it a necessary precaution," Manders sighed and put down his glass. He looked at Bar with an air of frankness. "You see, Slocumb, Guy Wilkins was a most trusted employee. I know of no possible motive for his murder. Unless, of course, it was one of those senseless acts of violence.—What do you plan to do with that knife?" The question slid out sharply. "It does belong to me, you know."

Bar waited while he finished his drink. "Quite. But I believe the police ought to see it."

Manders rose and looked rather menacing, tall and obviously muscular. "It *is* my property, Slocumb."

"But I do feel that the police should know of its presence here —unexplained."

A long moment passed, while Manders stood perfectly still. At last he shrugged.

"If you feel like that, certainly. I'm sorry, Slocumb. But—yes, naturally I wish to know who has managed to get into my house and remove a piece from my valuable collection. Very valuable, if not always quite authentic." He started for his coat.

Bar said quietly, poking at the fire, "You do not approve of the Judge's action, not only in contriving the parole of Jones but in taking him into his own house?"

"Why—I—why, no! I do not approve!"

"You remember the case of the Jones murder?"

"Oh, yes. I was in the city at the time. It was in the newspapers. The man, Jones, was convicted. I remember. I was very much surprised, I must say, at the Judge's recent action."

"But the Judge wouldn't act in such a way unless he felt that the jury was mistaken in convicting Jones."

"The jury!" Manders' eyes were as black and bright as bits of obsidian. Otherwise he showed no anger. He said, icily, "The Judge is certainly mistaken in having that man here. The evidence must have pointed to his guilt. The jury couldn't have been so shockingly mistaken in its verdict."

"That has been known to occur," Bar said mildly.

"Not this time! No, no, Jones killed that—that woman, his wife. And now the Judge has gotten him out of prison and—it seems incredible that Jones is actually a guest of the Judge's. Somebody said he is to assist the Judge in writing his memoirs. What a notion! I doubt if Jones can more than write his name."

"Oh, come on, Mr. Manders! Jones was a broker. He had to write at least."

"Listen to me, Slocumb. That man is a murderer. Now two men have been murdered!" He went to the door, jerking on his fur coat. "It can't be coincidence! Jones here in a peaceful community of law-abiding citizens, and then two murders! Get rid of Jones. Tell the Judge that. And get my knife back to me."

"Certainly," Bar said agreeably. "I'll try to see that it is returned to you. After the police have considered it."

"When do you think that will be?" It was a rhetorical question, for Manders had opened the front door. Cold, darkness and snowdrifts, but no shadow of anybody or anything huddled near the door.

"I don't know. Do you need a flashlight to see your way home?"

Manders was not to be outdone in courtesy. He waved one hand and shoved it into a heavy glove. "Not at all, my dear fellow. Not at all. Thank you for the brandy." He remembered his manners sufficiently to give a rather half-hearted bow in Emmy's direction, and left.

The pup uttered a small but threatening growl, as if to say, don't come here again!

"No more than I expected," Bar said. "Good for you, Mop. Bite him if you get another chance."

"I don't like that man."

"Neither does the pup. Manders is not real somehow. He may have been putting up some kind of carefully thought-out front. Does he seem right to you?"

"That man! He's as phony as—as a—" She could not think of an adequately descriptive word.

Bar laughed shortly. "Phony, yes. I have a notion that he has carefully cultivated all those fine manners of his."

"He was—I can't describe it, but he seemed very cautious about drinking his brandy."

"Still he did drink it."

"Convinced against his will that it held nothing?"

"No knock-out drops?" Bar said but rather cheerfully, "No cyanide?"

"That's exactly what I mean. So his past—"

Bar unexpectedly yawned. "Sure. But I'll tell you something. I'll bet all investigation, every single bit of it, about his past will show him white as—as snow. On the other hand—" Bar slouched back in his chair, his eyes half-closed. "Suppose for a moment that he was telling a very plausible lie. Suppose—" He waited a moment and then resumed. "Yes. If he was telling a fine lie, the truth just might have been this: He decides to leave that knife here. He wishes to threaten you—or he intends to use that knife—"

Emmy cried, "Oh, no! Not the way Belle—"

"I'm only saying suppose. Suppose then that he gets to The Barn, slices that wire with his fine knife—it's really very sharp, you know. Thus he turns off all the alarms in the Village, including his own. Then he runs over here, knowing that my alarm is off. He tries to get in the house. That"— he opened his eyes and smiled—"that fine big watchdog of yours hears him and carries on. You get up. Manders hears the pup, knows he can't—"

"He *can't* have tried to murder me!"

"I'm only supposing, remember." But Bar's gaze was very intent. "Suppose the pup scares him away, but he leaves the knife. Inside the house. While the alarm was off and he knew it. Then he plunges back to his own house. His alarm is still turned on when I get the electric wire connected. He is getting back to his house as fast as he can. He has left the door to my house open. So my alarm goes. And his alarm goes until he can get into his house again, turn it off and phone the police. Think about it."

Emmy thought. "It sounds complicated."

"Not at all. He's a healthy, youngish man, in perfect physical condition I'd say. No problem for him to sprint to The Barn, slice the wires, get over here, open the door a little. The pup gives an alarm, he drops the knife—"

"You *can't* mean he intended to murder—" This time her throat choked.

"Not then. Remember he must have believed that I was here, in the house. No—he could have meant that knife only as a threat."

"A threat—"

"To stop your dangerous digging about the Jones case."

"But that would mean that he knew and killed Belle—"

Bar sighed and rose. "All this is hypothetical."

Emmy said suddenly, "He was very violent about Jones."

"I thought that, too. There might be something, some connection. Otherwise he might not have been so quick to accuse Jones of murder and the Judge of what he called foolishness. But, don't worry, Emmy, I'll not let Manders or—or anybody touch you. Believe me—"

"I—oh, of course, I believe you. But—"

"But you are still scared. Trust me, Emmy."

She went to the fire and warmed her hands, which felt uncomfortably chilly and uncertain. "Perhaps, somehow, somewhere I *have* happened upon something about the Jones murder."

"Or perhaps somebody believes that you have. Now then, in the morning we'll take steps. I don't know what, but steps. Go to bed, Emmy."

It was an odd kind of night, changing in temperature. Emmy woke several times, aware of a peculiar kind of drip, as if a faucet had been left on in the bathroom. It became so stubborn that she got out of bed, turned on a light and went to look in the bathroom. Everything shone white and clean, but the drip continued. Presently she recognized it as a drip from the eaves of the house. So a thaw had stealthily and suddenly set in.

When she fully awoke, she found that she had shoved the warm eiderdown away. It was on the floor and the pup stretched out luxuriously upon it.

The radio weatherman announced cheerily, indeed as if he took pride in his forecast, that a sudden surge of warm air from the south had taken over. Basements were flooded. The thaw was almost as destructive as the blizzard.

Breakfast was beginning to be a kind of domestic, quiet meal, although Emmy and Bar did talk briefly about the events of the night before. After breakfast, when Bar opened the door in order to survey the dripping, steaming Village, the pup darted out, made for the nearest snowdrift and quietly, as if following a mandate, lifted his leg.

Bar grinned from ear to ear. "Good for you, Mop! Good dog!"

Mop came back with a satisfied air. "He's got to be older than Kate thinks," Emmy said, drawing upon her long-ago knowledge of the canine conventions.

"Whatever, he's a good dog. Just keep it up, Mop. Although, come to think of it, that may no longer be a good name for him."

"Listen," Emmy said firmly. "After last night—he wakened me, he growled, he barked—after last night, I'll call him anything big and brave—"

"There now, Emmy. I do believe it was only a threat, leaving that knife! But all the same, I'm not going to let you stir out of my sight. At least," he added more prudently, "out of this house."

"The Judge keeps saying that I'm in danger," Emmy said slowly. "Maybe—"

"Sure, perhaps he's right. We'll just have to wait until the roads clear and the police come back. And trains to the city start running from Appledown."

"What do you intend to do in the city? I can't imagine—"

"Neither can I, precisely. But there are one or two—call them paths of inquiry—I feel I'd like to pursue. Not at all dangerous," he added hurriedly as Emmy felt herself turning rather cold.

"What?"

"This and that. My efforts may come to nothing and—there's the phone."

Kate was on the telephone. "Oh, hello," Bar said. "No—we're quite all right . . . Yes, certainly, we knew the electricity was off." There was a pause. Then Bar said, "The lead wire had been cut. I fixed it. That's all, Kate—"

There was apparently a torrent of questions and self-made answers from Kate. Emmy could hear the staccato notes of her clear voice across the room. Bar said at last, breaking into her words, "It's all right now! I have no idea who cut the wires but—yes, only somebody living here in the Village would be likely to know just where the main wire comes into the Village but—No." After listening for a moment, Bar shouted, "No, Kate! No use in reporting to the police. The roads are slushy . . . Then suggest a way—" He held the receiver away from his ear and at last brought it back to say pleasantly. "Great news about the pup, Kate . . . Don't you want to hear? . . . I thought—"

He put down the telephone with a heavy sigh. "Dear Kate! But any news about a pup sidetracks her. Good boy!" He bent down to ruffle up the dog's ears. The pup looked up at him as if gravely considering this encomium. At last he decided to wag his tail in polite reply. Bar laughed. He sounded for a moment like the boy in his teens and the carefree young man Emmy had loved.

He sobered, however. "Nothing else to do right now. We might as well have another go at your notes, Emmy."

This, however, was barely begun when Kate telephoned again. This time Emmy, being near the telephone, answered it. Kate cried, "Emmy, is that you! Oh, Emmy, the most horrible thing has happened."

"Kate—"

"Wait, I'll tell you, no, you'd better let me talk to Bar. He'll know what to do."

Emmy shouted, "What do you mean? What are you talking about?"

"It's horrible. My gun—"

Bar snatched the receiver from Emmy but held it so she, too, could hear Kate's voice. "It was my gun! They found it."

"Kate, make sense." Bar was trying to be calm and finding it very difficult. "Take it easy. Tell me—"

"It shot him! My gun—the man on the truck. It shot him just outside Manders' house. I tell you it was my gun."

"Wait now, Kate, what truck?"

"The trash truck! The garbage truck! There are two men on it always. Young fellows. They managed to get here this morning and went around the houses. And it happened right outside Manders' place. While the man—one of them, his name is Sam something—was stooping over trying to make room for the garbage they had already collected. After all this time, you know, there was a lot of it and—" Kate gave a gulp and shrieked, "Sam was terribly hurt. He may have been killed by my gun."

Fifteen

"How do you know it was your gun?"

"The Judge said so. He—Manders—called him. The Judge went over to see. Manders called the doctor from Appledown. He's on his way. My gun!"

"How does the Judge know it was your gun?"

"Oh, I don't know! Bar, come here. I don't know what to do."

"Neither do I," said Bar, but tensely as if thinking hard.

"You've got to come. You're a lawyer, aren't you? Well, I'm employing you. To represent me and to—to advise me. Suppose he dies!" Kate's usually steady voice broke.

"But I don't see why—"

"Oh, Bar, can't you see that now everybody will say *I* killed Mac and that—that Guy Wilkins and—you've got to help me. Come here. Hurry."

Bar put down the telephone. "Emmy! You heard—"

"Kate's gun! She didn't shoot anybody!"

"Put on a coat. We'll see Kate and the Judge."

As she got into her coat the pup came in and sat, watching her, seriously.

"Just stay here," she told him.

Bar was sufficiently sensible to strew the kitchen floor with papers and shut the pup inside the room. "Now then, let's go."

It was very misty; the air was very much warmer, so faint steam from the thawing snow was stealthily rising from all the roofs and the melting drifts. Bar locked the door behind them. "Not our usual custom here."

Kate was waiting for him. She was pale but her eyes and chin were determined. "I've got to find out what exactly happened. Where they found him—when—thank heaven you are with me, Bar. I don't mind saying that I'm scared. I did not kill that man."

"He is still alive." Emmy linked a hand through Kate's arm. "You wouldn't kill anybody."

The sudden thaw left puddles and patches of watery, dirty snow along the road. When they reached the curve, they could see a cluster of cars and people around the door of a house at the far end of the road.

It was larger than most of the houses, like the Judge's house in size.

As they splattered along the road, an ambulance, white against the grays, its red cross gleaming, pulled away from the Manders house. A small coupe followed it.

"M.D. license. A caduceus on the car," Bar said. "So he's not dead, Kate."

But there remained the heavy garbage truck and a police car and a small crowd of people, who all turned and stared at them. Their combined regard was accusing, Emmy thought; so all of them knew that the Judge had said it had been Kate's gun.

The Judge was in the doorway of the Manders house, talking to Manders. A policeman stood with them.

Kate advanced bravely upon the Judge and Manders. Another man stood at the edge of the step, looking sick. He was wearing workman's clothing, a stocking cap; Sam's partner, probably. He rubbed gloved hands across his eyes. "I had no idea Sam was leaning over the truck at the back. We were right here where the truck stands now. The gun went off and then—" He choked.

The policeman patted his arm. "You'd better go back to Appledown. See his wife. Tell her everything is being done for him. Make it as easy for her as you can."

"Oh, yes, yes. Good neighbors—" He brushed his hand over his eyes again and stumbled out toward the truck. As he drove away, everyone watched. Then the Judge turned to Bar. "So you came."

Kate replied. "Certainly. He is my lawyer. He will represent me. Any questions you have—"

"Oh, come on, Kate," the Judge said gruffly. "Nobody thinks you shot him."

"Will he live?"

"They hope so. The doctor got here and the ambulance and we'll soon hear from the hospital. Don't take it so hard, Kate. He's not dead yet."

Kate moistened her lips. "Judge, tell them any expense! Anything in the world! I'll at least pay all that—oh, God," said Kate, and permitted herself a strangled sob. "I hope he lives!"

"Yes." Manders said. "We all hope so. I really think from what the doctor said that he has a fine chance, Miss Kate. It's very good of you to pay all the medical expenses."

"Good of me?" Kate flashed. "When I was so careless about my gun! Good of me!"

The Judge was more cautious. "It may run into money, Kate. Can you sell anything just now—"

"I'll sell anything I've got to save that poor man. My gun!"

The Judge said uncomfortably, "Yes, I'm afraid it was your gun. The police"— he indicated the man standing beside him—"have it."

Bar asked, "How did you happen to recognize it?"

In the same instant, Manders said smoothly, "We'd better go inside."

"Thank you, Mr. Manders—yes—" It was the Appledown chief of police. Emmy suddenly remembered his sturdy figure and his troubled yet determined face. He looked particularly exhausted.

Several of the men down in the road exchanged low words and trudged away. Only Mr. Clements and old Mr. Green came up to the door. "Thank you—thank you—" said Mr. Clements. "This is really too much—" he muttered.

Manders led them, not to the study with its rack for knives, but into a large living room.

Bar repeated, but politely, "Will you, Judge, please tell us just how you happened to recognize Kate's gun?"

The Judge shrugged out of his coat. "Kate showed it to me some time or other. I recognized the make and the size and—"

Bar said, "Is that all?"

"That's enough, isn't it?" The Judge's mustache bristled. "I know that it is Kate's gun."

"Will you show the gun to Miss Brace, Chief?" Bar turned politely to the chief of police, who drew out from his coat a revolver, wrapped carefully in a strip of plastic.

"Certainly. Please don't touch it—"

Bar looked. "Is this really your gun, Kate?"

Kate strode toward him, gave the gun a piercing look and turned her blue gaze to the chief of police. Kate couldn't lie. In any event, her gun would be registered; Kate would never have a gun in her possession unless it was legally registered. "It is mine," she said, "but I did not shoot that poor man."

Bar intervened. "How do you know that it is your gun, Kate?"

"I just know," Kate said conclusively. "And, of course, there are the numbers—I told you it is registered. Also, sometime or another, I scratched my initials—see?" She started to take the gun for Bar's examination but the chief stopped her.

"We believe you, Miss Brace. Thank you." He took the gun again. "But have you any idea how the gun got into that truck?"

Kate said sadly, "I ought never really to have had a gun! Stupid of me! And since I did have that thing, I ought to have taken better care of it. I'm so very sorry; I'm ashamed. Didn't the other man see anybody?"

The chief replied, "He says he didn't see anybody. He says Sam had gone around to the back of the truck after he picked up the garbage from Mr. Manders' trash cans. But the other driver, name is Rudy, didn't look back toward him. He was expecting Sam to get back in the cab when all at once there was this shot. He knew right away it was a shot. He was in Vietnam. So he jumped down and ran back. He saw Sam. He didn't see any footprints, anybody. He thinks whoever shot him just got out of the way as fast as he could."

Manders said, "I heard the shot. I ran out. Saw that Sam was seriously injured. Phoned the police and the doctor. Lucky the roads are better."

"Miss Brace," the chief said, "please tell me when you last saw the gun. I mean when you were last sure that it was in your possession."

"Oh," said Kate. "That." Trust Kate to tell the truth, the whole truth and nothing but the truth. "It's rather a long story."

"Go on," said the chief courteously. The Judge got an end of his little mustache in his mouth and gnawed it.

"The night my sister arrived, Bar here"— she indicated Bar— "saw, or thought he saw, someone hanging around the house. Matter of fact somebody got hold of a suitcase belonging to my sister and searched it. Bar came back to the house, asked me to lend him my gun and ran out to find out just who was dodging around the place that way—"

The chief interrupted. "Did you find anyone?" he asked Bar.

"No. But I did borrow the gun. I kept it that night and returned it the next morning."

The chief shifted his observant eyes back to Kate. "He returned it to you, right?"

"Oh, yes. That is, he said he did. The door to my house was open. I often leave it open, that is, not locked. It is quite customary around here. Or has been," she added, "until recently. Yes, Bar said he walked into my house and put the gun in the drawer where I usually keep it. However, it was not there." For a second Kate did falter. "I suppose I ought to have searched more thoroughly for it, but I was sure it was somewhere in the house."

"Didn't you feel, say, uneasy about it? Especially after—"

"Yes," Kate replied precisely if reluctantly. "And I did look for it. I didn't find it."

There was a slight pause. Then the Judge said, "But, Kate, my dear, surely you realized that a gun, any gun, I mean, after the murders—"

"Of course, I realized it. But I had no reason in the world to think that my gun—my gun!" Kate said again with a kind of horrified dismay, "could be used"— she paused, took a breath and added in a low voice, "in that dreadful way."

There was another pause. The chief stroked his cheek thoughtfully. Finally he said, "We can't be positive of anything until the surgeon gets out the bullet."

The Judge was certainly not accustomed to browbeating the

police, he had better sense than that, but he had to ask questions. "When will that be, Chief?"

"Soon. They'll work fast. If that is all you can tell me now, Miss Brace, I'd suggest that you think over everything you can remember about the gun and its disappearance and everyone who"— his voice became rather grim and commanding—"might have had opportunity to enter your house and take that gun. Please do that. Now, then, I'll have to get back to Appledown. Thank you, Mr. Manders. Glad the roads are much better so we could get a doctor and ambulance here."

"How about Sam's family?" Kate said. "Wife? Children?"

The chief's face did soften just a little. "We'll see to all that, Miss Brace. Our job. The citizens of Appledown are most generous and neighborly." He nodded at Manders, the Judge, everybody, said politely, "Thank you all," and walked swiftly out into the hall. A minute later, the outside door closed.

Manders sighed. "Tragic. But I feel sure they'll save that man. However, following Guy's murder and the guard's—by the way, Miss Kate, you did get a guard for night duty, didn't you?"

Kate was taken aback. Unbelievably she began to stutter and excuse herself. "I didn't. I don't know why I simply didn't think of it. I—but then—" She pulled herself together and checked an incipient wobble of her fine chin. "The roads—but I'll see to it today."

"Good." Manders glanced at the door where there was the tinkle of china and silver. "I believe Mrs. Clark has made some coffee for us. Thank you, Mrs. Clark." The vigorous little woman who had spoken up for Manders during the meeting at The Barn came in, placed a silver tray on a table near the fire and asked if she should pour.

"Thank you, Mrs. Clark, I think Miss Kate or Miss Emmy can do that for us."

Kate didn't seem to hear. Emmy took one look at her troubled face and went to the table.

The coffee service was beautiful; Emmy looked at it absently but could not help observing the gleaming silver, the exquisite porcelain cups, Minton, surely. Mr. Manders had taste and obviously the money to gratify that taste. Somehow none of the beauties in his house, rugs, polished tables and chairs, had that rather shabby but cared for look of inherited and beloved objects.

Everybody took coffee. The Judge sank down in his chair, sipped from his cup and brooded. A little color came back into Kate's face.

Nobody spoke for a moment. Then everybody spoke at once. "A terrible thing," said Manders.

"Crime," said the Judge. "But I trust not an attempted murder for which I have the least responsibility."

Manders' dark eyes narrowed. "You are thinking of your protégé."

"My guest," said the Judge warmly. "Kindly remember that. I must remind you that we have laws of slander."

"But, my dear sir—" The ruby lights glowed in Manders' dark eyes.

The Judge interrupted. "I must tell you that Mr. Jones is a very peaceable and kind man. No violence in him."

"Dear me," Manders said as pleasantly as a snake just might politely hiss before striking. "I wouldn't suggest that Mr. Jones had anything to do with violence. Yet I can't help noticing that in a strange way violence does seem to accompany him."

"Look here!" The Judge half rose and put down his coffee cup with a force that made Emmy wince. However, the cup proved itself tougher than the Judge and did not so much as shiver. "I understand you perfectly, Manders! So does everybody in this room. Witnesses, I might remind you. And"—the Judge was triumphant—"I might tell you now that at the time this shocking accident—not murder—"

"Not murder yet," said Manders.

The Judge went on, "—occurred, Homer Jones was having breakfast with me and my wife. What do you think of that?"

Manders said softly, "Not much, Judge."

"Now, see here—" The Judge was bristling with fury.

"No, no, I don't mean I doubt your word. That is, not exactly."

"You'd better explain yourself."

Manders waited a moment, his white hand caressing the polished arm of his chair. "I'm not sure I can," he said placatively, as if he were puzzled and admitting it.

His manner baffled the Judge who stared, got out his spectacles, put them on his nose, stared and returned the spectacles to a pocket.

"I don't think I understand you, Manders."

Manders smiled thinly. "I'm not sure I understand myself, Judge. I only say that violence does seem to attend your Homer Jones. His wife—"

"Ah! So you remember that tragic case?"

"Certainly, I remember it. A shocking and terrible murder. For which, Judge, you, yourself, sentenced young Jones to prison. But now you have contrived—I must say I can't understand just how, but undoubtedly your record as an honest man and a deserving official and—oh, well, your standing must have helped greatly in getting him paroled."

"The jury was wrong! I'm not going to argue about that with you. Or anybody!" The Judge gave what amounted to a forbidding glare all around the room. There had been a time when Emmy might have at least partially wilted under that glare. She didn't then; the Judge could be wrong.

Manders asked the Judge smoothly, "More coffee, sir?"

It was so clearly a false politeness that the Judge turned bright red. "No, thank you. I'm leaving. If you have any doubts of my own integrity you might inquire of my wife just where Homer Jones was at the time of this terrible event. I'm going now. Emmy —Kate—" He summoned them as if they were children.

Bar went with them. Bar was still in sufficient control of himself to thank Manders for the coffee. As the four of them left, Manders stood in the doorway watching them, an elegant figure in his red lounge coat.

The sudden thaw had turned the morning almost as balmy as spring. The sky, however, still lowered. The Judge turned off at his own house without a word and left them to continue on their way. Kate said, suddenly, "Why, there is China! And Archie! And Jones himself!"

The three were standing huddled together at Kate's doorstep.

Archie gave a kind of jump and started to meet them, stumbled in a puddle and fell ludicrously backward. His cap came off, his bald head shone, his legs waved and struggled in the air. Kate, usually sympathetic to anybody in trouble, went stonily past him.

China's pretty voice wailed. "What happened? Is it true? Not that man with the garbage truck—"

Kate said icily, "Shut up, China. He's still alive. You can all come in if you must." She fumbled for her key; Jones went to assist Archie to his feet.

"Thank you," Archie babbled. "Thank you—" and stumbled toward the door which by then Kate had opened. A bark came out but a decidedly lonely bark. China thrust out beseeching hands toward Kate. "Tell us, Kate. What do the police intend to do? Are you sure it wasn't another murder?"

Jones, hovering forlornly at the door, shivering with cold in his long, dark, but thin city overcoat, said miserably, "They'll say I shot him. Everybody thinks I killed those two men. Everybody hates me. Everybody is afraid of me. I've got to leave—"

Bar went to China's assistance, for China had managed to get herself hopelessly entangled not in sables this time but in a down-filled coat which was far too big for her.

He said quietly, "Mr. Jones was with you at breakfast, wasn't he, China?"

"Yes!" China turned her wide eyes up to Bar. "Oh, my, yes! Didn't the Judge tell you that? I mean, didn't he tell the police? Mr. Jones and the Judge and I were having breakfast when somebody phoned—"

"Who?" Bar asked.

"Why—why, I don't know!"

"Manders," said Jones. "He's down on me, you know. Hates me. I don't know why, and I feel sure that he objects to my presence here. Probably everybody objects. I should leave—"

"You can't just now, Jones," Bar reminded him.

China clung to Bar's arm. "Bar, darling—it *does* matter to me what Mr. Jones does. I don't want him to be accused of something he just didn't do, but I'm scared. I'm afraid of every sound at night. I'm afraid of—why, afraid of everybody! Except, of course, you, Kate. And Emmy and—Bar, please take me away. Now."

Nobody seemed to pay the slightest attention to China's plea. Homer Jones stared at nothing, which seemed to be his usual attitude. Nobody really could blame him, however, for having learned stoicism in a very hard school.

She took a long breath. Bar said, "Are you all right, Emmy?"

"Yes. I mean, no. I mean I couldn't remember how to turn it off—"

Two policemen came splattering through the wet puddles. One was the chief of Appledown police.

"False alarm," Bar said. "Accident. Sorry. Nothing wrong—"

Kate took over. "My sister was upset. Couldn't remember how to turn off the alarm." She addressed the chief of police. "But I believe you want to question her, so there she is. I'll stay, too."

"No, you won't," Bar said. "Thank you, Kate. But not now. Thank you, Judge—thank you—" He looked over their heads. A number of dim figures and white inquiring faces emerged from the gloom. Bar shouted. "A mistake! Everything is all right. Thank you very much."

"Needn't overdo it," the Judge growled. "I'm staying here."

The chief took matters in hand. "Thank you, Judge. Thank you all. I'll just take a few moments, Miss—Miss Brace. Thank you."

He was young but he had authority. Even the Judge, muttering, hesitated. The pup, in the kitchen, added a menacing wail and then he, too, was silent.

It was very unfortunate timing from Emmy's point of view, for just at that moment a long limousine and a following van turned up at the path. Car lights streamed out through the fog beside Bar's car.

Hubie shouted from the limousine, "Found your house, Emmy! Here we are!"

Eighteen

There was, not remarkably, a certain confusion. Hubie, smiling, confident, and instantly discerning, spotted the police chief. He took him aside where he waved his hands and talked fast. The little fringe of coated and curious figures drifted away into the fog and darkness. Even Kate seemed to find it expedient to leave abruptly. The Judge remained, shooting baleful glances at Hubie and Bar and, certainly, at Emmy.

But then, almost magically things seemed to sort themselves out. Emmy and Bar and Hubie were alone in the house.

Even the Judge had gone. The camera crew had departed, too.

"Hungry," Hubie explained. "I sent them off to Appledown for food. And a motel. Anyway they'll want to get some pictures there. Now then," said Hubie, making himself at home in a lounge chair, "what happened during the day?"

"How did you get rid of the police?" Bar asked shortly.

Hubie stretched out his legs, comfortably. "I told the chief that the camera crew was on the way to the police station at Appledown, to get pictures of everything. He felt this required his presence. Simple and sensible," said Hubie with a gleam of triumph. "He said he'd had a long day, anyway. But he'll be back tomorrow." He looked around him approvingly. "Luxury is the word for this. I call it a truly magnificent love nest."

Kate shoved her cape onto a chair and jerked off her scarf. Archie was wiping at his wet coat but paused to stare incredulously at China.

Kate, even at this tense moment, automatically reacted to anything disorderly. "For goodness' sake, Archie, if you have to shed water like that, get out to the kitchen. Oh, my! My dog—"

One pleading bark came from the other bedroom. Bar said absently, "I'll see to them, Kate. How many are left?"

"Only the mother!" Even then she could not suppress a tone of triumph. "I am convinced she's a thoroughbred—well, a thoroughbred something. Seems a pity whoever owned her just dropped her off here."

"Maybe she didn't like her owners and left them," Bar said over his shoulder. A grateful bark met him as he opened a door and the four-legged mother thudded into the hall, paused inquiringly at the living room door, saw no one who interested her and made for the outside.

"What's her name, Kate?" Emmy said.

"Never mind," said Kate.

"You can't just point at her and say, 'you,' " Emmy objected.

"I can do anything I want to do in my own house."

Bar followed her to close the outside door. He came back into the room and then just stood there with a peculiar look on his face, a kind of inner excitement. It was a very odd look, as though all at once he were intently following some new train of thought.

Kate said, "Oh, by the way, Emmy, you can come and stay with me now. That room has been thoroughly cleaned."

China's eyes widened. "Why, Kate, do you mean that your cleaning woman got here through all this dreadful blizzard?"

Kate replied loftily, "I cleaned it myself. Did a good job, too."

"But Kate, that room needed scrubbing. I'm sure—"

"I scrubbed it. You never saw a cleaner room." Kate bristled. "Do you think my—our"— she included Emmy as an afterthought —"our pioneer foremothers simply sat and waited for somebody to do the work? Nonsense. They didn't have much, if anything, in the way of luxuries, no matter what kind of tales you hear. Believe me, they worked—"

"Yes, Kate." Bar looked at his watch. "It's only ten. I'm going into the city. I had a word with the police chief. The thruways are splashy but clear. Emmy can stay with you, Kate."

"I'm going with you," China cried and ran to thrust her arm through his. The magnificent ring gleamed on her hand. She had decided not to wear her precious sables out that dreary morning and on such a very dismal errand, but she had prudently clung to the ring.

That ring! Like a flash of lightning on a cloudy night, Emmy knew what she had meant when she had scribbled, "No Rg." in her notes. And hadn't she put a faint question mark there? She had. She had meant that pretty Belle Jones had worn no ring. Not even a wedding ring.

She searched her memory and was sure. In all the news items she had read there had been no mention at all of a ring on one of Belle's hands.

Naturally, with Homer Jones making as moderate an income as had been disclosed, Belle would never have had a ring anything like China's.

The Judge never had stinted himself or his pocketbook when he presented a gift. Even with Emmy and Kate, his Christmas gifts had been lavish and extravagant. It was a quirk of the Judge's character. He might withhold as much of their property as he legally could, but when it came to Christmas or birthdays he threw prudence to the winds. Even Emmy's first car had been a gift from the Judge on her twenty-first birthday. But he was still adamant about retaining control of her property until she reached twenty-five. That was, she had regretfully known, as her father had intended.

But she had written "No Rg." Certainly then, there was not the slightest reason to think of China's ring with even near recognition. It couldn't have been actual recognition; the whole point was that Belle had worn no ring at all at the time of her murder.

Her train of thought had gone as swiftly again as the flash of lightning. But the instant's apparent light had revealed another speculation which astounded her even as she denied its existence. Perhaps the Judge himself gave Belle Jones a ring like China's.

This was a perfectly preposterous suggestion. The Judge had never even known Belle Jones. He had never known Homer Jones until he came up before him in the courtroom. She was sure of that. There was simply no reason for such an absurd notion to flit across her mind.

The others had continued to talk rapidly, it now occurred to her. China was winding up, "—so you see, Bar. Now Emmy can stay with Kate, where she ought to have stayed in the first place."

Oh, not again, China! Emmy felt like shouting. However, she said firmly, "You have to go home, China! I am staying with Bar and—"

"Ladies," Bar spoke decisively enough but looked faintly amused. "I am flattered. Emmy, come with me. See you all later."

He had flung Emmy's coat around her and they were both out the door before China could do more than clutch at Bar's arm.

He banged the door behind them. Melting snow slushed around them all the way to Bar's house.

"Now, Emmy," he began as soon as they were inside. "I don't know when I'll be back. I'll make it as soon as I can. You're to stay right here, understand? Don't let anybody—not even Kate or Archie or—China, *anybody* into the house. Understand . . ."

He dove into his own room, emerged with a briefcase in one hand and kissed Emmy lightly (on the cheek, though, she thought swiftly, on the cheek, just another New York kiss of no special significance) and was out the door before she could question him. Still he had a curious look of a kind of excitement. Anyway, there was no sense at all in trying to question Bar if he didn't wish to be questioned. The regular beat of his car's engine died away. So much seemed to have happened that morning, yet it was not even noon. She couldn't expect his return before dark.

Nothing could happen before dark.

But something could be done, or at least attempted. The telephone rang. Emmy answered it. "Hello—"

"You locked the door. Open it. I'm coming to see you—" It was a kind of hoarse whisper, yet completely audible. A man or a woman or just a whisper?

"Who is this? What are you talking about?"

"You know too much about that Jones murder. I'm coming—"

"Wait—wait—" she cried. "Who is this? What do you mean?" The telephone clicked. No other reply.

There was no way to discover who had spoken to her—no, no, whispered. A whisper offers little means of identification. There was no way of so much as guessing who had been on the phone.

Whoever it was had known that Bar was gone.

But then anyone in the Village could have seen him leave.

Nothing could happen before dark.

Sixteen

Nothing could happen before dark! All right then, stop shaking like a fool, and do something. Turn on the burglar alarm, of course. She wished she had watched Bar turn it on.

There was a kind of box, very small, with numbers on it; a tiny green light showed above the numbered panel. That must mean that the alarm was off. Red, then, meant that it had been turned on. How?

There were no directions of any kind, no figures written anywhere near it, nothing to inform her. She went to the windows and looked out upon watery fog and gray sky. Yes, there was somebody; Archie was trudging along from Kate's house, bent over, his wool cap pulled down to that oddly snouty face, head lowered, as a ferret might seek cover.

She resisted an impulse to call to him. There was a sound reason for that. Archie himself might have been too involved in the Jones murder to permit details of that involvement to come out. Archie might even have murdered Bell Jones.

It was as preposterous a notion as that the Judge himself had somehow been involved with Belle Jones. All the same, Bar had said let nobody in. Emmy watched until Archie disappeared toward his own house, then she telephoned to Kate.

She found Kate's telephone number in the flat, red-bound book near the telephone, labeled Alpine Village. It proved to include the residents of the Village. There was even a number for The Barn.

Kate answered quickly, "Hello, this is Miss Brace. I'm so glad—"

"Kate, it's me."

"Oh," Kate's welcoming voice changed. "I was expecting a man from Appledown who thinks he may take on night-guard duty for the Village. Hurry up, then, Emmy, whatever you want to say. He promised to call me—"

"Kate, wait," Emmy cried desperately. "How do you turn on the burglar alarm?"

"Each alarm has its own set of numbers. There is something I want to discuss with you. China insists that she is going to divorce the Judge and marry Bar. Does Bar know that?" Kate asked with a sharply sarcastic note in her voice which Emmy knew far too well.

"No. I'm sure he doesn't."

"Are you positive of that? China seems very confident. Made quite a statement. She really is a most attractive young woman, you have to admit that."

"Very," Emmy said without choking. "But she's quite wrong about marrying Bar."

"How do you know? She was so certain. Of course I don't know how the Judge will take all this. And Bar doesn't have any money to speak of, either. Not like the Judge—"

"Kate," Emmy said, surprising herself. "China doesn't know what she's talking about. Bar—Bar is going to marry me."

There was a short pause. Then Kate said again, just as sarcastically, "And does Bar know that?"

Emmy swallowed but said firmly, "Certainly."

"When?" asked Kate.

"We—we haven't decided."

"Well, then you can't stay there with Bar now! Not if you are engaged. Not proper."

"I should think it would be far nearer to being proper than—"

"No," said Kate authoritatively. "No, it isn't. Now you come right over here and stay—wait, did Bar go into the city?"

"Yes."

"When will he be home?"

"I don't know. He thought before dark."

"What's he doing in the city?"

"I don't know. Kate, tell me how to find the numbers that turn on this alarm."

"Dear me," Kate said loftily. "You don't mean you are afraid to stay alone without the alarm set?"

"Yes. I am scared. I'm terrified." That whisper over the telephone! But if she told Kate about it, she knew precisely what Kate would do: call the police, force Emmy to come to her house to stay, make her own inquiries, in short take over. A self-appointed police chief, that would be Kate.

It was not the first time in Emmy's life when she had been forced to cope with Kate's sense of rightness. Anything Kate decided to do was, in Kate's view, the only sensible and accurate course of action.

Emmy persisted. "Have you any idea where I can find that alarm number?"

"Oh, I don't know." Kate had no interest in the alarm. "You come right over here, now, Emmy. You can't possibly stay there with Bar now—now that there *is* something—"

"Romantic?" Emmy asked, an edge in her own voice. Kate muttered something, and Emmy decided the only thing to do was to hang up the telephone, and she did so with a hard bang which she hoped would resound in Kate's ears.

She looked helplessly and rather hopelessly around the room. Writing table with a drawer: she searched that, no written notation suggesting numbers. Nothing but stationery and some extra envelopes.

Eventually she found a piece of paper with a series of numbers written on it inside the drawer of a small table near the door. This looked promising but her fingers shook as she tried the numbers on the tiny panel with green light—nine, three, nine, three. The small green light vanished and a tiny red one came on.

So that was it. That was done. Let anybody try to get in the house now and the entire Village would hear.

She sank down, not relaxed but listening and yet thankful, for she did feel safe. At least, she amended it, safer. Besides, on Sunday surely nobody would attempt to—face it—harm her! The whisper over the telephone had been terrifying.

It did strike her if only faintly that it was rather odd for the men to collect rubbish on Sunday.

Suddenly, she sat up, shocked. It was Monday.

Sunday had passed all too quickly. The whole weekend had gone! It had to be Monday.

And she had not turned up at the studio.

There was simply no forgiveness possible when anybody failed to arrive at the studio without even a telephone call to explain.

So, in effect, she had fired herself.

She ought to have realized that it was Monday when Bar started off for the city. He could have done nothing—whatever he intended to do—on Sunday.

Monday. All right, she'd still fight, even if the job seemed to have lost some of its importance. She went to the telephone again. She knew the number.

When it was answered she asked, with a tiny glow of pride, for her own extension.

A man's voice answered. She recognized it at once.

"Hubie!"

"Huh—oh, Emmy! What's wrong?"

"Why are you there—I mean—my phone—"

There was a short bark of laughter from Hubie Naylor. "You're fired, didn't you know? And just now I've been handed your work —on top of my own, too. Until they can fill your spot here. Why didn't you phone in or something?"

"But, Hubie, you're too important to take over my job!"

Hubie laughed shortly. "Nobody is too important to do anything. Where are you?"

"Oh, never mind, Hubie. I didn't mean to be fired. It's the blizzard and—oh, never mind." Better not mention the Judge's high-handed authority. "I meant to come to work. I didn't realize it is Monday. And anyway, Hubie, the blizzard here has been terrible. Roads were all closed—"

"Phones are working," Hubie said shortly. "Weather suddenly like April! I've got to move fast on this Jones case. Don't you have some notes?"

"Yes. That is—yes, but—oh, Hubie, that was *my* story!"

Hubie was not unkind, he was only a keen, cynical, hard-working man. "Can't be helped now, Emmy. I'm sorry but the powers that be handed it to me. Not precisely on a platter. I must say this Jones story doesn't seem to have any sort of ending. He's in prison and that means—"

"Oh, no, he's not in prison. It's not over yet. You haven't got the latest—" It came out before she could stop herself.

Hubie, however, was instantly alert. "What do you mean, not over yet? Isn't he in prison?"

There wasn't even a short struggle between her recently acquired professionalism and her long-time affection for the Judge, in spite of her disagreement with him.

"Well," Hubie said impatiently. "What's the dope? Come on. What have you got on this? I need it. Where is Jones if he's not in prison?"

Affection for the Judge was stifled. "Right here."

She could almost feel Hubie's ears perk up. "Where's here?"

"Here. In Alpine Village. Staying at the Judge's house. He's supposed to help the Judge write his memoirs."

"What Judge? You can't mean Judge Doane who sentenced Jones? Now wait a minute, Emmy, just what are you talking about? This is all new stuff, if it's true. I mean, you're not kidding, are you? If Jones has been let out of prison—"

"He has been paroled. The Judge arranged it, I don't know how—"

"I know how he might have done something about it. The Judge is on the Parole Board now, isn't he?"

"I don't know. But the Judge got him out of prison."

"Alpine Village, you said? Where in the hell is that?"

"Hubie!" It was far too late to put such an experienced newsman off the trail. "Hubie—it's all—mixed up. Please just forget—"

There was something like a wave of electricity coming over the wires from Hubie. "Alpine Village—Alpine Village! Now what do I—hold on, Emmy. Don't leave the phone—"

She thought she could hear a rustle and scrabble of papers. Hubie came back on the telephone, his voice crackling with excitement. "Emmy, I saw it yesterday! A small item! But is there a kind of town near there called Appledown?"

"Yes," Emmy said feebly now, regretting what had seemed a mandatory impulse.

"Then that's it. Listen—two men shot—accidental. Accidental? Alpine Village—sure, that's why I remembered Alpine Village. Shot there—" He was reading swiftly and speaking in very revealing snatches. "Nearest police station—Appledown—not far from Mt. Kisco and White Plains—condominiums—that is, it seems to be houses, set apart—sure. Luxurious—exclusive, prices from five hundred thousand to a million—" he paused. "It does say a million! Is that true, Emmy? If the Judge paid a million for this place, he must have dough."

"Oh, come on, Hubie! That's a wild exaggeration!"

"Allow for inflation," Hubie said. "Both in fact and in print. Very choice residents—here are some names, Emmy! Do you mean to say that Manders has a house there?"

"I didn't say that." And I wish I hadn't said anything.

He was still reading. "Police could make no statement—blizzard checked inquiries—Emmy, how do I get there?"

"No, no—"

"Never mind. I'll get a car. Cars—"

"*Don't come.* Things are in such a mix-up. It's true that the police haven't been able to do much on account of the bad roads. We really were cut off for—" Days? "Since Friday night. So there's no use in trying to get a story."

"By God, Emmy, Jones' parole has to be an ending to this story. And a fine dramatic ending at that. How did you get in all this? Never mind, don't answer. This whole thing is news. I'll bet Appledown is already full of reporters."

"Hubie, listen! The Judge did see to Jones' parole. The Judge will be furious with me because I told you—that is, if you are going to use that—"

She could almost feel his tough, rapid-fire mind darting to a conclusion. "The Judge must have had this Jones on his conscience."

"Of course, he did! He said he felt all along the jury had been mistaken in their verdict."

"So he got him paroled. H'mmm." Hubie paused for only a second or two before he said, "I wasn't thinking of the Judge's conscience in that way. Seems to me the Judge might have had reason to *know* that Jones didn't murder his wife. Is there any chance the Judge knew Belle Jones?"

"None at all! You must believe—"

"As soon as he can," Hubie went right on, "he gets Jones out of prison and takes him into his own home. Now, if the Judge himself murdered the girl, Belle, then he'd have plenty on his conscience—"

"Hubie! No! The Judge is not like that! Believe me I know! His action in getting Jones out of prison only goes to prove that the Judge is a man of character, honesty, a—a firm defender of what he thinks is right and determined to right any wrong. Don't you see—"

Hubie's laugh was short and sharp. "Oh, Emmy, you're living in a world of illusion. The Judge had some urgent reason for getting Jones out of prison, believe me. It may relieve his conscience but not in the way you see it. Don't bother—we'll be there—" There was a firm click of the telephone.

Emmy shouted uselessly, "Hubie! No—"

Now she had really made a frightful mistake. The Judge hadn't murdered Belle Jones. That was perfectly, completely impossible. His reason for getting Jones released was in the hope of righting a wrong. The Judge would never murder anybody!

Hubie was hard-thinking, fast-thinking, implacable. The Village would be swamped with newsmen, cameras, publicity.

The thaw which had begun so quietly in the night had already turned the drifts of snow into grayish heaps of snowy puddles. The wind had come swooping in from the south. So now, not only Appledown would be full of reporters hunting out a story, but Alpine Village would be overwhelmed.

She had inadvertently done precisely what the Judge had accused her of planning to do: offered the studio the final, dramatic conclusion to the Jones murder story.

She hadn't meant to tell Hubie all that she had nevertheless let slip. The fat was in the fire, no question of that.

Once she wondered, wildly, if the residents of Alpine Village retained enough of long-ago Colonial measures to tar and feather anybody! She really must try to think logically.

The Judge had arranged Jones' parole; he could not have hoped to keep that fact a secret; somebody sooner or later certainly would have nosed it out.

Besides, if the Judge felt as strongly as he obviously felt about Jones, then he had nothing but praise coming to him, not censure.

But there would inevitably be a certain amount of publicity for which the Judge would rightly blame her.

It was done, nothing she could do now could change the predictable result. Hubie, cameras and publicity! But all that would have come eventually from Appledown.

But Hubie's cynical suggestion as to a reason for the Judge's conscience-stricken act was preposterous.

She didn't know how much time had passed when she decided that, in fairness, and in memory of many past kindnesses on the part of the Judge, the least she could do was to warn him, even if it meant confessing to what he would consider a gross disloyalty.

She braced herself, looked up the Judge's number in the little book and dialed it. The Judge himself answered.

"Uncle," she began and was annoyed to realize that her voice wavered. "Uncle, there's something I think you'd better know."

The Judge was quick, too, as Hubie was quick. "What have you done?"

"I—I told a man at the studio—you see, he's working on my assignment . . ."

"But you're fired! You are not working on the Jones affair."

"No, that is—but he is, you see. And—"

The Judge leaped to the correct conclusion and thundered at her, "You told him I got Jones out of prison! You can't have told him that Jones is here!"

"I—yes—yes, I did—"

"Emmy! If you told any newsman in your studio about these terrible murders—You did! I can tell. Emmy, you are nothing but a—a female scavenger. Disloyal to—to Kate and Bar and everybody here in Alpine Village! And more than anything you are disloyal to me! Your oldest friend. Your most faithful friend." His voice broke. However, the Judge was not entirely averse to a very convincing show of emotion. She knew that and steeled herself.

"But, Uncle, they already knew. There was an item in the papers yesterday. They had talked to the police in Appledown—"

"Got nothing from them," the Judge cried. "They haven't been able to do anything at all in the way of inquiry—"

"But they will. The roads are clear enough. Everything is dripping with the thaw and the police will be back soon."

"All due to you—"

"No, no! That's not fair."

"You told them about Jones."

"Uncle, it—it just came out. The story needs just that happy" —she nearly choked on the word—"happy ending for Jones. Can't you see that it does you credit?"

"I see that you are an ungrateful, self-centered young woman. I knew you would change. You've been seeing too much of a hardhitting world—" He put down the telephone with a bang.

At any rate, the worst was over. Or more likely beginning. However, she had confessed to him and no matter what he said, she was right. The whole story would show the Judge in an admirable light.

Of course, the two murders were shocking enough in themselves to attract the newspapers. The fortress, if one could call it that, would soon be besieged.

The siege began sooner than she expected with another telephone call. It was Hubie. "Emmy, is there a hotel anywhere around there?"

"No, no! Hubie, please don't send—"

He cut in. "I've got the dope directly from the Appledown police. Two murders *and* an attempted murder this morning!"

"No, no! That was called an accident."

Hubie paid no attention. "We're sending our camera crew. I'm coming along with script writers. Roads are clear. We'll be there as soon as possible. Don't let any other newsmen talk to you! You are our source, don't forget!"

"You said I was fired." Emmy spoke into a perfectly silent disconnected instrument.

An hour or so later there were angry thuds on the door and repeated shrills of the doorbell. Emmy went to the window. By pressing her nose against it, she could see the Judge, certainly still in a rage because he was pounding at the door with furious swings of his heavy walking stick with one hand, and jabbing the doorbell with the other. The pup didn't like it and set up a wild barking.

Bar had said not to let anybody at all into the house.

She certainly didn't want to face the Judge in what she knew to be his present mood.

He shouted, "I know you are there! Emmy, open the door at once."

It was easier simply not to answer. Besides, she'd have had to shriek above the barking of the dog whose instincts told him that all the evil in the world was threatening the house. And Emmy herself as well, she thought swiftly, her heart softening again for the valiant little dog who almost barked himself sideways in his determination to defend his home and owner.

The Judge shouted, the dog barked and the telephone rang again. This she answered, and it was Kate.

"Whatever are you doing, Emmy? Can't you answer the phone? The police are here again at The Barn. They have begun the serious inquiry. At last," Kate added sourly but, being Kate, added fairly, "They really couldn't do much before, I suppose. But now the roads are mostly clear, even though they're flooded in some spots. And then this horrible thing this morning. I've been on the phone to the hospital. Thank God, they think Sam is going to make it. The police have to question everybody in the Village. Do you hear me, Emmy? What on earth is that sound?"

"The Judge," Emmy said bleakly. "He's in a state—"

"Mad at you? Why? Now if it's Bar he's after, I can understand that. China makes no secret of her intention about Bar. But why is the Judge after you?"

"I'd better tell you. Newsmen and camera crews—and we'll be deluged here in the Village. You should let other people know."

Kate was as quick as the Judge, or as Hubie if it came to that. "You told somebody at the television studio. How could you?"

"They'd know anyway. The papers had it yesterday. The Appledown police were interviewed. There is simply nothing we can do to stop news."

That had been almost the first rule she had learned: news cannot be stopped; it's got to be accurate but news is news. What happened, when did it happen, where did it happen, who is concerned, why did it happen? The first rule of reporting: oh, she knew that.

The Judge pounded the door so hard the panels quivered. The dog yelped. Kate all but yelped, too. "What are you doing to that puppy?"

Seventeen

"Nothing. He's doing it for me. He thinks he's guarding the house."

Kate couldn't help being a little smug even at that moment. "I told you—I told everybody what fine watchdogs they would be. Don't forget, Emmy. They'll expect you—I mean the police will—at The Barn." She hung up. The Judge apparently gave up and went away.

But Emmy had promised Bar not to let anybody in the house and not to go out of the house. She wouldn't go to The Barn. She'd have to go if the police summoned her.

She resolved to wait until a policeman came to see her.

Time had passed: her thoughts circled around and around the same paths. The pup put a beseeching paw on her knee and wagged his tail. Food, of course.

Such a valiant little defender had certainly earned his keep. She laughed at him, and he wagged his tail happily and again displayed quick thinking for he led her toward the kitchen and the source of supply. She recklessly thawed out some steak from the freezer and minced it up for the pup while he watched, brown eyes eager, tail beating the floor and then, politely tasting each mouthful, he ate. He drank some milk but without much zeal. He'd prefer meat.

Eventually the early winter dusk began to crawl into the corners of the rooms. Twice someone came to the door, knocked loudly, rang the bell and at last went away. Once she thought it might be China but she wouldn't go to the window and peer out. A third time, however, it was Kate who shouted through the door, "Open the door, Emmy. But turn off the alarm unless you want all the police here." Emmy hunted around for the paper where she had found the numbers for the alarm and when she couldn't find it at once, Kate yelled impatiently, "I think it's nine, three, nine, three. I'm not sure but try it." Certainly; she remembered it then.

Bar had certainly never meant for her to keep Kate out. Emmy pressed the tiny buttons, nine, three, nine, three and the red light vanished. The small green light came on, and she opened the door but not only for Kate. Homer Jones was with her, looking thoroughly soggy. Kate, however, was looking as if the thaw had given her a fresh glow. She flung down an enormous rain cape and said, "Come on in, Homer. Nobody is going to bite you."

He was already in, apologetically huddling near the door as if he expected to be thrust out any moment. He stood looking at Emmy diffidently. "If Miss Brace, that is—you know, Miss Brace, I'm not really welcome anywhere," he said desolately.

Clearly he meant Emmy with the first Miss Brace, Kate with the second. However it was, Homer edged further into the room, shed his damp, black overcoat, sat down suddenly on a bench near the door, put his face in his hands and burst into tears.

Emmy was too embarrassed to speak. Kate was in full control. She put a brisk hand on Homer's shoulder. "Now, now, no use crying. Sit up and act like a—"

Emmy knew what Kate was about to say, act like a man. Kate bit her lip and substituted, "Act like yourself."

From the little she had seen of Homer Jones, that did not seem to Emmy much better. Homer Jones had never impressed her with his hearty manliness.

Homer said between his spread, thin fingers, "Before I came here everything was peaceful. And now—oh!" He lifted his red-rimmed eyes to Kate. "That poor man yesterday! I tell you I'm not welcome at the Judge's or anywhere—"

"Well, no use in calling yourself a Typhoid Mary," Kate said firmly. "You didn't shoot Sam. Besides he's better. But I hate any sort of violence. Don't forget they say it was my gun—"

"But they don't think you shot him," Homer said and sobbed.

"Don't choke yourself." Kate could be bracing but also brusque. "Straighten up! How about a drink, Emmy? He's been with the police and of course they know his—his history." Kate said kindly but exactly, "I'm afraid they made it rather tough for him."

"I didn't even know that poor man!" Homer was trying to stop his convulsive sobs; his voice shook.

"You didn't know Mac, either," Kate said.

Homer looked puzzled and then identified the nickname. "Oh, you mean the guard. No, no, I didn't know him. Exactly. Of course I had seen him, at the gate—"

"And you certainly didn't know that man Guy Wilkins."

Homer put his face in his hands again. "Oh, no! How could I have known him or anybody here except the Judge?"

Kate went to shove more logs on the fire, then sat down. The pup sat down nearby but merely looked at her.

Kate glanced down at him. "No gratitude in that dog, Emmy. All the time I fed him and the rest of those pups—"

"Kate, forget the puppies. What will you have to drink, Mr. Jones?"

Homer looked at her vaguely. "Oh, I'm not sure I ought to drink. Might be held against me. I do wish the Judge's wife liked me. She hates me. I can tell. She wants the Judge to make me leave —and she's so pretty," he said with a sob in his voice again. "So pretty. So graceful, so—she reminds me of—" He covered his face with his hands again but the words got out "—Belle. I loved her so. She was everything in life to me—"

What should I do? Emmy thought; he's going to have hysterics. Kate intervened. "Stop that, Homer. You'll just make yourself sick."

"All that time in prison I couldn't stop thinking of her. I can't stop now. She's always in my mind. I loved her so—"

"Well," Kate said reasonably, "even if some people still think you killed her—"

"No—no!" Homer cried.

"You can't be tried again, even if somebody thinks up—I mean invents—some kind of evidence against you, you couldn't possibly be tried again for the same crime."

"Oh, I know that! I was told that. The Judge—many people have been so helpful. But mainly the Judge. It's only his wife who—who hates me. Honestly she does."

"Don't give it a thought." Kate was in the dining room. Emmy heard the splash of liquid. No, liquor, she amended hastily. Kate walked quickly into the kitchen; turned on a faucet, came back with a glass. Homer gave her one look and shrank as if from poison. "I'd better not drink. I told you—"

"This is for me," said Kate, downed some of it and turned to Emmy. "It really has been hell at The Barn. It's a roundup of the whole Village. Somebody was sent to get you. They said you were gone. At least you wouldn't answer the doorbell or even pounding at the door and yelling."

"I didn't hear any yelling. But no, I wouldn't have opened the door for anybody but you. Bar said not to."

Kate eyed her over the glass. "I met China outside. She is still determined to leave the Judge and marry Bar. Makes no bones about it."

Homer muttered, "So lovely. So beautiful. So like—" He stopped himself as Kate gave him a stern look.

"We know, Homer. We know what a tragedy that was. That is, we don't know exactly, never having had the experience of being tried for the murder of somebody we—but we understand. Perhaps you loved her too much, and she—I mean—" Kate began to flounder.

Emmy said it for her. "She just might have had, say, some other admirers. Or even—"

"No!" Homer started up; his thin face white. "No! There was nobody. Except that Archie Callser."

"Oh!" Emmy was surprised. "You knew about him?"

Homer made a sound like a moan but no other reply.

Emmy turned to Kate. "And you knew about him, too. Who told you?"

Kate smiled. "Archie, himself. He was upset. Sure you or somebody would say he had something to do with the murder of poor

Homer's wife. But Archie—heavenly days! Archie wouldn't kill anything."

Homer said humbly, "I don't think he would. I don't think he could. Besides, believe me, he just wasn't on anything but the barest friendly terms with my Belle."

"How do you know?" Emmy asked irresistibly.

Homer opened teary eyes. "Why, I met him. He came to the apartment several times when I was there. Belle explained that he had been very kind to her—somewhere—" He added vaguely, "I think he shared his taxi with her on a rainy day or something, and then he became our friend gradually. At least I thought he was a friend, but now he avoids me. He thinks—they all think in spite of what the Judge has done, all of them think I'm a murderer."

Homer's explanation of Archie's friendship with Belle did not square with Archie's admission of a pick-up in a bar.

But the ring, or rather no ring! Emmy had to go on with her lightning flash of memory. She said swiftly, before she could reproach herself for further torturing Homer Jones, "Did Belle ever wear a ring? Any ring—"

A swift glimpse of something like pride crossed Homer's face. "Her wedding ring. She always wore it. She loved it. I couldn't get her a big handsome ring, or any kind of engagement ring. I didn't have the money. As soon as I got some money, I was going to get her the prettiest ring I could afford. But—but I never did." His voice sank again.

"So she wore her wedding ring. Always," Emmy said thoughtfully.

Homer gave her a vaguely teary look. "Oh, yes, she was very proud of it. Never had it off her finger. Said she never would remove it—"

He was going to cry again, Emmy thought, but she had to go on. "There was no ring on her hand when she was found. Did you know that?"

Homer's eyes opened widely. "Oh, no, that couldn't be—"

"Fact," said Emmy, ignoring a disapproving look from Kate.

"But—but—oh, I don't know! I can't remember—I didn't look at her hand. I didn't—all I could see was—"

"You can't say what might have happened to her ring?"

"No! No!" Homer cried and put his head in his hands and sobbed wildly.

That man, Emmy thought, could do with a psychiatrist. He was at the breaking point. Kate, however, with the uncanny perception of a sister, guessed her thought and gave her the sisterly look which meant shut up.

Emmy felt she really ought to try to calm Homer as gently as she could. "You didn't notice whether or not she wore her ring, naturally. Of course, you were in no state to think of it. There couldn't have been anybody she'd have given her wedding ring to."

He lifted his face. "I don't know what you mean! Give away her wedding ring? Oh, no!"

She wasn't doing very well. She said carefully, "I only thought that somebody—a thief perhaps, or somebody might have been—someone you thought of as a friend. Or even a friend of Belle's. Someone you may not have known—"

"No! No!" Homer sobbed. But Emmy finished, "No one in your apartment, of course, but perhaps just leaving or—"

Homer cried, "I've told them! Over and over! I didn't see anybody! Anybody at all. I can't stand this—"

Kate took over efficiently and kindly. "What you need," she said to Homer, "is a good hot meal."

"No, no! I *can't* go back to the Judge's now. His wife is cooking, you know—and she—"

"She'll not really put poison in your soup," Kate said. "However, you can come home with me. I'll give you some food and come on, get into your coat. Things will be all right." She turned to Emmy. "Put your alarm on again. Call me if you get upset about anything. I think the police at The Barn are just about finished with the entire roster of Village residents. All of them," Kate smiled, "very, very indignant! Come on, Homer—"

She got an elbow under Homer's arm and propelled him along with her. Emmy was thankful to see them go and yet—and yet the dreary and dripping dusk fell upon her and the entire Village. Very few lights shone through the heavy fog.

She remembered, though, to put on the alarm again, nine, three, nine, three. The tiny red light seemed to mean safety.

She hadn't intended to wound Homer so painfully. But she had certainly persisted. Yet now she was grateful for Kate's common sense and kindness.

The thaw was, in an odd way, more disheartening than the snow had been for it had come too suddenly, melting the drifts of snow, creating puddles everywhere, causing a constant dripping from eaves and trees and shrubs. She thought she could hear an occasional dreary plop of melting snow from the roof. There was no way to tell when Hubie and his cohorts would arrive. Probably, they had gone first to the police.

She was not tough enough to be a real reporter. And just perhaps, said a vagrant little notion in her mind, it was just as well. Now stop that, she told herself, at once! She could claim she was going to marry Bar, but that didn't mean it was a fact so she would have to give up her treasured job.

She couldn't put Homer Jones out of her mind. He was a tragic figure, convicted for the murder of his wife, whom he all but idolized. If Hubie or Bar turned up any other man whom Belle had been seeing, it would really break Homer's heart. Unless the murder had already broken his heart as it had obviously broken his nerves. The Judge, she decided, not for the first time, was truly a good, perceptive man.

If the police were still in The Barn—no, there would be someone at the Appledown police station to inform Hubie and all the others of the plain facts.

The early winter twilight increased. A steaming fog misted the lights over the whole Village. Still no police came to the door.

Emmy wished that Bar would return soon. She wouldn't put on any lights in the house. Let everybody think she had gone. The pup would bark but that need not mean that she was in the house. Only Bar would know of her presence.

It was almost entirely dark when the telephone rang. It was a dismal darkness. By then she was half afraid even to answer the telephone yet she hoped Bar was calling.

She was right. "Everything okay?" Bar asked cheerily.

"Yes. That is, no! Everything's all wrong!"

"What do you mean all wrong?" His voice sharpened.

"I mean—oh, Bar, I did a terrible thing."

"Well, now—how terrible?"

"I told Hubie—that is, he is a man at the studio, a writer and a famous reporter and—oh, Bar, you see he was asked to do my work temporarily. Just until they can get somebody else—and I told him about Jones and the Judge."

"That can't hurt anybody."

"You don't understand. There was an item in yesterday's papers from Appledown. Hubie got in touch with the police. He's sending a whole crew of cameramen and writers here and—"

"Nobody can keep two murders a secret."

"But the Judge blames me—"

"Let him. News is news. Emmy, I'm in a phone booth at a filling station. I only want to tell you I'm on my way home. And Emmy! I think I have news!"

"About Jones?"

"Sure. You wrote 'No Rg.' No ring. Not even a wedding ring."

She broke in. "I know! At least all at once I remembered. So I asked Jones. Kate brought him here awhile ago. He went to pieces. He said she loved her wedding ring and always wore it but he couldn't remember; he never looked when he found her body. He doesn't know whether or not she had it on."

"Now that is interesting," Bar said slowly. "The man at the newsstand, you remember, where she bought her hometown papers? I asked him and he remembered her and said she always wore a very handsome, big, costly, he thought, ring. All green glitter—emeralds, I suppose, and diamonds. He noticed that. So one wonders where that expensive ring came from and where it went, if it comes to that. But wait, there's more. After Archie told us about picking her up in the bar—"

She broke in again. "Jones says Archie shared a taxi with her—picked her up yes, but in that way and then it seems Archie gradually got to be a kind of family friend. That's what Jones says. Not what Archie said at all."

"All right," Bar said after a slight pause. "I'll talk to Archie again. But listen to this. We thought that if she picked up Archie in a bar—as Archie says—then she might have picked up somebody else in a bar. So I made a circuit of neighborhood bars, near the Jones apartment, I mean—I don't know why the police didn't do this, but evidently they didn't bother because the case was so open and shut. Anyway, Archie was *not* her only pickup. What do you think of that?"

"Who?"

"Do you have any photographs of the Judge?"

The Judge! "Yes, I suppose so. Somewhere. But the Judge couldn't have killed her."

"Somebody did. Can you get hold of those photographs?"

"I think they must be in my apartment in my desk or a trunk or—I tell you the Judge is not the kind of man who would pick up a woman in a bar, even if she was pretty and young."

"That's why the bartender remembers her. She was so pretty and so young. He did describe Archie—that is, he said a fattish young man, bald, looked sort of like a rat."

"Archie doesn't look like a rat!" Still he did have that snouty look that she'd noticed lately. He was bald. And plump.

"But he wasn't the only one. The bartender couldn't describe the other man very accurately, seems he thought she didn't meet him often after the first several times. They could have met in other places though. Now listen, I remember sorting out my mother's letters and papers in her desk. I believe there was a kind of group picture of the residents of Alpine Village, I'm not sure. It wasn't a very clear picture but possibly clear enough to show to the bartender."

"You mean for identification."

"Sure. Oh, by the way, tell Kate not to fuss about her gun. I think it'll be all right. That is, not all right exactly. It did damn near kill somebody."

"Kate phoned the hospital. He's going to live."

"Good! I've got to go. There's a woman waiting to use the phone and she's beginning to look dangerous. Besides—"

A clear businesslike voice cut in. "Your time is up. Please drop in—"

"Never mind, operator. I've finished. Fix some dinner for me, Emmy. I haven't had a bite to eat—"

The telephone went dead as the operator obeyed the rules.

Emmy put down her own telephone desolately. He must have called from New York. It would take time for him to reach Alpine Village. She had hoped that he would arrive before Hubie. She didn't think she could face Hubie and the cameramen and crew and the writers alone.

So Bar wanted a photograph of the entire group of residents of Alpine Village in order to induce the bartender to identify Belle's second pick-up. Or third or fourth, she thought sadly, thinking of the pretty girl Belle had been.

It was a remote chance that some man from Alpine Village had met Belle. On the other hand, Archie had certainly picked her up.

The Judge had liked pretty young women; no question of that. He had married China and loaded her with very costly gifts.

Belle had habitually worn a ring, a big, handsome ring of emeralds and diamonds. But in all the accounts of Belle's murder there had been no mention of any rings—which had seemed to Emmy odd enough to warrant a scribbled question mark to that effect.

So then, someone had taken the ring. Jones could remember nothing of any ring at all. None had been found in the apartment. If so, it would have been mentioned in the newspapers.

Dinner! China would have prepared a perfectly superb dinner, out of nothing if it came to that.

The cupboards, the refrigerator, above all its freezing compartment did supply a generous amount of food, in spite of her having denuded the freezer of one small steak. She searched out a wrapped package of filets of beef; they could be broiled. She found potatoes in a bin; these could be baked. At least she could bake a potato and make quite good coffee.

By the time Bar arrived the steaks should be just right for broiling. Scouring potatoes was a curiously comforting chore. Pioneer foremothers, Kate had said indignantly, wouldn't have waited for someone to come and help. It would be rather comfortable to believe that some strain of pioneer foremother blood had descended to her, Emmy. She went to hunt out the group picture Bar had mentioned.

She found it almost immediately but it was not very revealing. It seemed to have been taken at the Village swimming pool on a sunny day. Water reflected the sun, and the people standing, sitting or lounging around the pool were only dimly recognizable. The sun was in their eyes, so everyone seemed to be squinting—also laughing. China's face was a mere blur; however, her bikini displayed her lovely figure. Her hair was tossed back. The Judge's mustache identified him but he wore dark glasses. Few of the faces were known to her. There was Kate, however, her strong features and short black curls unmistakable, as was her no-nonsense skirted bathing suit. Emmy thought that one slim, darkly handsome man standing half in the shadow was Manders. Archie sat dabbling his feet in the water, wet, curly fringe of hair, hunched up and squinting in the sun.

If the bartender could make anything at all of that photograph, she felt coldly, no jury would accept such identification.

She put the photograph safely away. As she did so, there was another thunderous pounding at the door. She closed the drawer of the desk swiftly.

But she wouldn't open the door. Then she heard Kate shouting, "Emmy, open this door at once! Emmy!"

Kate was safe; and it was like her to pound on the door.

Emmy opened the door, forgetting the burglar alarm completely until an instantaneous ear-splitting sound came from above her head.

Kate yelled over the noise, "Turn off the alarm."

A man in a blue uniform stood beside Kate. "Please, Miss," he shouted. "Turn off the alarm. You'll have the whole force here."

"And everybody in the Village. Hurry up, Emmy!"

Emmy was confused by the shriek; she couldn't remember, *couldn't* remember which little buttons to push. "Kate," she screamed, "What do I do?"

And what a fool I am, she thought ashamed.

Kate did not hear her. Nobody could hear through that horrible, repeated shrieking. Probably people were running from all over the Village.

She was fumbling at the buttons on the panel, trying to think which button, this one, that one, she heard the Judge roaring, "Turn that thing off, Emmy—"

She thought she heard a car dashing up before the house. Finally, she heard Bar shouting quite near the door. He must have shoved the others aside. He flung the door open, and in one movement turned to the tiny panel near the door, pushed the correct buttons and the scream stopped.

Bar had started toward the dining room and drinks, Emmy knew. He turned back at that. "What did you say?"

Emmy hastened to introduce them. "This is Hubie Naylor from the studio. Barselious Slocumb."

Hubie got to his feet and nodded in a friendly way. Bar glared and offered no hand. "Did I hear you say love nest?"

"Why, yes. Indeed, I'm pleased—if a bit surprised—to know that Emmy at last—"

"How would you like your teeth knocked down your throat?" Bar asked in such a mild way that Emmy was astonished to see Hubie sink back into his chair.

Hubie, however, had not heard that threat infrequently during his days of reporting. "I wouldn't like it at all. If I've made a mistake—but I thought—Emmy here, you see and—"

Emmy saw thunder clouds gathering in Bar's face. She said swiftly, "We are going to be married."

She didn't dare look at Bar after what seemed a necessary, if mendacious, announcement.

Hubie surprisingly disclosed himself as equally conventional as Kate. He sat forward, frowning. "Really, Emmy! Then you *shouldn't* be living here with that man. It's not a bit nice!"

"Hubie!" Emmy cried, astounded. "You *can't* be so old-fashioned. Such a—such a throwback. Or something," she finished inadequately.

Hubie was not affected. "I can be anything I want to be. I am thoroughly sick and tired of all this living together just to see if you like it. Not for you—"

Bar, Emmy knew, was about to explode.

She cried, "Wait, Bar. Let's have something to drink. We'll explain all this to Hubie."

The idea of drinks seemed to strike Bar and Hubie as welcome. Both men quieted down a little, although she felt that Hubie was simmering at the idea of her love nest and Bar was simmering for the same reason. Unless, of course, he was simmering at Emmy's decidedly inaccurate claim.

Yet underneath, in an instinctive way, she knew that the two men had a kind of instantaneous liking for one another.

Bar departed to fetch the drinks and Emmy thought of the filets she had left out to thaw. A good thing she had put out the whole package, for it was certain that Hubie would invite himself to dinner. He never had a qualm about asking for anything he wanted.

Bar had gone into the kitchen. There was the tinkle of ice cubes below the happy greeting of the pup.

Hubie lifted his eyebrows. "A dog and all! How very domestic! I really wouldn't have thought this of you, Emmy. Staying here with an old friend, that's all right. But I didn't know there was any —any romance about it. It simply is not proper at all—"

"Oh, Hubie, you sound like my sister. Kate—" A mischievous purpose suggested itself. "You were planning to stay here tonight?"

"Sure. I thought you'd take me in but as it is—"

"There's no room here," Emmy said wickedly. "But my sister Kate has an extra room. I feel sure she'll let you stay there—"

Bar returned, balancing a tray with decanters and glasses. He had overheard. "Why, sure." All at once he grinned, quite like himself. "Kate will be delighted to make you welcome. Kate," he added, "is running for office. I expect you'll be glad to do her the favor of a few words of praise during her campaign. On your program, I mean. Scotch or Bourbon?"

"Bourbon, thank you," said Hubie. Emmy had never before seen him outmaneuvered. He took the generous measure of Bourbon and, as Bar waited, he said, but rather feebly, "And branch. Please."

So that settled that, Emmy reflected with a mean kind of pleasure.

Bar gave her a tall glass and asked quietly, "The picture?"

She nodded. But Hubie, recovering, perked up his ears at once. "Picture?"

Bar nodded. "Something that belonged to my mother. Cheers."

"Cheers," said Hubie thoughtfully. What picture? he was clearly asking himself. Something concerning the small world of Alpine Village. Hubie would pluck that fact out of the air. He was experienced in just such nuances.

He made up his mind. "Look here, if that picture, whatever it is, has anything to do with this—this Alpine Village, I really would like to see it. Just to inform myself a little. We've got to make a story of this, you know. News is news. Can't be avoided. How about it?"

Bar drank, thought and said, "I don't see why not. Let's have it, Emmy, please."

No reason not to give it to Hubie. He was well-informed about all sorts of oddments of news. She got the photograph and handed it to Bar first, who gave it a long look before he gave it to Hubie. To Emmy's astonishment Hubie got out some spectacles which seemed to magnify, for after one look at the picture through the heavy glasses he said, "Interesting. Who's the pretty girl in the bikini?"

"That's China," Emmy explained. "I mean the Judge's wife."

"Ah," said Hubie and let his gaze enjoy China for a moment. Then he nodded. "That's the Judge all right. Stern as if he were sitting on the bench. Crusty old duck. Oh, I beg your pardon, Emmy. Isn't he some sort of connection of yours?"

"Uncle," Emmy said briefly.

Hubie's gaze fastened again upon the picture, then sharpened. Hubie, the imperturbable, sat up with a jerk that unshipped his heavy eyeglasses and stared. "Is that Manders? *The* Manders?"

"Sure," said Bar. "Has a very luxurious house here. Full of interesting collections. At least one collection. That is, knives."

"Did you say knives?"

"Yes. That is, I believe now he has put them away somewhere—"

"You *saw* them?"

Bar nodded. He didn't add, "we found one of them here in this house." Instead he said, "What do you know about him?"

Emmy swallowed some of her drink.

Hubie sighed. "Not much. In a general way just what I expect a lot of people know. He's quite a big shot financially. But however he makes his money, he does it within the law—at least as far as anybody knows."

"What are his business interests? I really never heard of him until I found that he had bought a place here."

Hubie was still examining the picture. "Hey, there's that little guy Manders calls his secretary. Vague rumor has it he does Manders' dirty work for him."

"Not anymore," Bar said dryly. "He was one of the two men who were killed last Saturday."

Hubie darted a piercing glance at Bar. "If you ask me what the dirty work is—was—I don't know. Manders does seem to be financially interested in many things. Nobody has ever said anything specifically about anything illegal like dope running or gun running, but there have been hints. It's very likely that he is simply very, very smart about making money. There are men like that. Of course, he is a mystery in a way. Doesn't give press statements. Doesn't want his picture taken. I'm surprised he permitted this."

"It's only a snapshot. My mother took it one day at the swimming pool here in Alpine Village."

Hubie was distracted sufficiently to raise his eyebrows. Bar said, "Oh, sure. Olympic length—"

"It would be," Hubie muttered.

Bar went on. "Two tennis courts. Golf course. The works."

"So Manders makes his home here. At least one of his homes." Hubie squinted into space. "Seems to me he has a big apartment in New York. He does collect pictures, too—as well as knives apparently. Seems to have his fingers in quite a number of successful enterprises. But I'll tell you now that every one of them is sure to be perfectly solid and legal. There could be some other reason for Manders' making a mystery of himself. No wife—or, for all I know, he has had a dozen wives. But this secretary—"

"His name was Guy," Bar said. "Guy Wilkins."

Hubie sighed. "That's just all I've heard about Manders.

Bar said vaguely, "He drives in one of those cars with blacked-out windows."

"How long has he had it?"

"I don't know. Seems to me somebody, Kate perhaps, said about a week, maybe less. Does it make any difference?"

"Who knows," Hubie said and then shook his head. "There was a kind of fad for those cars for awhile. I believe now they are very much frowned upon by the powers that be. Still, blacked-out windows do suggest that whoever has such a car is afraid of something. Or somebody. Certainly your Manders is publicity shy."

"He has another car, a long white—"

"Who drives that?"

"He drove it. Sometimes. Guy Wilkins sometimes. Do you recognize any of the other people?"

"Only the Judge. And Manders. He's a good-looking son of a gun, isn't he?"

Both men oddly looked at Emmy as if a woman's judgment were needed here. She said, "Yes, he is. That is—I'll see to dinner. Bar, it might be a good idea to tell Hubie what we know about the murders."

Bar said calmly, "You mean *everything?*"

"Yes," Emmy said firmly. "Begin with the Judge telling me I am in danger about the Jones murder. Hubie is doing that piece now. If the Judge is right, Hubie is in danger, too."

Hubie jumped quite out of his chair at that. "What the hell—"

"Show him the knife," Emmy said and gave Hubie a long, level look. "Hubie," she added, hoping she was correct, "can be—is—very discreet. He can keep any secret he wants to keep a secret."

She left a very thoughtful silence as she started for the kitchen. Then she heard Hubie say, rather feebly, "Did she mean one of Manders' knives?"

"He says somebody got into his house and stole the knife. If you are taking over the account of the Jones murder, and if the Judge is right, then you are in danger, too."

There was a sound as if Hubie had collapsed into the chair again. "You'd better tell me about the knife—" he said in a very peculiar voice. Hubie, who was never discomposed by anything!

"I'll show it to you," Bar said.

She closed the door to the kitchen. She couldn't rival China but she could cook potatoes and broil steaks.

In the end it wasn't a bad dinner. Cooked string beans with some almonds found in a cupboard took the place of a salad. Dessert was canned but cold apricots, over which she spooned kirschwasser which she found in the dining-room cupboard.

When she called the men to dinner, Hubie was rather pale. "That's a terrible knife."

"I'll put it away again." Bar did so, wrapping it carefully under Hubie's fascinated gaze.

The food seemed restoring. Both men sat at the small kitchen table with her and ate hungrily, almost wolfishly. This gave Emmy some slight satisfaction. They didn't talk much, although Hubie was still white and inclined to look nervously toward doors and windows. Bar was very quiet. The pup got a scrap of steak which he wolfed down, too.

Emmy made coffee and they took their full cups back to the living room and began an exhaustive retracing of all the events since Emmy had arrived in Alpine Village. No, she amended that much later, not quite everything! Nothing was said of China's determination to leave the Judge and marry Bar. Nothing was said of the curiously excited look of aroused interest in Bar's face when he had found whatever he found or saw or merely thought in Kate's bedroom, the dog-room, Emmy labeled it, something which had argued that Kate need not be too troubled by the fact that her gun had been used to shoot Sam. Otherwise, listening, it seemed to her that Bar had left out nothing.

Finally, Hubie put his chin in his hands. "I don't know—I can't —I don't know—what's your opinion, Bar?"

"I haven't any," Bar replied gloomily, "that is, not a firm idea."

"What about Jones? How does he take all this?"

"Feels the murders happened after his arrival—well, of course that's true. Feels he is not welcome at the Judge's house—that is, that the Judge's wife doesn't want him there. That's true, too."

"He was here," Emmy said. "He nearly had hysterics when he spoke of his wife, Belle."

"He was here!" Hubie cried.

"Oh, yes. Kate, my sister, brought him in. He looks awful, pale and thin and he cried, talking of Belle. He really must have felt that life held nothing for him after her—after that terrible murder."

There was a short silence. Both men looked serious, imagining perhaps the ugly scene when Homer Jones came home and found his wife.

"He's had a rough time!" Hubie rose. "Emmy is not going to like this, but I can't help feeling that the Judge may have had more than a wrong verdict on his mind when he got Jones paroled."

"No!" Emmy began but Bar said, "Yes, I thought of that, too. Especially since it seems that Belle Jones had a way of picking up men in the bar. Such as Archie—"

"From what you told me about Archie, he's not much help, is he?"

"There's one rather odd thing, though," Emmy said. "He and Homer Jones tell different stories of their acquaintance."

Bar nodded. "Interesting. I didn't get to that. Tell him, Emmy."

"Archie said it was a bar," Emmy said. "Homer says that Belle was waiting for a taxi sometime, on a stormy day, and Archie happened along in a taxi, saw her plight and gave her a lift. After that, Archie became a sort of family friend, Homer said. Archie doesn't say that at all."

"Well, now. That is interesting." Hubie eyed the ceiling. "Your friend, Archie—"

"Oh, no!" Emmy cried. "He *couldn't* have killed Belle. He is just not the kind—"

"People always say that," Hubie said skeptically.

"Yes, I know. But you see, we—Bar and Kate and I have known Archie since we were kids. We really do know him. Don't we, Bar?"

"Yes," Bar agreed but rather reluctantly. "At the same time, I would like it better if Archie's story and Jones' story agreed."

"Do you think Archie killed the girl?" Hubie asked bluntly.

Bar thought for a moment. "I'm not sure that anybody can say with certainty what anybody else would do in a—oh, in an emotional storm of some kind, for example. Yet I truly cannot see Archie getting into a murderous state—no, I feel positive that Archie didn't kill Belle."

"I'd like to see this Archie," Hubie said. "Now, the Judge—look here, Bar, how long has the Judge been married?"

Emmy replied. "Two years—a little over."

"So," Hubie said, "the Jones murder took place just over two years ago. Jones served close to two years on his sentence. Then was paroled. If the Judge actually had something going with poor Belle Jones and wanted her out of the way so he could marry your friend China, then he'd have a real reason for killing Belle. That is, if she proved hard to get rid of. And now a reason for getting Jones out of prison. Conscience, sure. I've said too much. Emmy won't listen to any such idea. See here," Hubie actually seemed rather diffident. "If there is anything in the world I can do for you both, only let me know. I mean—"

Bar took him up at once. "There is something you can do and

something important, I think. You have ways and means of finding out things about people, don't you?"

Hubie's lips tightened. "That's my job."

"Then could you look into Manders' affairs? And then—if you don't mind leaving what seems to have become the murder capital of the world—"

"No, no," Emmy said under her breath.

"If you'll take this snapshot to the bartender and get him to take a good look at everybody in it—"

"Certainly, I can do that."

"It means leaving your story here."

"Maybe I'll get a better story," Hubie said but not really very hopefully. "It's all right. Give me the picture."

"You see," Bar said, "I don't want to leave Emmy alone again. Not the way things are. And the police, I'm sure, won't let me take her to town and lock her up somewhere—"

"Give me the picture. Better wrap it in something so it won't crumple. And the address of the bar. That's all," he added as Bar folded two heavy envelopes around the snapshot. Hubie put it carefully in an inner pocket, took a long breath, straightened his shoulders and unexpectedly leaned over and kissed Emmy. "I hope you'll be very happy," he said. "You've got a good man here. Now I know you don't like to consider this, Emmy, but I know something of the Judge. Believe me, if he wants anything or wants to do anything he'll get it—and do it. I've seen him in action—just remember that, Emmy. He may be right about the danger. Now I'd better go."

"*Now?*" Emmy cried. "But it's so late—"

Bar said, "Bars stay open late."

Hubie gathered up his raincoat. "A lot to do. Some friends to get hold of. Don't hope for too much, but I'll do my best."

Bar went with him to his car which must have left swiftly for when Bar came back he was brushing splatters of muddy water from his coat. "Your friend doesn't take long to get off the mark."

"Hubie is like that. One reason he is so good at his job. But the Judge didn't kill that girl."

"Your friend, Hubie, said you'd insist on that. But I don't know, he's got a point there."

"Not the Judge. I tell you I know him."

Bar rubbed a hand across his eyes. "Sure of that, aren't you?"

"Yes. Oh, Bar, can't you see—"

He locked the door and turned to put on the alarm. Over his shoulder he said, coolly, "So you told your friend Hubie that you and I were going to be married. I heard you."

Nineteen

She could feel color come up into her face. "I had to. Because he was so sure we were living in sin."

"Why? Nobody calls it that nowadays," Bar said, but absently.

"He thinks it's sin."

"Oh, come on, Emmy. He is a very observant man. He'll adjust to the mores of the present."

"Oh, no, he hasn't. He thought I was living with you and that—well, he'd always thought of me as being conventional and—and proper, doing what was expected of me. He was disappointed. I could see that—so I thought I'd make it all right by telling him we were engaged."

Bar sat down heavily in a lounge chair. "And did it make it all right with him?"

"Well, no. He really is a fussy old—old dodo!" Emmy said angrily. "He said that made it wrong for me to stay here with you. Honestly!"

"He's in love with you," Bar said flatly.

She stared. "Hubie! Oh, for heaven's sake! No!"

"Yes. I can tell."

"But, Hubie—I don't think he could ever be in love, not really in love with anybody. Unless he's in love with his job. He's really very good, you know. Very near tops—"

"He's in love with you. How do you feel about him?"

"Why, I—why, I like him. I admire him. I know I can count on his friendship and loyalty—"

"See him often?"

"Why, of course. At work—"

"Not in your apartment?"

"No. That is, sometimes, at a little party."

"Sometimes?"

"Bar, he is too important to run around, attending little parties."

"But he comes to your place."

"Sometimes, I told you. Not often. But I do count on his friendship."

"Maybe you are in love with him and don't know it. You should tell him, of course, that you are not engaged to me or anyone—"

"I won't. That is—oh, forget it—"

"Sit down, Emmy. You are hanging onto the back of that chair as if I might spring at you and eat you. I told him about China and the Judge—"

She stared. "You told him that China keeps saying she's going to leave the Judge and—and marry you?"

"Does she tell everybody that? Dear me! Anyway, in the course of the story I told him before dinn—by the way, Emmy, that was a very good dinner. I didn't know you could cook."

"I can't. I mean not like China." China, again. She must try to keep China out of their conversation and her pretty, appealing presence out of their thoughts. "I'm going to bed and for heaven's sake don't let Hubie know that you think he likes me—"

"I told you to sit down." There was a snap in Bar's voice.

"You sound like an army sergeant." But Emmy prudently sat down. It occurred to her belatedly that perhaps—just perhaps—Bar was a little jealous about her friendship with Hubie. If she had proper feminine good sense, she ought to encourage a possible jealousy. But considering Bar, it was an unlikely basis for coquetry.

Bar said, "If only I *were* just for about a minute and you were a new recruit—oh, never mind, Emmy. I know it's my own fault that I lost you. I was in love with you. But then China came along and—that was that. She didn't love me. Doesn't really care for me. She wants the Judge."

"She says it is you—"

Bar shook his head. "She's only working on the Judge's feelings. He'll probably come across with some very extravagant present. No, China doesn't mean what she says."

She had thought many times of what she would like to say to him if she ever had a chance. Words that would hurt, words that wouldn't be so much reproach as justifiable anger. He had led her to expect a marriage proposal from him. She had expected him at least to keep in touch with her—especially after China's marriage to the Judge. But now the opportunity came, she couldn't say any of the scalding words that had occurred to her in the months after Bar's departure from her life.

There they were, demanding speech: "But you were cruel to me. You were mean. You let me think—and then all at once you just paid no attention to me—you went for China—you didn't even see me—you . . ." Not a single word of any of it could get past her throat. She stood up.

Bar rose from the lounge chair with a swift swoop of his long body. "You are an idiot," he said and took her into his arms.

He kissed her, too, and put his face beside her own and held her and her whole body seemed to leap into being as if for the first time. She tried to speak but he kissed her again. So she still couldn't say a word but for a different reason.

Suddenly, though, his arms dropped away from her. She leaned against the chair beside her. Bar said, "Go to bed, Emmy, and rest. Tomorrow will be the deluge; every law-enforcement agency in the state will be here now that the weather is better. Not to mention all the newsmen and cameras and—" He finished, wearily, "inquiry, everything. Go to bed." He eyed her for a moment. Then he came to her again, put his hand under her chin and lifted her face. She thought he was going to say something but he didn't. He only kissed her again, but lightly this time and turned her gently but finally toward her own room.

The pup, watchful as a little tiger, shot ahead of her.

The night was long and quiet except for the continuing drip of the thaw. For Emmy it was anything but a quiet night. After what seemed a very long time she decided there was simply no use in thinking of Bar.

Eventually however, she did drift off to sleep. The pup was gone when she awoke at last. Bar must have quietly let him out. She dimly began to realize that it was very late in the day.

Archie had arrived for lunch. He and Bar were cozily seated in the kitchen. Bar gave her a friendly smile and said rather pointedly that she must have slept well and what did she want for lunch.

"I'll make some toast. Thank you."

"As you please—"

Archie's bald head was shining. "Emmy, practically the whole of the state's crime detecting force is here. Has been here all morning. Also cameras and newsmen, and they say you let the television people know about the murders—"

"They already knew. There was a piece in the Sunday paper, from Appledown. Hubie saw it."

"Hubie?" Archie's scant eyebrows shot up. "Who's he?"

"A friend of Emmy's. A newsman," Bar said. "She told him everything she knew of the murders."

Archie's pale eyes were wide with shock. "You did that, Emmy! How could you?"

"Why not?" Emmy said crossly. "They'd have found out anyway. And besides, Bar told him more than I did. Archie—"

Bar intervened. "Archie sticks to his explanation of meeting Belle in a bar."

"But it's true," Archie cried. The red wave came up over his face and then faded away again, leaving only pink rims around his eyes.

"Homer Jones says that you were often at their apartment." Emmy sipped some coffee.

"Well—well, once or twice," Archie said feebly, "but I don't remember ever even seeing this Jones—until, of course, the trial."

Emmy drank more of the heartening coffee and insisted, "But Jones did claim friendship, Archie. I heard him."

Archie blushed vividly again and looked down. His lips quivered. "I suppose Belle told him something or other."

"Belle told him that you had given her a lift in a taxi. On a stormy day. When she was trying to get a taxi and couldn't." Emmy spoke coldly; why, I sound like Kate, she thought.

Archie stared at her. "But that's not true. Why would Belle tell him anything like that?"

Bar said, "But you did meet him in the apartment. Didn't you?"

"No!" Archie flashed. "No! I told you. He's lying. I saw him only at the trial. Not much of a man. But I felt sorry for him."

Bar went on, quietly, almost soothingly as if speaking to a recalcitrant witness. "Why did you feel sorry for him?"

"I just—just did," Archie said weakly.

Emmy said, "Homer says that now you act like you don't even know him. He said that you were a kind of family friend when Belle was alive."

"That's not true, I tell you! We met at Kate's for the first time. The night of the murders. We were both embarrassed. At least I was." Archie hesitated and added miserably, "I *had* picked up Belle in a bar. I *had* gotten into the apartment with the police. I *had* seen what they saw. The whole thing was a terrible shock. I can't tell you what a shock. No, I didn't want any of it brought back again. It was dreadful even to see him so unexpectedly. I don't suppose you can understand that."

Bar poured more coffee for him. "All right, Archie. I don't see why Jones would lie about your meeting with Belle."

"I do," Emmy said and could almost feel Kate nudging her on. "Belle told him that. She must have had to make some kind of explanation for—for seeing you. And," Emmy added remorselessly, "probably some other men, too. The taxi story was what she told Jones. But didn't you ever wonder about—well, about another man?"

"No. That is—no."

"Or," said Emmy boldly, "other men?"

"No! Oh, perhaps!"

Bar gave Emmy an odd look. "You sound more like Kate every day, Emmy."

"What's wrong with that! We are sisters!"

Bar nodded, his lips looked as if he wanted to smile, but he had other things on his mind. "Archie, you were in that neighborhood very close to the apartment where she was killed. Did you see *anybody—anybody* at all on the street—or—oh, anywhere—who just might have known Belle?"

Archie wiped a hand across his eyes. "Anybody could have done it. You don't know, you can't imagine how horrible it was."

"Didn't you see somebody—say, leaving the place or on the street or—"

"Oh, of course, there must have been people. I only saw the police and then—and then Belle."

Emmy leaned forward. "Archie, think. Usually she did wear rings, didn't she?"

Archie nodded. "Oh, yes. Only a wedding ring at first and then later a big flashing ring, an emerald, diamonds, something very valuable but—who was I to question where it came from! I—I only thought, if I thought about it at all, that her husband had given it to her."

"He didn't," Emmy said flatly. "And in all the accounts of the trial there was no mention of a ring. Did you see her hand? Didn't you—"

"Emmy, don't!"

"You did look at her—"

"Don't!" Archie cried again. "Yes, I do remember her hand, so little, so white and helpless and—"

"She was wearing no rings."

"No. I think I'd remember that. I don't think I'll ever forget any of it." Archie gave a gigantic sob.

Emmy rose. "Stop, Archie. I'm not going to have two men weeping on my shoulder. That is, not literally but it's almost the same thing," she said defiantly to Bar, who was clearly astonished and disapproving.

He rose and put his hand on Archie's shoulder. "All right, Archie," he said firmly. "It's in the past. You must put it all out of your mind."

"I can't!" Archie cried. "I can't! She was so lovely—"

"But Archie— she lied to her husband. She accepted a ring like that one—"

"Stop it, Emmy," said Bar, who meant what he said.

Archie, however, took up her defense. "No, Bar. Emmy is right. Belle—poor Belle, no she couldn't have been the kind of girl she looked. I mean—she was so pretty, so sweet and—" But Archie added drearily, "She did pick me up at the bar. She could have picked up other men. Sure. She must have picked up somebody who could afford to give her a ring like that. But I'd rather not remember that," he finished with a pathetic dignity.

Emmy was about to cry herself; she had been cruel, hitting Archie when he was down. But Archie said, oddly, "Never mind, Emmy. I know you're just angry about something. China always getting after Bar when you—well, probably you want him yourself and—oh, dear! I've said too much. I don't know anything about it. I'd better go—"

Go he did, scrambling out the door, clutching coat and woolly cap as he went.

Now she was crying, tears rolling down her cheeks. Bar said, "That wasn't like you, Emmy. You hurt Archie."

But he hurt me, Emmy thought, and wiped off the tears hoping that Bar had not seen them.

He said, "I really don't care for it when you behave so much like Kate. I feel uneasy when she goes on a rampage."

"I didn't go on a rampage."

"No? It sounded like one to me. Eat your toast. It's getting cold."

"Belle couldn't have been loyal to her husband—"

Bar interrupted. "But I don't think she was exactly a tramp. I think she was a very pretty girl, naive perhaps—"

"Naive?" Emmy muttered through her toast.

"You'll choke on your toast. And not a bad thing if you are turning into a shrew. No, listen, Emmy. She was a young pretty girl, probably a little on the dumb side, married to a man who couldn't give her the—oh, the fine clothes, the luxuries, the jewels she must have wanted. Then, she *could* have met somebody who would, probably the man in the bar. Or for that matter, don't say it, I will—there could have been several men. We'll know more when your friend, Hubie, gets back."

Unexpectedly stung by Bar's reference to Kate, Emmy mumbled, "It's just the way they used to say to me when I was little, 'Why can't you be a good girl like your sister Kate?' Over and over and—"

Bar did not smile but amusement was in his voice. "So you decided you'd die before you'd be like your good girl sister. What kind of mischief did you get into, Emmy? Something very dreadful?"

Emmy was still upset and cross. "There wasn't anything very

wicked to do. But"—she cheered a very little—"I did get myself a job. I wasn't going to sit around and"—and try to forget you, she thought—"and interest myself in thises and thats, like Kate, and just live on whatever income the Judge let me have. So," she was defiant. "So I got a job."

There was a pause. Bar cleared the table while Emmy finished her second cup of coffee. At last he said, almost idly, "You'll enjoy being with your friend Hubie again."

"Yes!" Emmy understood too well her own unhappy reactions, but was defiant. "Yes, of course. I'll like working with Hubie. Is there more coffee?"

"You've had enough," Bar said with finality. "We'll have to see the police. I don't want a nervous, yelling termagant."

"Me!" Emmy cried with astonishment.

"Yes, but only for the moment, I sincerely hope." He did smile, only a little, as he came back to the table and sat down opposite her. "I think that we ought to tell the police every single thing we know or suspect. We are amateurs, trying to do something that isn't in our ability to do. And besides," he added. "That chief of police from Appledown. He's really a very good guy. Probably a little awed by all the official help he's getting today, but all the same in my opinion he's an honest man, and very capable. So I'm in favor of telling him every single thing—the knife we found, the ring business, your notes, everything from the beginning. Even the Judge's opposition to your work on the Jones case. Everything."

"Bar, I *was* dreadful! Poor Archie! I made him cry or—I'm so sorry."

"What do you think of my idea of going straight to the Appledown police chief?"

"Oh, yes. But wait a minute, do you really think I'm so like Kate?"

"Why, I—well, yes. That is—since you were a child you've been very defiant about Kate. You've tried, you say, to be everything Kate is not. She is bossy, no doubt of that. You're not bossy, but you do have a certain drive and—but don't go too far, Emmy. Actually I can't imagine any man falling in love with Kate! She was certainly well-named."

"She's not—not really a shrew."

Bar shook his head. "She needs a man who'll take a cane to her or even his fist if she needs it. But, Emmy, you are so silly. You are upset, angry, but in fact you did ask questions which ought to be asked of Archie. And that, I'm afraid—I know the police will do when they get the whole story. Poor old Archie!"

The pup shoved a cold nose at Emmy's ankles. She rose and found that Bar had already prepared some chopped-up meat for him. The pup fell upon it with a happy little growl.

"Funny," Bar said suddenly, "how Kate's instinct for helping others, even puppies, has complicated this ugly affair! Kate didn't shoot that man, but she *was* careless with her gun. She'll get a well-deserved reprimand for that—more, unless she can prove that she took better care of that gun than she must have done." He rose. "Come on, Emmy. Get on your coat. It's already afternoon. We'd better go to The Barn and see the police. They'll be sending for us soon. We may as well go now. I'll try to get hold of the Appledown chief. He's the one to talk to.

In the mirror, Emmy straightened her hair, put on lipstick, adjusted the neat white collar of her blouse. She shouldn't have hurt Archie. But then, she told herself again, he had hurt her and had done it purposely. No—no, not purposely; Archie was merely saying what came into his disturbed and saddened mind. He really hadn't paid much attention to his accusation concerning China. Belle couldn't have been very true to her husband; yet she might not have been, as Bar said, a tramp. Bar had been far more perceptive and, if it came to that, more generous than she had been. But Bar wasn't thoroughly upset by—by a few kisses. Damn it, said Emmy uselessly to herself.

She flung on her coat and went out with Bar, who closed the door behind them.

It wasn't going to be easy to speak to anybody alone and discreetly that day. Nothing was going to be easy. The whole place had changed.

People, uniforms, cars, an official-looking van, activity of all kinds was going on; there was almost a hubbub in the once-quiet Village.

The Judge was standing in the doorway of his own house and saw them.

"Going to see the police?"

Bar nodded.

"I've been there." The Judge seemed rather pleased with himself. "Knew some of them. Took me back, it did indeed. And they knew me." He seemed to preen himself a little about that.

"I'm sure they did," Bar said.

"Yes, oh, yes, people do remember me. Look here, Bar, all this is going to make it hard for you to sell your house. That is, if you really mean to sell it."

"I don't know." They had stopped at the steps to the Judge's house. "It may work the other way."

The Judge bristled. "What do you mean the other way? My God, two murders—"

"Lots of people like publicity. Judge, how many people who read the papers or watch the television news ever heard of Alpine Village? Why, this is as good as advertising."

The Judge tugged his moustache, his eyes very keen but startled. "I must say I never thought of that. No, you can't be right, my boy."

"We'll see. Come on, Emmy—" Bar was smiling to himself.

She knew the Judge stared after them digesting this strange idea of the profits of publicity as they splashed through puddles toward The Barn.

Here, however, while there were people everywhere, Emmy soon perceived an ordered confusion. There were many uniforms, different somewhat in their stripes and sleeve symbols. There were bright spots of the police's orange storm coats tossed here and there; one hung on the Christmas tree, a bizarre decoration. There were tables set up, holding telephones or computers or various mechanical-looking boxes whose purposes she could not even guess at. None of the policemen seemed to look at them when they entered The Barn and felt a wave of rather damp heat. But unexpectedly Manders came from a group huddled around another table and a man tapping busily into a computer while another man talked urgently but very quietly into a telephone.

"They've found the gun," Manders said.

"Not Kate's gun—"

"I don't mean that one." Manders waved a hand. "I mean the gun that killed poor Guy."

"When? Where?"

"I'm trying to tell you." Manders was very much in control of himself and his calm voice, but he couldn't quite conceal the ruby gleam in his dark eyes. "It was dug out of a melting snowdrift, there at the clump of firs where Guy was shot. Guy and—" he turned politely to Emmy—"and your friend, Mac, the guard. In fact they found two guns. Both had been fired. Three bullets gone from one. Four from the other."

"Whose guns were they? Do the police know?" Bar asked tautly.

Manders' eyes were black and steady. "One belonged to Guy. I had given it to him. The other belongs to the Elsters. They left it in their house when they left for the Bahamas a month ago."

"Then, you mean, somebody knew of it—"

"Certainly. I knew of it," Manders said. "Elster told me. He said he wouldn't think of bothering with a burglar alarm while he had a gun and could use it. He just left it in a drawer in the house when they went away. Someone obviously knew about the gun—as I did. Elster made no secret of his decision, but I did not enter his house and take the gun, and I did not kill anybody either!"

"The Elsters' house is very close to yours," Bar said altogether too quietly.

Manders lifted shoulders which were neatly clad in a fine suede jacket. He wore a red sweater and red scarf and did indeed look handsome. "But I assure you I did not take the gun. Why—" He nodded at the clusters of police. "They already have been on the phone to the Elsters. Old man Elster was very shocked, but they have the most complete alibi, naturally, for the entire week. Also, obviously he had no motive for shooting not one but two—"

"Somebody had a motive," Bar said. "What do the police say about the post-mortem?"

Manders ran a white hand around his sweater collar. "They say they have only theories so far. They seem to think that the guard —your Mac—was simply a victim of crossfire."

"Cross—" Bar began.

Manders nodded. "Seems likely. They think that Guy and whoever killed him were shooting it out. There by the road. Your Mac came along, heard the gunfire and—tragically—felt he had to help, investigate, stop the shooting."

Bar said, slowly, "Yes. Mac would have felt it his duty to stop anything wrong—"

Emmy felt the now familiar and painful lump in her throat. "Yes," she said. "Mac would have done his best."

"So," Manders said smoothly, "the police think that he was merely caught in the crossfire."

Bar nodded. "Yes, that makes sense." His eyes hardened. "You put away your collection of knives, didn't you, Manders?"

Manders lifted sleek black eyebrows. "After seeing that knife that was brought to your house and frightened Miss Emily? Yes, I put them away and locked them up. No more temptation for anybody, no possibility of another knife's being taken for any—" He looked into Emmy's eyes. "No chance for anybody at all to get hold of one. So forget about them."

"Ah," Bar said and disappeared into the clusters of men. Mr. Clements came over, fussing, angry and excited. "Manders," he said, clutching at his sleeve, "you're sure about the revolver? The Elsters' revolver, I mean? My God, this is terrible."

"Yes," said Manders, detaching himself from Clements and returning to the police; Clements gave Emmy a hurried and rather harried glance and waddled away again. Bar returned accompanied by the young police chief from Appledown and said very quietly, "There is a police car available. Come with us, will you, Emmy."

The chief, beside Bar, touched his cap and then removed it. He looked better; there was some color in his face, the tired black shadows around his eyes had disappeared. He was shaven and alert. He said, "I do hope you can help, both of you. This way—I believe you wish to be private and—no, no, it's quite all right. Nobody will mind—" He glanced at the array of forensic apparatus and added, "Nobody will miss me. And if you can help—"

There was no bitterness in his statement; there was indeed a note of hope. He preceded them outside into the damp, foggy air and led them to what proved to be his own car, with its lights now shut off.

"Not too crowded here," he said politely, "you might sit in the back, Miss Brace." Bar had gotten into the front seat beside the police chief. "My name, by the way," said the chief, "is George Walsh. Now—you thought I might be interested—"

"Yes," Bar said definitely. "And actually, since this is your case—"

"Well," Chief Walsh said, "not entirely, you know. The state—"

"Never mind. You can report anything you feel ought to be passed along to anybody else. Now then, I'll begin at the beginning! That was when Emmy, Miss Brace here, arrived. She went to have dinner with Judge Doane and his wife. She met Homer Jones there but did not hear his name and did not recognize him until the Judge explained his presence later. Judge Doane knew that she was working on the research for a television piece, or a series of pieces, about recent, famous murder trials, specifically the Jones murder. So the Judge had her fired."

This startled Chief Walsh. "How did he do that?"

"The Judge is a man who knows the people who know the right people. I believe in this instance it was some of the topnotch men at the television channel. Anyway, he said that he had control of Emmy's affairs through a power of attorney and somehow—through sheer determination, I think, or magnetism, or the fact that he is still a very well-known person—they concluded that Emmy was no longer needed. The Judge told Emmy that. They quarreled—"

Chief Walsh jerked around to stare at Emmy in the back seat. "*You* quarreled with the Judge?"

"Yes. I was so angry that I left the house, without my suitcase or purse, and went to my sister's—Kate Brace's house and then Bar came and took me over to his house because Kate's house was full of puppies and then—"

The chief took rather a long breath and turned back to Bar. "All right. Just take it slowly, please."

"Miss—that is, Emmy, had made notes during her research into the Jones murder. His wife—"

"Yes, I know all about that. At least a hundred—well, ten people have told me of it. Nobody seems to like having this Jones in Alpine Village."

"That's putting it mildly. The Judge gave him a job. Jones had to have a job as part of the parole agreement. He couldn't find a job with his record, so he appealed to the Judge, who hired him to help write his memoirs. However, the night Emmy arrived, Friday, her suitcase was searched. Her notes were in her handbag. When it was brought to her the next day, the notes were soaked and wet and—but I must tell you, Chief, she used her own system of shorthand. Nobody could possibly read those notes."

"I could figure them out if I had time, I'm sure," Emmy said softly. Neither man bothered to look at her. Bar went on. And on.

When he got through with Archie's disclosures, with the deciphering of Emmy's notes about the lack of a ring, even the wedding ring the dead woman had always worn, when he went on to the bartender's evidence and the evidence of the man at the newsstand, Chief Walsh stopped him. "All right. You do realize that I'll have to report all of this, Mr. Slocumb. Have it checked out—"

"Yes. But I told you since it began as your case—"

"That is very fair of you, Mr. Slocumb. But it is no longer entirely my case, as you saw. You know that some evidence has been found about the guns."

"Manders told me. Two guns. One was Guy's. The other was apparently stolen from a closed house here."

"Seems," said Chief Walsh, "that neither the murderer nor Guy Wilkins was a very expert shot. So many bullets. Your guard, they —we think—unfortunately got in a crossfire—"

"Yes," said Bar. "And the murderer apparently wasn't even touched!"

Chief Walsh nodded once. "You do understand that the bullet that killed Mac, the guard, came from the gun that was stolen here in the Village."

"Yes," Bar replied. "Chief, Manders himself *could* have had a motive for killing Guy Wilkins. If, say, Wilkins knew something or other that Manders felt to be a threat."

The chief brooded for a moment, then he turned to Bar. "Do you believe that?"

Bar hesitated. "Not really. No. I think Manders is too smart for that."

"Ah," said Chief Walsh thoughtfully. He added, "Is this all you have to tell me?"

"There was a knife—" Bar went on again: The knife, Manders' denial, then the gun.

The chief interrupted again. "But you know about the gun."

"I mean Miss Brace's gun. The one that shot Sam. Kate's gun. It's true she was careless with it but—"

"But since it was her gun, how—"

"That man, Sam, had just picked it up along with the other trash. And some bunches of damp papers. You see, Kate had been paper-training some puppies."

"Huh?" said the chief in a startled way.

"Never mind," Bar said. "It will be difficult to prove but I think that is what happened. Thought of it when I went into what had been the room where the puppies were living and it was all cleared up, no more papers, so something had to have been done with them."

Chief Walsh rubbed his forehead in a bewildered way, as a car driven as if for a race jammed to a stop beside them. Hubie scrambled out. He saw Bar and Emmy; he recognized the chief. He came splashing through puddles. "The bartender identified the men! In the snapshot! Two of them. One was Guy Wilkins—the other was Manders. And that's not all, Bar. Manders changed his name some years ago. He's been in hiding."

Chief Walsh took in the statements as if, now, he was prepared to believe anything. "What's he hiding from?"

"Wives," said Hubie. "Too many wives."

Twenty

After a moment, Chief Walsh said, "You'd better get in here." He leaned back and opened the door of the back seat. Hubie squeezed in beside Emmy. "I didn't waste time, did I?" he said rather smugly. "Good thing I got busy right away! However, I did have help. The bartender was on duty late last night. A friend of mine tracked down Manders. His name was originally—well, it's unpronounceable but here it is."

He hauled a wrinkled piece of paper out of a pocket. The chief took it and scrutinized it. "Looks like Chekoverly—can't be—"

"That's near enough. He had it changed legally. It's on record," Hubie said. "Wow, I'm tired."

Bar said, "How many wives?"

"Two, just now. Not for long perhaps! It does explain his determination to avoid publicity like a plague."

"Where are these wives?" Chief Walsh asked.

"Oh, I did some checking. Rather my friend did. Funny nobody ever really dug into Manders' past before."

"Where are the wives?" the chief repeated.

"My friend wasn't sure. He thinks one was somewhere in South America—I don't really know why he got that impression. The other, he didn't know about, he only knew that she was married to this Chekoverly, or whatever that name is. Fact is, he, Chekoverly—Manders—must be a bigamist. So he had plenty of reason to keep out of sight and hearing of either wife. It's funny in an odd way," Hubie said, the newsman in him coming to the surface. "Old Handsome Face—hiding wives and going around with Belle Jones."

"Belle Jones?" The chief jumped around to stare at Hubie. "How do you know that?"

"I told you. That is, I haven't had time to explain—"

Bar intervened. "I had a snapshot which my mother had taken. Alpine Village people around the pool. A good picture of Manders. Not so good of Guy. Was the bartender certain of Guy, Hubie?"

Hubie was still a little breathless. "He recognized Manders, and Guy, too. Seems Guy had visited the bar several times and had had drinks with Belle once or twice. But then all at once Manders turned up and—right away, the bartender said—seemed to take a fancy to Belle and—" He paused.

"And after that?" Bar nudged.

"That's simple. After a few times neither Manders nor Belle came to the bar again. So," Hubie said soberly, "my guess is that they met in more private places."

The chief said soberly, "We can't be sure about that. Let me think a minute. Manders didn't kill either of his wives."

Hubie sighed, rather reluctantly. "No, seems he didn't. But somebody killed Belle and I have a notion that she was the clinging kind. I mean," he amended it hastily, "I don't mean to blame poor little Belle. She was really more sinned against—but never mind that. Possibly Manders killed her because he wanted to get rid of her. That may be true but somehow—it doesn't square with the fact that both Manders' wives are still alive and apparently flourishing."

"We can't be sure of that either," the young chief said soberly. "Not until we find the wives. You do realize, Slocumb, that I'll have to report every word of this in detail. That is, if your friend—"

Emmy had to speak up. "He is Hubie Naylor, Chief."

"Oh!" Chief Walsh took a long, respectful look at Hubie, who dug his hands in his pockets and yawned.

"Long night. And day," he mumbled.

The chief said, "Never would have recognized you, Mr. Naylor.

An honor to have you here. But we do have to check on all this and—"

"No problem," Hubie yawned again. "Oh, by the way, Bar. What reason did Manders give for sending this man Guy down to the guardhouse?"

Bar looked startled. "I think he said it was something trivial he wanted Guy to tell Mac."

Hubie yawned again. "Not so very damn trivial. Staying in a motel near Scarsdale. Frightened off by the blizzard. Very good looking—"

"You can't mean a third wife!" Bar cried.

Hubie sighed. "Not yet. But it seems she was on her way here when the blizzard got too heavy. She had told Manders to expect her."

There was a short, rather stunned silence. Then Chief Walsh said, "How do you know all that?"

"Had to stop for a reviving drink in the motel. A handsome young woman was there. She asked me if I knew the way to Alpine Village. And then if I knew Mr. Manders. I really don't know how it happened, but all at once she was telling me that she was his fiancée and they were about to be married. Now, I'd like some food—"

Perhaps Hubie really didn't know just why people confided in him; Emmy thought of his superb interviews. "Where is she now?" Chief Walsh asked sternly.

"Still in the bar is my guess. But Manders must have been trying to get away from her. Sending Guy to tell Mac to stop her, is my guess."

"Three wives," said Bar blankly. "That is, only two at the moment but the prospect of a third. What will you do about this, Chief?"

"Can't say offhand. But thank you, Mr. Naylor. All that evidence may help."

"Look here," Hubie said. "Somebody tried to arrest me on the Hutch—I mean, the Hutchinson Parkway. Officer, do you think you can fix that? The summons, I mean—"

"I might be able to," the chief said. "Not the thing to do, you know, but still—"

"I've really worked like a dog. Hard and fast. I haven't had a bite to eat—"

"All right, Hubie," Emmy said. "We'll go back to the house."

"Might as well." The chief began to bundle himself out from under the wheel. "Come with me, Slocumb. This all requires—yes, I'm afraid you'll have to repeat all this—"

"I know." Bar crawled out of his side of the car and glanced at Emmy. "See you," he said and slouched around the car to join Chief Walsh. The two men, both young, both lithe and strong, strode along the brick path toward The Barn.

Hubie sighed. "I didn't get much thanks. Or did I?"

"Yes, oh yes, you did. Hubie, you really did talk to that woman—the third?"

"Do I ever invent a story?" He gave her an injured look then said hardily, "I'll have to get back to my research job on the Jones murder after I have some food. Are my boys doing all right?"

"They are all over the Village. At least they are part of the incoming flood of cameramen and reporters and—I don't want to talk to anyone. Not now—"

"I'll see to that." Hubie gave his face a rub and got out of the car. He took Emmy's arm. "Just show me the way. Don't say a word. Don't mind any cameras. They have to use flashes on a day like this. Light is too bad. Just keep your pretty mouth shut and hang on to me and—here we go."

It wasn't really too bad; there were a few derisive whistles and a few sharply sarcastic comments, intended to be overheard. "Hubie—hey, Hubie—why are you hiding her? Hubie—give us a line—just a word—come on, Hubie, don't be mean. Let us in on this. You'll have to later on—"

"That," Hubie said savagely in Emmy's ear, "was my own cameraman, my favorite, too."

As he spoke, there was a bright flash in Emmy's eyes.

"Just shut your eyes," Hubie said. "You look like death warmed over anyway—that is, I didn't mean to say that. Hurry along now. There. I think we can make it to your house."

"Bar's house," she said, but Hubie paid no attention.

"I really did do quite a good job," Hubie said. "Of course, meeting that woman was sheer luck. Reporter's luck, maybe. But

I couldn't have done anything without that friend of mine. He's great on hunting out statistical facts or—oh, hunting out anything. If you were coming back to work, Emmy, I'd give you his name. Introduce you. He's really great for snooping. That is, gathering information. Too bad you're not coming to work again."

"But I am," she said, although rather feebly, and opened the door to Bar's house. The pup fell upon her, muttering, scolding and pleased at the same time.

"Nice dog." Hubie shed his raincoat. "Now, Emmy, I'll have a real drink. With your permission . . ."

She showed him the cabinet in the dining room. Later, she broiled lamb chops, which had turned up in the freezer and obligingly thawed while Hubie drank.

Kate telephoned as she was about to put the chops in the oven. "Emmy," Kate cried. "You were at The Barn. What are they doing now?"

"I expect just the same thing they were doing when you were there this morning. Or were you there—"

Hubie had coolly taken a position very near the telephone and listened. Kate's voice was always very loud and clear.

"Oh, yes. They questioned me again about my gun. Bar said I needn't worry about it. What did he mean? I am very upset about it."

"Oh." In his long recital to the chief, Bar had barely begun to talk of Kate's gun. He had said nothing of Archie's tormented sorrow for Belle. And nothing of Homer Jones' almost-hysterical grief. Hubie shoved an ear closer beside Emmy's ear.

Kate said impatiently, "Answer me, Emmy. What about my gun?"

"He said it was picked up, wadded into damp newspapers. Accident."

There was a pause. Then Kate said, "You mean somebody hid it in a lot of puppy papers! Heavens sake, Emmy! Who did that? Can't you get anything out of Bar? Does he know that you say you're going to marry him?"

"Good-bye, Kate." Emmy dropped the receiver with a thud. Hubie went back to his drink. "I could hear most of that. Kate sounds like a fine woman. You must be a little like her, Emmy. Of course you *are* sisters. Natural. I'll help myself to another drink," he added and did. "A long night and a long day. But I did accomplish a thing or three, didn't I?"

"Yes." Emmy put the chops in the broiler.

Hubie ate hungrily. He had spotted Bar's room and afterwards took himself there without any apology.

The telephone did not ring again.

Bar did not return.

Time passed and it was a good thing she had not put on the alarm for suddenly the Judge opened the door and walked in. "Thought I'd find you here. Where's that man—that friend of yours from the studio?"

"Shhs. In there. Asleep."

"Nothing better to do?" the Judge asked sarcastically.

"As a matter of fact, he left here last night and worked—"

"He's back now, and his men are all over the place. Emmy, I've got to get something clear with you." He settled down comfortably as if he owned the place.

"Don't shout. Hubie has earned some rest."

"That may be." The Judge cast a skeptical glance toward the closed door of Bar's room. However, he did moderate his resonant voice a trifle. "There's something I've got to talk to you about. I don't believe in apologies, but I want you to understand that my motive in getting you out from the Jones murder piece was that I've loved you since you were a kid. You were not always lovable," he said sharply. "Kate always behaved herself. Like a lady. You did not, however—don't interrupt. I'm doing the talking. My reason for getting you out of danger, if possible, was quite sincere. You see, once Homer was paroled, the real murderer might be obliged to take steps. Now I could get a private detective agency, and I know some good ones, which would undertake to dig considerably deeper into the Jones case than had been done. But I didn't want you to have anything at all to do with it. I mean that, Emmy."

She believed him, yet there was a trace of doubt remaining too. "Did you set a detective agency to work?"

"Not yet. There wasn't time. Before I could more than get the boy properly clothed and settled in my house I found that you were working on the trial and all the evidence and—Emmy, I was frightened." He meant that, too. "You were always a kind of stubborn kid. Hell bent to do what you decided to do. Not like Kate. She always did what she was told to do."

"I can't have done anything very bad!"

"N-no," the Judge hesitated. "In a way, yes. You wouldn't take advice, you know. And while you did go to the school where I sent you, you left it whenever you liked to go off dancing or—oh, anything you wanted to do."

She risked it. "China went with me."

"Yes." But his face softened. "I realize that. China—but it's you I'm talking about. Truly, believe me, I was afraid you would get into this more deeply than you ever could have dreamed. There must be a real murderer somewhere, I told you that over and over. He must have been alarmed at the announcement of so widely seen a report of the whole case. He must know that, somewhere, there are facts leading to his exposure. But I meant it for the best. Getting you fired, I mean. I hope you'll believe me."

"Oh, yes, I believe you. I always have believed you."

"You haven't always followed my advice, but it has always been the best advice I could give you. That's all, Emmy. Just do try to keep out of this—this ghastly affair."

"Thank you, Judge." She lifted her face as he got out of the chair, came to her and quite gently kissed her cheek.

He went away, looking curiously older. He had kept himself in such fine shape that up to then he had looked and certainly acted far younger than his years.

He had barely gone, however, when China burst in without knocking. "I knew you were here. I knew the Judge was here. Never mind that." She flung aside a scarlet rain cape. "You've got to understand one thing. You claim you are going to marry Bar. You are *not* going to marry Bar."

"Don't shout!" Emmy took a firm grip on her anger. "Sit down, China. Let's talk about this."

"That is why I came here. You are making a fool of yourself. Claiming to marry Bar—"

"Don't you think that you are being a bit of a fool yourself, married to the Judge and insisting on keeping Bar on—on a string —in case you should happen to want him."

"Well, really!" China looked astounded. "I never thought I'd hear such words from my oldest friend. Why, Emmy, we were in school together. You—"

"You can't have both men, China. It isn't done."

"I need Bar," China said; her voice became very soft and treacherously disarming. "I do need him, Emmy. Please—"

"If—I mean when I marry him," Emmy said between her teeth, "I'll not let you work on his sympathy for one minute. You have done exactly what you wanted to do. Married a man who is really, truly in love with you. The Judge even overlooks all your silliness—"

"Did you say silliness?" China forsook her soft pleading and bit out the words.

"Oh, forget it, China. I know you. But I think you are beginning to know me. Of course we are old friends—were old friends. Schoolmates, all that. I was very glad to see you when I arrived Friday night. But frankly, if I never see you again it will be too soon—"

China shot up from her chair. "I cannot believe it is you saying such dreadful things—"

"Oh, it's me all right. Just let Bar alone. I tell you, you cannot have two men the way you want them. Bar is no rug to trample on and cast aside but keep on hand in the event you want him. Not Bar!"

China had flung herself out of the door. All the same, Emmy felt better. She hadn't done China any good—or perhaps she had, in the end. But she had certainly done herself a world of good.

After a moment, Hubie poked his ruffled hair and sharp face out the door of Bar's room.

"Well, well! Didn't think you had it in you. Hasn't Bar come home yet?"

"No. And it's getting dark. Time for him."

"I think I'll just saunter down to that Barn place and find out what's happening."

He emerged wholly, looking rather disheveled but with very intent eyes. "See you—" he said and went out the door, banging it behind him so the pup uttered a startled little yelp.

It was getting dark. The early December dusk was already settling down over the Village.

Bar did not return. There seemed no need to put on the burglar alarm, not with policemen flooding the whole place.

She thought of going to Kate's, only for company and Kate's always-bracing if bossy conversation.

Kate, however, telephoned. "Bar back yet?"

"No."

"Funny. Guess what the police just now asked me. How long has Mr. Manders had that car with the blacked-out windows."

"Oh? How long—"

"Four—no five days exactly. I remember people objected to it."

Emmy thought for a moment. "Why did the police want to know that?"

"I thought you could tell me."

"I don't know anything about it."

"I saw that friend of yours, that television man hustling past. What's he doing?"

"I don't know."

"You don't know much, do you?" Kate was not actually insulting, merely matter-of-fact and put down her telephone.

Kate, as usual, was right. But Emmy believed the Judge. She felt a kind of glow for having stood up to China. She was not even interested in how long Mr. Manders had driven a car with blacked-out windows, and actually he hadn't driven it himself the night she had seen it. Guy Wilkins had been driving it, Manders following in his long white car. She remembered Mac's expression of puzzled surprise when both cars came up beside Emmy's car and then went swiftly on.

Lights were beginning to dot the foggy dusk. The police would certainly question her again, question everybody, over and over again. She hoped they would send Bar for her. She turned on the lamps in the room and instantly the outside world became blacker.

The radio borrowed from Bar's room provided little comfort; the thaw had already done great damage; roads and many basements were flooded; people again had had to take refuge in nearby schools. She turned the radio off.

Mop proved himself again a dog of remarkable learning ability; he went to the door and scratched it.

"Good dog," she said. She ought to go outside with him. He really was still a pup in spite of his suddenly grown-up manners.

She took up her coat, opened the door, watched indulgently as Mop shot out into the night, and went forward a few steps, into the path of light from the open door. From the dusk a man spoke to her. "Miss Brace? They want you at The Barn. The chief—" The path of light showed up his blue cap and his bright orange storm cape.

"Oh! Let me put the dog inside—"

The dog scrambled to her as she called him but refused to go inside the house. The policeman said impatiently, "This way" and turned down the path—and down the path and off to one side of the path.

"But this isn't the way to The Barn."

"Short cut. Hurry up." He shoved his arm under her arm. "They are waiting for you."

He was very strong. She was strong herself but no match for the sudden strength which pulled, dragged, scuffled her along until they were behind some of the enormous boulders, off at one side of the Village.

"I tell you this is not the way to The Barn!" she gasped.

"Short cut," he repeated.

It couldn't be the way to The Barn. Yet a policeman ought to know. She stumbled along beside him; suddenly there was no path at all. She could barely see the gleam of his orange coat and then that disappeared into the foggy darkness. She hit a toe on a boulder and gave an involuntary cry. He seemed to whirl around; she could see the white oval of his face. "Short cut," he said again and took her elbow. They were off any path there had ever been. They were heading toward the entire mass of huge boulders, shielded by firs and growth.

This was not a short cut.

He was not a policeman.

She pulled back hard and he grasped her arm.

"No!" she cried and then screamed.

Rather she tried to scream; a hard wiry hand came down over her mouth. An arm shot out around her.

She pulled against it, she kicked, she tried to wriggle away from that wiry hand and very strong arm and couldn't. Someone must see or hear, I'm in sight of the Village, she thought wildly. But she was not in sight of the Village. She wasn't in sight of anything or anybody in this foggy blackness.

He's going to kill me.

It was a clear, perfectly certain realization.

She wondered if he intended to use a knife. She fought, she kicked and they were both behind a big boulder and all the far-away glimmering lights of the Village were shut off.

So—so now was the time. "But why?" she cried against his moist palm. "I didn't—I don't—"

Another wiry hand traveled to her throat and gripped, cutting off speech, cutting off breath, cutting off life. She struggled and kicked and writhed and could not escape that murderous, relentless grip. An odd kind of hovering blackness seemed to come down upon her senses. She must not faint. She must get some air. She must scream, something—

A furious high-pitched yelp came from the mask of darkness and the hand shot away.

"Damn dog—" The voice squeaked angrily. There was a swift motion and a sharp wail from the pup.

"Nipped me on the ankle," the curiously high voice came through the darkness. "Damn dog—"

The pup gave another shrill yelp. In the same instant a furry little body hurled against her. She clutched at it and still had no breath. But her ears had not been shut off. An eerie, loud shriek arose from the darkness, from somewhere, from everywhere.

The dark figure stood still for a second, then released her throat and simply vanished.

She could hear nothing but the pup's whimpering close to her face, and the alarm from the Village. But all at once lights came up from everywhere, flashlights, floodlights and the welcome sound of racing engines and voices calling her.

"Emmy—Emmy—" That was the Judge.

"Emmy! Where are you?" That was Bar. She couldn't move. She was still frozen with terror. But then lights came nearer, a strong light beam struck her and she blinked and tried to say, "He's gone —he's gone—"

Bar carried her back to his house. The Judge sat down beside her and took her hand in his and, she was sure, almost cried into it.

Kate appeared from somewhere. There were police. China huddled near the Judge.

The room was full and yet not full. Manders was not there. Archie was not there. None of the other Village residents was there. There was by then actually only a sprinkling of police but among them was Appledown Chief Walsh. He was soberly watching Kate, who had the pup on her lap and was feeling it all over as the pup gave little whines when she apparently reached a sore spot. Emmy tried to speak and found her voice hoarse and her throat hideously painful. She put her hand up to her throat and Bar said, but very gently, "He tried to strangle you. We saw in the flashlight. When he heard us coming, he let go and ran away."

Manders thrust open the door and strode in. He was no longer handsome. He looked white and frightened but he was in command of himself. "I'm sorry," he said to Emmy. "I'm afraid I am responsible for two murders."

Hubie emerged from the dining room with a glass in his hand. "Give this to her," he said to Bar.

A policeman, orange-coated, face harshly gray, came into the room without knocking.

"Chief—we got him. Out on the main highway. Trying to thumb a ride. He had this—"

He held a shining, sharp knife toward the chief, who said grimly, "See to him. Probably needs restraint—I'll be there shortly—"

China started forward, peered and gave a horrified scream. "My very best carving knife!"

"Quiet," said the Judge and China was quiet.

Emmy nearly choked on the brandy, got it past her painful throat, wondered how she could have been so easily deceived by an orange storm coat and a blue cap. Yet she had expected a policeman.

Manders said again, "I am very sorry about leaving a knife here, Miss Emmy. I do apologize. I rather think your lawyer friend here, Bar, is smart enough to have surmised just how I did that."

"Yes," Emmy said huskily.

Manders said politely, "I only meant to stop your delving into the Jones murder."

Bar interrupted. "How did you know that she was working on the Jones case?"

Manders replied smoothly. "Why, Guy told me. We saw a strange car, yours, Miss Emmy, at the gate when we came back from the city Friday night. Guy had made it rather a custom to go down to the gate and chat with Mac. The guard enjoyed the company. And frankly, I liked to know something of what was going on in the Village. A whim," said Manders. "The guard told him all about you." He looked at Emmy. "He was very proud of you. Guy knew, though, that you were a danger to him and to me."

Bar said, "So Guy sneaked around, watched the Judge's place and saw his chance to get Emmy's suitcase when her sister dropped it."

"Yes, that is a fact. Guy told me. He searched it, also told me he had searched her handbag, quickly of course. But he found only some scribbled notes. He had a flashlight but he couldn't make sense of them so, he told me, he simply dropped the bag behind the nearest shrub and came home. Poor Guy! I really do apologize to you, Miss Emmy. I did want to stop you delving into the Jones case, especially after what had happened to Guy. I knew that Homer Jones—at least I thought he was very dangerous to you—"

"And to you," Bar said.

Manders lifted a sleek eyebrow but accepted it. "And in a way to me. So I tried to frighten you, Miss Emmy. I even phoned a threat to you. I had to get you away before you explored the Jones murder too dangerously. I tried to get him out of the Village. I had to keep myself out of publicity or involvement! After he shot Guy, I knew I was next. Good Lord, I had even gotten a car with blackened windows to protect Guy and me, too." He turned to Bar. "You knew that."

"We knew that you had ordered it, bought it, just after he came here to stay with the Judge. So you were scared."

"I made a terrible mistake." The Judge's voice shook. "I thought I was right. I thought I was only undoing harm that had been done to an innocent man." He put on his spectacles and looked around the room. "I was a fool!" he said loudly, took off his spectacles and went on unsteadily, "It was no coincidence, Homer Jones turning up here with his story of failing to find a job and suggesting that I write my memoirs and let him assist. I agreed. But I see now that while he was in the city, he was looking up Manders and Guy Wilkins. Manders has a place here—"

He shot a glance at Manders. The Judge said, "He made up that whole story to get a chance at you and Guy. He knew. A man with one idea! All that time, only one idea of revenge! He blamed you, not himself. I'm not sure he wasn't right—"

"But he murdered his wife," Bar said.

"I was a fool," the Judge said. China slid swiftly to the Judge and snuggled against him, comfortingly. In that second Emmy forgave China; this might have to be reconsidered later but not just now.

"Homer Jones!" Emmy said hoarsely. "Why did he suddenly decide to kill me?"

Kate looked up from the pup, her face was strongly outlined because she was so pale. "Remember how you kept questioning him, Emmy. And he got so scared he had hysterics. You simply got too near the truth. He was terrified—" She turned to Bar. "Why did he hide my gun in those papers?"

"Remember he was here, the night of the two murders while we were all at The Barn. He must have found your gun, took it because Manders was to be his next victim—"

Manders did slightly shudder. "I suspected that, of course."

"And then—" Bar went on. "We returned and he had to hide the gun and there, in the room with the dogs, were hordes of newspapers to be bundled up and thrown in the trash. So he must have simply wrapped the gun in those papers. It is only your—our good fortune that Sam was not killed as he was adjusting the trash bags and the gun went off."

The Judge said, desolately, his head down, "The death of two innocent men."

"Dear," murmured China, her head against his arm.

Manders said, "In a way Guy was innocent. I sent him to tell Belle that it was all off between her and me. And to get the ring I had given her. Unfortunately she resisted and in his haste he snatched both the rings off her hand. And tragically Homer Jones came into the apartment house just after Guy had gone. He must have seen him leave. Guy was afraid of that. Guy hurried to tell me and we—we tried to take protective action. Guy said he didn't like the look on Homer's face. Next morning there was the account of Belle's murder, so we knew who had killed her—savage, beside himself with jealousy—"

Kate put the pup down on the floor. "Homer almost had hysterics here as we talked. I could see he was getting very worked up and nervous—scared, I know now. But I never thought he was so dangerous—"

The chief stirred. "Yes. After the murders Jones must have dropped the gun he stole. Then hurried back to your house, Miss —Miss Kate, to ask to rent a room. Thus he hoped to establish a sort of alibi. No use trying to put it all together right now. Thank you all very much. Do you want a doctor?" he asked Emmy.

Emmy shook her head. "Oh, no. I'm here. I'm safe."

The pup scampered to her and nudged at her legs.

Bar picked him up. "You are a hero." His voice was very unsteady. "You bit, he yelled, the alarm went—"

"Oh!" China lifted her head. "I did that. I knew Homer Jones was not in the house and I was scared of him so I—well, I just set the alarm and opened the door."

"*China!*" Emmy cried. "Oh, *China!*" Somehow she stumbled out of her chair, ran to meet China and they hugged, cried, hugged. "You saved my life! You saved my life—" Emmy couldn't stop crying.

Someone, Bar, Kate, Hubie, everybody got her back to a chair.

"Darling." The Judge pulled China to him, again.

Manders said, quite politely to Hubie, "I suppose the whole thing—Belle Jones, Guy, Homer and—and myself—all this will be in the papers. All the media."

Hubie eyed him. "Can't keep the news out. And by the way, you did send Guy down to the gate, didn't you, to discourage the expected arrival of your present—she says she's your fiancée. She's still in Scarsdale waiting for you to come for her, I suppose. Anyway, waiting. A powerful woman," Hubie added. "All-in wrestler from her looks, but handsome."

Manders did not change color; there was only a dark glow in his eyes; he spoke so simply that it was almost disarming. "My weakness is, I like women."

Bar, however, did not seem impressed. "What are you going to do about your wives?"

Manders drew himself up. "Pay, of course. Money is all either is interested in."

"But isn't there a charge of bigamy?"

"Oh, no." Manders almost smiled. "You see, the second one—she only thought she was married. The divorce decree from the legal wife has just been granted. So—" he shrugged. "I'll get rid of her, the second one. Give her all the money that seems reasonable."

"What about your—the lady waiting in Scarsdale?"

Manders lifted his eyebrow. "I'm not sure, really. Something. I'm sorry about Belle, really sorry."

"But you got Belle's ring," Bar said. "Thrift is said to be an admirable trait."

Manders' dark eyes flashed. "Idiot! Belle never knew my name. Didn't seem wise to tell her that! So don't you see that the only possible way she had of ever tracing me was through that ring. Jewelers, all that. Not that I expected to need the ring again—not just now—"

Kate was shocked. "But you *can't* be thinking of marriage again!"

Manders looked at her very seriously; the ruby glint came back into his eyes. "I wouldn't quite say that, Miss Brace."

Kate unexpectedly blushed to the roots of her pretty black hair. Without warning the door flung open. Archie fell into the room. "What's all this? Police—alarms—everybody carrying on—what happened?"

No one replied. Bar said, "But we do have the real murderer. Manders."

"*What!*" Manders looked astounded. "You can't mean me!"

Bar turned to Chief Walsh. "Isn't a threat with a deadly weapon illegal?"

Chief Walsh's eyes flashed. "Certainly. A knife—"

Hubie, ever quick, said, "I can't quite believe that you changed your name, Manders, entirely to escape wives! I have a friend who is now very much interested in your various undertakings. He does thorough research and while I don't say, yet, that he'll find anything illegal, all the same I believe he will. And besides, thanks to my news story, your face, the account of these murders and the reason will be seen and heard all over the country. You'll find nobody who will trust you about any kind of business dealing. But then—depending on what we find—maybe you'll be in prison, so that won't matter much to you."

Manders' eyes shot ruby flares. "I am perfectly safe—"

Bar was stern and solemn as even the Judge. "You were responsible for three murders, Manders. Belle Jones, your own front man—and our friend, Mac."

"But *Jones* shot those people!" Manders edged toward the door. Chief Walsh had already quietly moved between Manders and the door.

Bar said, "Jones held the trigger. But you were the one who turned him into a living weapon!"

The Judge leaped to his feet. He jerked out his spectacles and stared through them icily. All at once the room turned into a courtroom. He said, "I don't understand your reference to a knife. But I do suggest you take him in custody, Chief, until this gets straightened out."

Suddenly Manders seemed to realize that Chief Walsh had his arms in a hard grip. He made one frantic effort to wriggle away. "Now, now, Mr. Manders," the chief said. "I suggest you leave, Judge, you and your wife. We'll see about all this tomorrow." Suddenly the chief and Manders disappeared as Archie flung open the door for them.

The Judge said magisterially, "Right. Certainly. Come China, Archie—"

"Tomorrow and tomorrow and tomorrow," Archie chanted inescapably. "I'll just go with you, Judge!"

All at once the room was very quiet. Then Hubie put a friendly hand on Emmy's shoulder. "I'm very thankful, Emmy! I was scared when we heard the dog yelp. Thank God, China turned on the alarm—"

"Yes," Emmy said. "Oh, yes!"

Kate started for the kitchen. "You can stay if you want to, Hubie."

Bar called after Kate. "By the way—or not by the way at all,

Kate, you should know that Emmy and I intend to marry—" He looked down at Emmy. "Right, Emmy? Can you give up one job —but take me for another?"

Emmy took a long, shaky breath and got herself upright. "Yes. I already told Kate that, so just try to get out of it. But let's not sell this house. We'll make out."

Bar laughed. The tenseness, the rigid muscles in his face all changed to warmth. Kate said from the kitchen, "Then you can address some of those leaflets for me, Emmy. And help trim the Christmas tree in The Barn."

Bar laughed again but gently for he knelt beside Emmy and took both her hands. "My darling. I just couldn't try to go back to you —after all the silly hoopla with China! But now, with all my faults—"

"Oh, yes," Emmy said. "I love you still. What on earth do you want, Hubie?"

Hubie was hunting for matches. "I want to light a fire for this domestic scene. Why do you suppose your sister blushed so much when Manders seemed to be considering another marriage?"

Kate called from the kitchen. "I heard that. No reason at all! After Belle and—and all those women! And causing murder and —the very idea! I'll bring the leaflets to you tomorrow, Emmy. Oh, you can help me now, Hubie." Hubie got a sudden and surprising gleam in his eye and positively pranced for the kitchen.

Bar grinned. "Just the man for Kate. Oh, never mind anybody else. Tomorrow."

Tomorrow and tomorrow. Her head against Bar's shoulder, his arms around her, Hubie and Kate, perhaps very friendly indeed, in the kitchen, peace with China and the Judge. There was nothing else in the world at that moment that Emmy could want. There was, however, a small addition; the pup wriggled up on her lap.

About the Author

MIGNON G. EBERHART'S name has become a guarantee of excellence in the mystery and suspense field. Her work has been translated into sixteen languages, and has been serialized in many magazines and adapted for radio, television and motion pictures.

For many years Mrs. Eberhart traveled extensively abroad and in the United States. Now she lives in Greenwich, Connecticut.

In the seventies the Mystery Writers of America gave Mrs. Eberhart their Grand Master Award, in recognition of her sustained excellence as a suspense writer, and she also served as president of that organization. She recently celebrated the fiftieth anniversary of the publication of her first novel, *The Patient in Room 18.*